LASERA

To: Christine

Watch
for
Mer!

Till my soul is full of longing
For the secret of the sea,
And the heart of the great ocean
Sends a thrilling pulse through me.
~ Henry Wadsworth Longfellow

LASERA

BOOK ONE OF
THE MER ARCHIVES

DANIELLE MATHIESON PEDERSON

OTHER WORLD PRESS

Published by Other World Press
Kamloops, BC, Canada

This novel, by definition, is fiction. If you've purchased this novel via accepted channels, many many thanks to you. Supporting both the arts, and the artists, is one fantabulous way to be awesome. If you didn't, thanks for the compliment of saying my book is good enough to steal. What'll happen if you buy ripped off copies or don't buy additional ebook copies? I'd like to say I'd hunt you down like you were a Siamese twin from Saturn and force you to do a contemporary dance piece, but alas, that's not going to happen. Readers? Stay awesome.

Library and Archives Canada Cataloguing in Publication

Mathieson Pederson, Danielle, 1987-, author
    Lasera / Danielle Mathieson Pederson.

(Book one of the Mer archives)
Issued in print and electronic formats.
ISBN 978-0-9947841-0-0 (paperback)
ISBN 978-0-9947841-1-7 (pdf)

    I. Title.

PS8626.A8323L38 2015   jC813'.6   C2015-903776-X
                                    C2015-903777-8

Printed in the United States

Cover design by Deranged Doctor Design.
Formatting by Polgarus Studio

To Tim, for being the rock to my crazy.
And for loving me so completely.

To my parents, for their enduring love.
Mom, thank you for the love of reading.
Dad, thank you for your quiet strength.

To my friends and family, for their relentless enthusiasm.
And for their (sometimes needed) swift kick to
get me back to writing.

And to Harry Potter, for the laughter, the tears,
and the imagination.

Wyn's Choice

Water surrounds me, holding my form in its cool grasp, but it feels off: wrong and harsh. Saturated with poisonous chemicals and lacking salt, it leaves its mark. The dulled colour of my scales is proof of this. Starvation makes me weak. My strength and speed are not what they were.

Blurred forms above the surface try to help the girl.

The screams are more disturbing underwater.

What have I done?

My family, my people, my world—all are now at risk. But failing to act would have gone against my core. To turn aside would have been cowardice.

Perhaps it will not matter. If things do not soon change, death will claim me as surely as the moon shapes the tides. But perhaps that would be best? If I die they cannot question me and discover what I know. If my life is prolonged, we are all exposed. Everything—everyone—that matters to me could suffer because of my choice. They may grow to hate me, their son and brother, because of this—because of *her.*

The water swirls around me in the deepest corner of the pool. Her body is pulled up through the water and she is gone.

There is nothing to do but wait. My tail flicks and thrashes uncontrollably. Image after image passes through my mind. Worry gnaws at me. There are so many things I might have done differently.

Yet I made my choice. What will the consequences be?

-CHAPTER ONE-
Saved

The accident that changed my life was as unexpected as it was terrifying. That single moment stole away, perhaps forever, the one thing that still made me happy. If the fates, or gods, or whoever, had plotted the event and the complete upheaval of my life, the least they could've done was warn me about it.

Instead, the day that changed everything started out completely normal. The shrill ring of my cellphone woke me. My coach's voice blasted through the speaker demanding to know why I wasn't at diving practice already. Provincials were just three short months away, and I had two events: three-metre springboard and the five-metre platform.

I groaned, told him I'd be right there, and went and worked my butt off as promised, because the Olympic trials were within reach. Then I went about my regular day—six and a half hours of dreary gym and social classes, along with a course involving ridiculous numbers that the horrible government required. I was a solid B student, but math was so dang elusive. By four o'clock, however, I was back in my native habitat, sitting in a plastic beach chair by the pool, slurping a fruit smoothie.

I couldn't hear the dripping of my wet swimsuit over the roar of those in the pool behind me, but I felt the drops as they splashed through the holes in the chair onto my heels. The smells of chlorine, water, and frying snack food were homey, familiar. The white noise of voices echoing off the concrete walls soothed my mind. My drink was sweet and icy on my tongue.

Two girls and a guy who didn't go to my high school blew past my table. Their laughter hit me hard, and tears pricked at my eyes. That used to be Zack, Heather, and me. Our little trio formed when Zack moved to town in grade four, and it survived seven good years, right up until May of last year, when I lost it and screamed at them in front of everyone.

"Stop trying to get me to talk about it!" The words haunted me *and* them. We still hung out occasionally, but they'd stopped coming to the pool regularly, and our visits were never the same.

Blinking rapidly, I checked the time on the digital wall clock and shook my head. My green plastic straw made a *scree scree* sound on the lid of my smoothie as I stirred it. Heather and Zack were late. Of course. They always were nowadays. Watching the entrance, I saw them finally come in. Zack was wearing a new golf shirt and jeans.

"Hey," he said as they approached my table and sat down.

"Took you guys long enough," I said. Zack raised an eyebrow; I raised one right back.

"I forgot how muggy this place is," Heather said, pushing her hot-pink bangs out of her green eyes and pulling her dirty blonde hair into a ponytail.

"You look nice in that suit." Zack nodded at the black and

green swirls. "It makes your blue eyes pop." He emphasized the pop with a flare of his fingers.

I shrugged, pushing a strand of my mud-coloured hair behind my ear. It was just a racing suit and he'd seen it before. "When did you guys go to the mall? Those are new." I pointed at his ensemble. The turquoise polo and dark wash jeans were at odds with the grease stains on his hands. Zack had always been a confusing combination of contrasts. He'd inherited the huge lumberjack physique of his dad's francophone side and the facial features and hair of his petite Japanese mother.

"Saturday. I scoped out grad dresses and Zack bought new pedals and shocks for his bike," Heather said.

"Missed you," Zack said. "It's been weeks since you came with."

"Yeah, and? It's been months since you guys came to the pool." Not to mention the fact that they'd also kept me waiting for half an hour today.

"Not the point. Point is, we hardly see you. Even then it's mostly at school. You don't do anything but dive. You're always at the pool. When are you gonna start to live again?"

I froze mid-slurp. *Don't even.* He was not talking about this.

"I mean it, Val. You're not yourself." He shoved a hand through his jet-black hair. "It's been a year, and if you're not diving you trudge like a zombie from those video games your brother Th—"

"Don't you dare say his name! I'm not ready to talk about it yet."

"Yeah, but if you'd get out of your own head for one minute you'd realize that I—"

"Zack, shut up." Heather glared at him. "What he means is

that we're seriously worried. We miss you. We want to help you."

My chair scraped across the concrete as I shoved it back and stood.

"I'm going to dive." I slammed my smoothie into the garbage and wove through the crowd toward the diving boards, not looking back. They'd come to the pool for the first time in months and *that* was what they wanted to talk about? Figured.

Shoving thoughts of Zack and Heather out of my head, I waited for the little girl ahead of me to work up the nerve to jump off the platform. When my hands gripped the stair rail, my heart jumped. No matter how often I trained, how many times I jumped or simply fell into the water, I never tired of it. I always relished the experience, the thrill.

Two boys behind me were talking about the latest version of Halo. *Theo had liked that videogame.*

A wall slammed down in a corner of my head and I threw the memory behind it. That was where I put *all* thoughts of Theo, constantly—if all too often futilely—striving to keep the canvas of my mind blank.

My hands pulled me up the stairs. I walked the length of the platform, my feet slapping the wet concrete.

I gazed at the clear rippling surface beneath me.

Think about the water, only the water.

This was home. This was where I belonged. This required no thought, no feeling.

I closed my eyes and breathed. Standing up here, I was convinced there was nowhere you could feel as comfortable or as relaxed. I pushed up onto my toes, brought my arms forward then fell straight down in a simple front dive. Air whistled past my ears. Cool wetness met my hands and I split the surface. But something was wrong. The back of my hand brushed something hard. Wood? My eyes whipped open and my chin jerked up. Instead of crystal clear pool water, muddy brown filled my vision. ...

With a blinding crash, my head slammed into something. Agony throbbed at my temple. My head, *my mind*, felt like it no longer existed.

Thought stopped.

Water.

Why so much? Where was the air?

Pain.

Deadened. Held back by blackness, a weight.   ·

My body was weightless in the water—a sensation I should have enjoyed. But something pressed in on me, a sense of ... unease. My mind and body should be doing something, or at least my mind should be *telling* my body to do something. There was a block somewhere.

All water, no air. I was drowning, dying.

My thoughts chased each other. I wanted to yell, kick,

scream. I might be dull, I might've made some stupid choices and huge mistakes, but I didn't want to die!

My body was not doing what it should; adrenaline should be rushing through me. My hands should be shaking; I should be screaming. But my brain was locked. Where were my eyes? Where were my arms? Where were my legs?

The blackness shoved against my mind, trying to make it succumb just as my body had. I had to move. I had to live. I heaved against it, trying to free my limbs, but it was like trying to lift resistance weights that had been increased by a factor of ten—impossible.

And suddenly, I had air. I was still surrounded by water. Yet I had air. I couldn't make sense of it. It didn't feel the way I expected, though. It didn't brush my cheek or swirl through my hair; it filled my lungs directly.

Forced in.

Some of the blackness receded as oxygen dispersed into my blood. Fresh pain swelled in my growing consciousness. It was wrenching. If I'd had control of my body I would've whimpered.

The pain surged again.

It hurt so much! Please let it stop.

Pain upon pain, pounding into me like a battering ram.

And then, so swiftly I was stunned, I knew where my mouth was, where my lungs were. I was bursting with the need to exhale. I focused on telling my mouth to open and found that I could. Bubbles streamed around me as I let go of the air trapped inside me. They sped toward the surface—the way I needed to go. I didn't know how far underneath I was, but I knew air existed above me. I needed to go up.

These realizations came one after another, and between the

next poundings of pain, I found my eyes. I was trying to open them when a new sensation reached me. My lungs were expanding.

Pressure was being exerted on my mouth.

By someone else's mouth.

I was being *resuscitated*.

I felt gentle pressure on either side of my ribcage, like a pair of hands.

There was a strange lifting sensation, and then I gasped.

Air. Pure air.

I coughed and convulsed. My shoulder blades hit something cold and hard. Pain exploded as my head hit something solid, but I didn't care. I could think. I could breathe!

I opened my eyes, was blinded by intense light, and squeezed them shut again. Cool air swirled over my stomach. Water lapped at my knees.

I opened my eyes again, slowly this time. Pain sickened me—but I could see.

My lower legs were floating in deep water; my back was propped on the edge of the pool. On my right side, close to the surface but fully submerged, was a face.

It had unfamiliar, slightly surreal features. Another smash from the ram of pain hit me, but I focused through it. Dark hair swirled with the movement of the water. Sharp eyes gazed into mine. The lines of the mouth and chin were angular. Shock flitted across the stranger's face, then smoothed again. ... His gaze intensified. Measuring something; my reaction?

After the next wave of pain faded, my mind caught what my eyes had already seen. The face was breathing underwater.

What? The thought confused my already foggy head.

Another hammering jolt of pain. That's when my ears began to work again and registered the shouting, screaming. When the yelling started, the face slid out of my vision and was gone.

More clamouring voices. Pressure on my shoulders and arms.

I couldn't shove against the battering ram anymore. I let it smash through.

-CHAPTER TWO-
Hallucinations

I opened my eyes to stark whites and pale pastels. I blinked at the harsh light. Everything came into focus and I realized where I was.

A hospital room.

My breathing accelerated.

My mind reeled and my heart raced.

The monitors attached to me with various cords beeped wildly. A nurse rushed in.

"Valerie? Valerie, calm down," she cried.

"No, no! I can't be here. Send me home. The wall's breaking—please. *Please.*" A flood of images overwhelmed me. That corner was locked. There was a wall!

"I need some help in here!" The nurse reached for me and tried to grab my flailing hands. Other figures pressed into my field of vision, but they didn't matter.

I curled up in defence and continued to thrash, trying to block the images. I dimly registered increasing pain in my head, but that was nothing compared to what I knew was coming. "Knock me out, use a sedative, do whatever it takes!" I knew I was hysterical. I didn't care.

"I'm sorry, Valerie, we can't do that. You've had a concussion. It's going to be okay, though. You're all right. You're all right." Her attempts to soothe me did nothing. She grasped my wrists tighter. More figures appeared. I didn't see them for long.

The horrible memories blocked out everything.

"I can't take it! No more. Please!" A wordless scream erupted in my head—one long screech of horror. Grandpa Leroy strapped to a stretcher being taken away.

Flash.

My sister Meredith laid out in a blue dress she hated, lifeless.

Flash.

Mother stiff as ice.

Flash.

Father pale as paper, his always-there smile gone.

Flash.

Theo's small, barely fifteen-year-old frame hooked up to dozens of machines.

My mental screeching ratcheted up to a frenzied pitch, but I don't know if any of my screams reached my mouth.

Theo. Oh, Theo!

Hot tears streamed down my face. My mind climbed, crawled, and clawed away from those images. I fought with all my might to force the scenes away, to lock them up again. To rebuild the wall. As the bricks slipped back into place, my screams faltered. *So they had reached my mouth.*

"Please, let me sleep ..." I had nothing left in me. I was spent.

"Valerie."

I turned my head the smallest of inches. I had no energy, but I knew that voice.

"What's my middle name?" Heather said. She was at the foot of my bed, gazing at me intensely. A rush of joy went through me. She was here when I needed her.

I sifted through my muddled brain, knowing I had to come up with the right answer in order to save myself from this nightmare.

"Eliza."

"And when are the Junior Provincial Championships this year?"

This one was easier.

"June third to the tenth."

"Her brain seems fine. Can you give her something to let her sleep?"

Heather knew and understood ...

Thank you, Heather.

"I'm her older brother and legal guardian. Go ahead and give her something." Josh's voice was clipped.

Josh is here? Of course he would come now, *after I hadn't seen him in months. How'd he, the obsessive almost-doctor, manage to leave his precious surgical practicum?*

Movement fluttered near the crook of my arm and then something new pumped through my bloodstream. I trusted it and hurried into the dark.

Days later I was leaning against the bricks that made up the outer wall of the hospital.

Through the sliding glass doors I saw one of the *doctors*—my mind cringed at the word, but I couldn't stop it from traipsing across my brain—speaking with Jocelyn and Andrew, my aunt and uncle. My six cousins were standing close around them, the younger ones clutching to pant legs and hands. Josh had left again right away—no surprise—and passed off helping with my recovery to my aunt and uncle.

I glanced at the—*cringe*—doctor again. He seemed to be describing something using his hands. I shuddered and looked away. I didn't want to know what he was going on about. I'd been poked, prodded, and x-rayed. I'd had enough.

I'm outside. I'm fine, I thought fiercely. I forced my gaze up and away from the doctor's flapping hands and my aunt's worried face. Clouds obscured the mountainous hills surrounding the three-armed valley that was Kamloops. With three major highways traversing it, three rivers running through it, and only four bridges crossing those rivers, it was a strange, stretched, conglomeration of a city. A mix of pine and leafy trees mottled the hills amidst a ton of desert-like grasses and plants I couldn't name. Years ago a film crew came to shoot scenes for a chick flick involving pants. They used our climate and scenery to replicate Mexico, and even incorporated some local girls as extras to play soccer.

I sighed and looked back at my cousins. Lisa had on the soccer jersey she rarely took off. A wave of guilt washed through me. Jocelyn had trundled all my cousins into the van so she could pick me up today and learn how to help me take care of my injury, and all I could do was sulk. It was a surprise to see Andrew here, too. I guess he occasionally felt some responsibility. I shifted away from the wall, irritated at myself and the entire situation. My head throbbed incessantly, a harsh reminder that even though I was loaded up on medication, a concussion was nothing to sneer at.

The lifeguards still didn't know how the toy wooden boat I'd hit had ended up in the deep end of the pool. It didn't really matter now. The outcome was all that mattered.

I can't dive.

The thought struck me again. Just as potent and horrifying to me now as it was when they'd first told me. If only I hadn't gone to the pool. If only I'd not taken that dive from that platform. If. If. If. My life wasn't going to be the same. Even if I was allowed to dive again, somewhere in the shadowy future, I had no idea how my injury would affect my ability. They couldn't even say if I'd be well in time to go to Provincials, which made my goal of the Olympic trials a hazy possibility instead of the bright light I wanted it to be. If diving was lost to me forever I didn't know what I'd do ...

But you're not dead. The fact popped into my head the way it always did when my pity party got too rowdy. And it was true. I could've died, but someone saved me.

There'd been a face ... and it wasn't just my imagination or the head injury talking. I was sure of it. It was either some guy who could hold his breath for an absurd amount of time, or I didn't know what ...

A hand touched my shoulder. "Andrew's getting the van, Valerie."

I jumped. I'd been so caught up in my thoughts I hadn't even heard Jocelyn come up behind me. My hand flew to my temple. The quick movement sent another sharp pang through my head.

"Oh, I'm sorry. I didn't mean to startle you. Is there anything particular you'd like for dinner tonight?" Jocelyn asked.

I shook my head. *Ow.*

"That's all right. How about some nice chicken noodle? Not too much for you?"

I shrugged. They were going to too much trouble on my account.

"Oh, there's Andrew now. Everybody in! Valerie, go ahead and have the front, then you can use the headrest."

"Thanks." I would definitely not refuse anything that helped my sore head.

I leaned gratefully against the seat, and worked to tune out my cousins' banter in the back. Moments later I heard nothing at all.

The next few days passed in a blur. I spent most of my time sleeping, and I had trouble remembering what I did when I was awake. I was subsisting and surviving, but my conscious mind was dormant. Whether that was to facilitate faster healing, or my brain's way of avoiding the alarming reality of where my diving career now stood, I didn't allow myself to contemplate.

Five days later, I was forced to go back to school. I had a spare block first thing. Normally I would've gone to the pool, but now what? I plopped myself in a back corner of the library, plugged headphones into my ears, and watched episodes of some random British drama on my laptop. Time passed too slowly. My spare came and went. Even in the next class, as I listened to the animated drivel of my English teacher, it was much too slow. Lunch was torture. My aunt wouldn't let me drive with the concussion, so I was trapped at the school like all the puny grade nines and tens. I so missed my pretty yellow Honda Civic I'd named Felicity, but I was in no mood to beg a ride off Zack or Heather just to escape.

I dug through a couple of extra swimsuits and spare towels stashed in my locker, forcing myself not to think about my now questionable shot at the Olympic trials. Beneath a few books on diving technique, I found a manicure bag. I chose an eggplant-purple nail polish from the multitude of bright bottles stashed in it, and slipped some polish remover pads, a topcoat, and a nail file into my jeans pocket. My eyes landed on some DVDs in the front pocket of my bag. I'd rented a ton while healing. Renting DVDs was a dying business, but I had to do something now that the pool was lost to me. Nail polish would only fill up my brain so much, so movies it was. I could've watched Internet shows again, but I was only so patient and streaming at school took forever.

I plunked onto a bench with my laptop in a corner of the Art hallway, my sandwich and a bottle of water balanced beside me. I blasted the volume of the first movie through my headphones and concentrated on making even lines with my polish brush. Being this close to the Art room was bittersweet. I used to spend a lot of time there, but now the only brush I would hold was for nails. It was unseasonably warm for early April. The single breeze came from the opening and closing of the door at the far end of the hallway, and bright sun poured through the east-facing windows. For most sane students, it was way too hot a spot to spend the lunch hour. However, when it came to heat, I wasn't most students. I liked the feeling that my brain was melting, that my body was close to overheating, and that all thought was slowing.

Zack found me near the end of lunch. Putting the polish brush back in the bottle, I waited for him to say something. I definitely wasn't going to start the conversation after what he'd brought up the last time I'd seen him. "Look, I'm sorry about how things went down at the pool," Zack said.

"Yeah, well, I felt ambushed. I hadn't seen you guys for ages and that's the first thing you want to talk about? Seriously?"

"I get how you feel." Zack huffed, his face conflicted. "I miss talking to you though—and I wanna say I'm sorry about your accident."

"Thanks." I nodded, and then grimaced at the movement.

"How's the head?"

"Sore—but I need less pain medication now, so that's good at least. I still have no idea if my shot at Provincials is screwed or not, though."

"Yeah, but Provincials are every year. It's not like you can't go again."

"Except Worlds are this year and if I qualify for Worlds and do well, I have a shot at the Olympic trials."

"The Olympics are really that important to you?"

"Of course. Diving's all I have."

"Not true and you know it." Zack glared. "You've got Heather. You've got me. Even if we fight all the time, you're one of my best friends and that's not gonna change."

I could see the sincerity in his face, and maybe it was the pain meds but my eyes were teary. "Thanks. I know I've got the two of you. But right now I've gotta focus on healing, so I can get back to my diving like *now*."

"Anything I can do to help?" he asked.

"Not really. I'm just going to go back to my movie, 'kay?"

"Sure," Zack said.

I watched him stride away, tall and confident, and turned back to the blare of Hollywood in my ears and the polish brush in my hand.

Zack turned the corner, using all his willpower to keep from slamming his fist into a locker. The metal would not be kind. He kicked out a foot instead, sending a garbage can skittering across the hall. Bad idea. He groaned and reached down to pick up the papers and Coke cup that had spilled. He glared at some minuscule grade ten who was staring, until the kid squeaked and ran away.

He'd just righted the can when a voice called, "Hey, Zack."

"What?" he snapped, and turned to see a thinnish guy with dark hair. Greg reeled back in surprise. "Sorry," Zack said. "Bad day. Bad year, really. You need help in math or something?" They had Calc together, but were definitely not on speaking terms.

"I, uh ..." Greg cleared his throat. "Are you cool if I ask your friend out? You're not an item or anything?"

Zack sucked in a long breath through his nose, then cursed, glaring. No way was he letting some punk kid ask Valerie out. He was still waiting for her to heal to make his own move. "What?"

Greg shifted and stared at some point on the wall over Zack's shoulder. "Uh, yeah, well, I know you and Heather are always together, but someone said you were just friends, so I"—he dared a glance at Zack's face—"thought I'd ask?"

Heather. Not Valerie. Zack's breath escaped in a grateful sigh. "Yeah, no prob. We're not a thing."

Greg's face was transformed by relieved disbelief. "Great!"

He started to scurry off.

"Oh, and Greg?"

"Yeah?" He looked back.

"Break her heart? Mess with her at all? My fist meets your face."

Greg paled, but Zack hardly noticed. His mind turned to his own romance troubles.

He had to get Valerie back to herself, but how?

The next morning I jerked awake, too early, to the loud ring of my cell. Coach Chase's voice buzzed in my ear, just like old times. "The local newspaper wants to interview you."

My mouth dropped open in surprise, and I resisted the urge to groan as Chase gave me the details. They'd heard about my accident, wanted to know how serious my condition was and whether I'd be competing in Provincials.

After scribbling down the particulars on the back of old math homework on my desk, I asked, "How much will they be asking about my injury?"

"I'm not sure," Chase hedged. "We can talk it through tomorrow. I hope you'll do it though. The team needs the publicity. Make sure you get lots of rest."

As Chase hung up with a click, I stretched long from my toes to my fingers. Press was always good, especially with Worlds and Provincials just around the corner, but I so didn't want to talk about the fact that I might not be competing. All the same, I'd look a lot better if my eyes didn't have bags under them.

"Coach Greene, how will it hurt your chances if Valerie is unable to compete as a member of your team at Provincials this year?" a low female voice asked.

"Well, Valerie is definitely one of our star divers and we're sorry there's a possibility she won't be competing—but she'll still be an asset to the team. She'll keep training as though she will be competing."

The interviewer was a local journalist named Poppy Snodgrass. I recognized her halo of curly orange hair. A memory from when I last saw her blasted my mind. *No. Stop.* I jerked my mind back to what she was saying.

"There's a possibility you won't be competing in Provincials—but you were the favourite to win this year after getting second place the past four years to your rival, a girl who has since moved up from the Junior Division. Are you still considering the possibility of training for the world qualifiers, and how do you feel about the entire situation?"

I so wanted to snort, but restrained myself. Chase wouldn't want me to be rude, but really? *How did I feel?* I felt like my feet had been cut out from under me. I was only a few key competitions away from the Olympic team and a chance at the podium, but if I didn't make Provincials my timing would be shot and I'd be another four years away from representing Canada. Not to mention the fact it felt like a train had smashed into my skull over and over again. Of all the ridiculous questions!

"Diving was—and is—a very important, very large part of my life. I still plan to train with Chase's help—"

"You mean Coach Greene, of course?"

"Well, yeah. His first name's Chase, so a lot of us call him that. But with his help, I'll keep working towards my goals for both Worlds and beyond." There, that didn't sound too angry or bitter.

The rest of the interview passed in much the same fashion. I answered Poppy's questions with some coherency, but it was hard to concentrate. The next morning would be my first time at the pool since the accident. Chase said I had to wait at least another week before doing any dry land training, but I'd already decided to go to practice anyway. My body was primed to wake up by a certain time every morning. I could either be awake and lying in bed at home, or awake and at the pool.

While absentmindedly listening to Poppy, I tried to decide what to do while at practice. I couldn't just sit and watch; it'd be torture. I could study technique books, but maybe I should bring a stack of movies and my laptop? I supposed there was also a third option: tackling the tottering pile of homework mocking me on my desk at home. While Poppy asked Chase a question about diving mechanics, I decided on movies—least amount of thinking.

When the interview concluded and the photographer with Poppy took a picture for their article with a click, I felt a sigh go through my body. I hoped I wouldn't be a news item for long.

That night I struggled to keep my pain from showing on my face as my ears were assaulted with the racket of dinner with my aunt and six cousins, aged one to eleven. I didn't have to eat with them, but I usually did. It was a delicate balance that I strove for—allowing enough noise into my head to keep it occupied, but not enough to drive me to insanity.

Splat. A glob of spinach and spit landed on my cheek—a projectile flung from eighteen-month-old Tristan's spoon.

"Oh, I'm so sorry! Here." My aunt fumbled as she managed to extract a napkin from the mess on the table and passed it to me.

"It's fine." I wiped the gluey mass from my face.

My aunt's eyes flitted to the clock again, as they had every few minutes since dinner began. My uncle was late. He was an associate chiropractor in an office with two others, and obviously his patients had run long today, but it didn't stop my aunt from fretting. I just didn't get her overt need to worry when her husband wasn't exactly on time. His lateness, however, made the ordeal of feeding the MacPherson clan impossible. Even as I put the napkin in the trash, I heard the unmistakable crash and splash of a glass being knocked over.

My aunt mopped up the juice, and I went and helped Britney take off her soaked shirt. It was no longer bright orange but a revolting brown thanks to the fluorescent green of tonight's Kool-Aid. I dropped the drenched shirt in a hamper at the foot of the stairs and glanced out the window. A car pulled into the drive. I flopped into my chair back at the table.

"Andrew's home," I said.

The rounding chorus of "Daddy!" reverberated off the walls and slammed into my head.

As Andrew came into the house, he gave my aunt a kiss on the lips, then herded my cousins back to their seats. He made a funny face at Tristan, who immediately stopped his wailing. The baby had been none too happy at being left in his high chair while everyone else rushed to greet Andrew. I studiously focused on not making eye contact.

"How was everyone's day?" Andrew asked, sidestepping as Britney raced back to the table in a clean shirt.

"I went on a field trip to the museum—" Lisa said.

Michael interrupted. "That's not interesting! My teacher told us all about chrysalis-es, and she's going to bring three caterpillars into class tomorrow so we can watch them become butterflies."

"My turn! My turn!" Britney bounced up and down in her seat. I put a hand to my head. They were all so loud.

"No! Wait until I tell Dad about my day," Sasha said.

"Don't be babies. Dad can't listen to everybody," Justin, the oldest, said.

I rubbed circles into my temples. It wouldn't be good if I snapped at one of the hellions, but little Tristan decided it wasn't loud enough.

"Dad! Dad! Dad!" He punctuated each word by slamming both hands onto his high chair tray.

I stood up, my chair shoving back across the floor.

"May I be excused?" I directed the question to my aunt. "I have a headache and just want to sleep."

"Sure, whatever you need," she said.

She gave me a small smile on my way towards the stairs. I tried to return one, but failed. Everyone probably saw through my forced conversation and mechanical responses, but that's the way it was. Diving wasn't even a refuge anymore, and the past was forever intruding. I didn't know how to act. Not since—

You idiot! Focus. Keep your thoughts tight. Don't think about it.

I trudged up the stairs to my waiting bed.

The next day, backpack slung over my shoulder and laptop in hand, I walked into the pool in my street clothes. *It was so wrong—and awkward.*

Jocelyn had dropped me off. I refrained from thumping my head on the window in protest as we listened to five different Johnny Cash songs on the way. All I could think about was how my usual morning songs sounded. How a loud beat would start pounding when I hit the bridge. How one song shifted from loud to soft and then back again as I turned a corner at the top of the hill. This guy was so messing with my diving mojo!

Resigning myself to the self-induced horror that would be attending a practice but not participating, I slumped over to the canteen area. Plopping my stuff on the seat of a chair, I dragged it with a loud screech to the edge of the Olympic-sized pool. I probably wasn't allowed to, but I didn't really care. I ignored the water and the athletes at the far end and ripped open my bag, pulling out a random movie. I was only about ten minutes in when the sounds of practice began to intrude. I struggled to shut out the echoing sounds. Did I want to watch? Would I be able to just sit by and observe when I couldn't participate? A part of me wondered how much it would hurt to do so.

To heck with it. I glanced up to see who was on the board. It was one of the twins, Leah or Maya. I followed her rotations, waiting to see how she finished. A dark shape was directly beneath her. *Oh, no.* Would she hit it and injure herself like I had? "Watch out!" I screamed, jumping out of my chair, clutching the laptop to my chest.

All heads turned to look at me as the twin entered the water, her hands splicing it cleanly, her form perfect—and uninterrupted.

That didn't make sense. Something had been there; I'd seen it. I scanned back and forth across the water, searching. I stared and stared, but no matter how hard I looked, the water under the diving boards remained blue and clear.

"Watch out for what, Valerie?" Chase said.

I tore my eyes from the water and looked at the coach. He looked confused and then concerned. His gaze shifted to the water just as a head broke the surface.

"How'd I do, Coach?"

The question fell over me as I sank down into my chair.

"You'll have to go again, Maya, sorry. I didn't see you finish."

I blocked out the rest of what Chase said. Was I hallucinating? Had my head injury been serious enough for me to start seeing things?

I looked towards the diving boards again, but as I focused on Chase and my teammates, my brain registered what my eyes had passed over. I glanced back at the centre of the pool. The shape I'd seen was closer to me now, past the bulkhead, about halfway down the lane. I stared and stared.

It was impossible.

NO!

I slammed my eyes shut and took a slow, deep breath.

You're hallucinating.

Count to five and it will be gone. Another deep breath.

One.

Two.

Three. Another deep breath.

Four.

Five.

I slowly opened my eyes. It was still there!

I whipped around and threw my things into my backpack. *Don't look back.* I hurried through the lobby until the pool was out of sight. I stood outside, leaning against the rough wall with my eyes closed. *Your head's still injured, that's all. Nothing to worry about. You're not going crazy.*

A car pulled up to the entrance, but I didn't open my eyes.

"Valerie? Are you all right?" I recognised Heather's voice, and my eyes popped open. Heather's ten-year-old green beater sat idling at the curb. She was out, running towards me. Zack was halfway out of the front seat, with the passenger door open.

"We stopped by your place to see how you were. Your aunt said you were here. Are you sure this was a good idea?" Heather asked.

"I'm fine."

"Liar." Zack's eyes searched my face.

"Hmpf." Heather's face said my lie was as clear as pool water and she saw right through it. "Come on! We're getting you out of here. You're paler than when I made Zack up as the ghost Jacob Marley in our grade six *A Christmas Carol* play."

I climbed into the back seat, careful not to think about what just happened, what I'd seen.

"Should we not go to school? I can skip Bio. I'm ahead anyway," Heather said.

"Yeah, I can blow off Bio. Who needs it?" Zack chimed in, turning to watch me.

"Seriously. Are you okay?" Heather's eyebrow rose in the rear-view mirror.

"I don't know yet. Just talk and fill up my head."

They both obliged. Heather babbled about her little brother Jesse's latest escapade on his dirt bike and the subsequent punishment. Zack told me about his excursion into the mountains and all the biking he'd done in the last couple weeks. I let their conversation wash over me and tried to relax.

One question broke through to me after a number of minutes.

"How can we help?" Heather asked. "Are we skipping with you? You've got a spare. Is there somewhere besides school you want to be?"

"Mac Park," I replied, after a moment's hesitation. "And I think I want to be alone. Thanks for the offer to skip, though."

"You got it. You'd do the same for me," Heather said, and then more of her chatter calmed me as the streets blurred past my window.

When we pulled into the park, Zack's face had a serious cast. "Don't forget that we're your best friends, Val. We're here for you." His eyes narrowed. "But you really need to—"

"Git yer butt outta my car 'fore ya make us late," Heather finished for him.

I raised an eyebrow and she laughed. "I'm practising my Southern. We're doing improv in Drama today and I feel like trying out a New Orleans big mama caricature who loves cooking greens and fried chicken."

I shook my head. Only Heather.

"Will you need me to pick you up later? Are you coming to school at all today?" Heather asked as I got out of her car.

"Don't worry about it. I'll walk to school or take the bus back to my aunt's if I don't go. Thanks for the ride. I'll catch you guys later."

"Yeah, no worries."

"Take care of yourself," Zack said, and then his mouth pressed into a thin line. He opened it again and started to say something else—and his window abruptly rolled up.

I caught the end of Heather's laugh before the window

closed and they pulled away.

I started to walk and tried to lose myself in the park's rich greens and bright colours. I headed towards the river, breathing the sweet floral air deep into my lungs, then stopped and plopped down on a small patch of grass across from the rose garden. The smell of the roses wafted over me, and some of the tension released from my muscles.

I pulled my laptop out, and then realized the grass was still dewy. Ugh. I rummaged for one of the towels I always had in my bag. That'd solve this "being wet when not in the pool" problem.

I finally found a scrunched up towel beneath the movies I'd rented and a pair of blue jeans. While the first movie was loading, I tried very hard not to think about what I'd seen at the pool.

Once the loud sound blared in my ears I felt marginally better. But after only a few scenes, the screen in front of me shifted out of focus.

And that's when *he* appeared. The underwater guy.

Why? Why was this happening to me? Did I actually see him? Or was my brain putting images in front of me that weren't there? He had scales! He *had* to be a hallucination. Okay. Two options: I could go back to the pool and determine whether or not I was crazy; or I could go back to my aunt and uncle's, hope my aunt would be cool with me skipping, and try to dislodge the images from my head. Neither option was appealing. I didn't want to confirm the fact that I was insane, but I also didn't feel like returning to my aunt and uncle's house.

Was there a third option?

A thought struck me. *Joshua.* Under the circumstances he was probably the best I could do. He'd tell me what I wanted to know. If he got too pushy or nosy I'd hang up. I yanked my cell out of my bag and searched through my contacts for the unfamiliar number.

It rang once, twice, three times. ... My hand itched to end the call.

Maybe this wasn't such a good idea after all.

"Hello?" Joshua sounded groggy, thick with sleep.

It wasn't that early, was it? Curses. Why on earth was he still asleep?

"Why aren't you up yet?" My voice was clipped and irritated. I pursed my lips, unsure. I couldn't afford to have him hang up on me, at least not until I got my answers.

"I worked late last night. ... Who is—wait a minute ... Valerie? What's wrong? Are you okay?" In the two seconds it took him to recognize my voice, I realized the assumption he'd jump to, especially considering my recent mishap at the pool. I concentrated on making my voice smooth and calm.

"Yeah—except I was just doing some research on the Internet about concussions, and there seems to be contradictory evidence about whether or not they can cause hallucinations." The lie came more easily than expected, probably because it was something I actually might've done. "What do you think?" *Open-ended question—that'll give me more info.*

"Well, I never saw your medical file, so I can't give you an informed opinion about your case. But in general, as concussions go, I would say no. Only if it had been a much more serious brain injury—but you wouldn't have been released so quickly if that were the case."

So quickly? Yeah, right. Three freaking days.

"So it wouldn't happen to people with more minor injuries?" It was getting harder to keep my voice neutral.

"I would say no, not that I know of, at least. But why do you need to know? Are you experiencing hallucinations?"

He was sounding more concerned by the minute. Good grief. It wasn't like he'd tried to be involved in my life. Even during this last year when most people would've tried harder, not Joshua. All he lived for was medical school.

Tell him or not tell him?

"Yeah, I am. And it's totally freaking me out. I saw a merman in the pool."

"A *merman*? Like a guy mermaid? You need to see someone. Immediately. How's your pain? I should've asked you days ago. But I've just been so busy."

"My head's all right. The pain sucks, but it's bearable. I'm *fine*." I didn't care if I started to see leprechauns and prancing unicorns. I wouldn't go back *there* of my own accord.

"If you're seeing things that aren't there, you're definitely *not* fine. Get an X-ray at the very least. You have to take care of yourself. You can't ignore warning signs."

"Yeah, yeah. Stop nagging me. Just because you're my brother, doesn't mean I won't hang up on you—" The phone was already away from my ear ...

"No, wait!"

I stopped.

"Just tell me how you really are. I was going to call soon anyways."

"I'm bored out of my mind, so bored I'm considering taking

up knitting actually. Jocelyn won't let me drive, which is irritating and incredibly stupid—and makes the fact that Heather's brother Jesse is going to help me put new wipers on my car next week totally pointless ..."

Even as I relayed all the mediocre details of my life to Joshua, I couldn't come to grips with what was happening. I shouldn't be seeing impossible things. My mind wasn't cracking. It was already broken. There was only one conclusion. I was going insane. *Straitjacket, here I come.*

And there was nothing I could do to stop it.

Perfect.

-CHAPTER THREE-
Acceptance

Eventually I told Josh I had to go. I couldn't keep up the small talk, not with something else taking up so much space in my head.

When I got to my aunt and uncle's house, it was strangely quiet, with only two of my cousins home. After a short explanation to Jocelyn, I went up to my bedroom and popped a romantic comedy into my laptop. I tried to relax and doze off, but every time my eyes closed, the man with a tail filled my head. The afternoon stretched slowly on.

As the rest of the children arrived home, the noise level increased exponentially downstairs, but I was grateful rather than irritated. They got me out of my head at least. The night was uneventful (other than two spills: milk and pot roast gravy) until Uncle Andrew asked me how school was.

"Oh, Valerie stayed home today," my aunt cut in, before I could say anything. "She wasn't feeling up to it and I told her that was fine."

Andrew's eyes narrowed and I had to work not to glare at him.

"She went to the pool early this morning, didn't she? So she should've gone to school." He turned to me. "If you're well enough for the pool, you're well enough to park your butt in class, understood?"

Of all the arrogant, presumptuous ...

"I've got a head injury and wasn't feeling well. Plus, Jocelyn said it was fine, so give me a break."

"If you're under my roof and not deathly ill, you go to school. You've got six cousins who watch everything you do. I expect you to do as I say, when I say it."

"Hell no!" I shouted—then glanced at my cousins and lowered my volume. "Who are you to contradict what Jocelyn says is fine? I'm only living here so I can graduate as a Bronco with my friends. You're not in charge of me. I live here, that's it. You never cared about my crap before, so get off it."

"You will watch your language. And you will do as you're told while you're here. I won't tolerate any—"

"Leave me alone!" I whirled and sprinted up the stairs, ignoring Andrew's protests. Flipping the sign on my doorknob to its Do Not Disturb side, I slammed the door and locked it behind me. That sign was close to sacred, my one and only condition upon moving in: no one was allowed to bother me, ever, when I had it up.

I picked up a random DVD from the floor and chucked it across the room. The plastic case hit the closet door with a *thwap* and ricocheted into my stereo. Of course Andrew wouldn't understand, and he'd be his regular dictatorial self. I threw myself onto my bed, snatched up my pillow and scrunched it against my mouth. I screamed loud and long into the fabric. Screaming wasn't enough, however, and I threw punch after punch into my bedding. I punched until my arms were tired and my lungs burned. Then I shoved in the closest action movie I could find and slammed off my light. Three mindless, zero-plot action movies later, when the last scene faded into credits with a ridiculous amount of stuntmen, I finally hit the power button and closed my eyes.

Sleep, however, wouldn't come. *He* appeared again. The many distractions of my cousins weren't enough. Fighting with my uncle wasn't enough. Three action movies weren't enough. He wouldn't leave me alone. His image kept chafing my mind, like a bad swimsuit. I flipped my pillow over and shifted my blankets. Despite all the practise I had at blocking images, I sucked at it now. I could have been underwater for how often the blue of the pool swam in front of my eyes. But I wouldn't acknowledge him. I struggled to keep the details at bay. A flash of dark blue scales. A long and powerful tail. I shook my head, refusing to let his image solidify and take shape. His reality meant my insanity.

If I was going insane, however, and this was it—well, maybe it wasn't so bad. I kept thinking about the same image over and over and over again; so what? What was the definition of insane? Did I fit the bill? I wasn't having any other hallucinations. At least, I didn't think I was. Everything else I saw seemed to be real. When I glanced around my room I didn't see goblins dancing in my mess of DVDs and clothes.

Why would I only get one hallucination? Was that normal?

The bright blue glow of my clock read four thirty.

I blinked a few times—my eyes were gritty—and rubbed my temples. Could I rub the image out? Not likely.

I rolled out of bed, slumped over to the window and splayed

my hand on the glass in the middle of the ink-black sky. The coolness of the pane seeped through my fingers. I stepped closer and looked down at the street. The moonlight made strange shadows on the cars and pavement as it mixed with the streetlights. The houses were lined up straight and uniform, like the curved backs of racers on diving blocks.

I sighed and touched my forehead to the chilled glass. The street scene dimmed, a haze of bright blue water formed in front of it—and *he* swam into view. Rich brown eyes, intense in their scrutiny, set in a face surrounded by dark hair. A lean torso, a shimmering tail of the brightest blue I'd ever seen.

My eyes closed against his image. Think about this logically, I instructed myself. *Think objectively.*

First: I had been injured. This injury, supposedly, didn't have hallucinations as a side effect.

Second: my body and mind were both extremely stressed. Stress of any kind, pushed too far, could cause problems.

Third: I could be experiencing a type of withdrawal. I had been diving for years. Maybe I had become dependent on it for emotional release.

Fourth: I had only seen one thing I labelled as a hallucination.

Fifth: *I* was the one who classified what I'd witnessed as a hallucination.

Was that the key? If I was truly hallucinating, would I *know* what I was seeing wasn't real?

I seemed to. I knew the merman wasn't real. Couldn't be real. Even as my brain had shoved his image at me, another separate part of my consciousness recognized it for what it was: imaginary. I sank to the floor, relieved tears wetting my cheeks.

I was sane. My mind was my own. I could still think logically. I was fine.

I got up from the floor, knowing I'd be able to sleep now. There was a rational reason for what I'd seen. He was either a twisted memory of some guy who'd saved me—or a stress-induced vision, my subconscious mind's way of scaring me so I'd stay away from the pool where I'd been injured. Well, I didn't need protection. I would dive again, and I was not going to let my fear control me.

I'd go to the pool tomorrow.

Saturday morning dawned—overcast and pouring. Gross. Water belonged in a pool. Water was wonderful in a pool: beautiful, clear, and still. Water *should not* fall from the sky, dirty and slimy, making the world dreary and grey.

Maybe it was an omen, a bad omen. Stinking precipitation. Why didn't it go to the coast where it always was? Or east to Alberta to feed farmers' crops? Rain turned the hills around Kamloops into a lush green everyone loved, but they'd be back to their usual brownish olive in less than a week, so why endure it at all? If we got enough small rainfalls during the night to keep the fruit trees thriving, so I could munch on apples in the fall, I'd be satisfied.

The bus I rode swished through the layer of water on the roads, its windshield wipers on full blast. I leaned back and closed my eyes, adjusting to the rocking motion. Not good enough. I shifted my weight and fiddled with my puzzle ring, taking it apart and putting it back together as I rode. It had been a gift from a trip to Europe that Mom ...

Stop.

Eyes closed. I wiped my mind blank.

Three breaths.

One.

Two.

Three.

I looked back down at my hands and focused on the puzzle again: six thin loops of metal that interwove and locked in one specific way to make a single ring. My fingers knew the trick well, and only a few solved puzzles later we were turning into the pool. The bus stopped near the entrance, and I bolted through the slick, disgusting sludge falling on my head. I shook off the excess water inside the doors, slung my bag over my shoulder, then hesitated.

Could I really handle this? What would I do if *he* appeared again?

What if he was *real*?

I strode to the large glass doors and windows that overlooked the pools, careful to look only at the children's area, with its bright colours and fun slides. A mother and two young boys played with a foam mat. Two older girls and three boys threw a ball around, trying to sink it in a basket. It was odd to see with no sound. A little girl with water wings sped down one of the waterslides, looking scared. Her father caught her with a big splash, and a wide smile spread across her face.

The smell of chlorine and chemicals was heavy in the air. As the scent settled around me I knew I was right, that this was right. I was ... I searched for the perfect word ... real. It didn't matter if everything went wrong and I ended up in a psych ward. This was *home*. I took a deep breath, exhaled it slowly, and closed my eyes. Then I turned swiftly and walked straight for the changing rooms before I lost my nerve. I flashed my pass at the women behind the counter and focused on continuing to put one foot in front of the other.

I had no idea whether I was allowed to go in the water and swim yet. I also knew, however, that I couldn't just sit beside the pool today. I had to do something.

In a changing stall, I pulled on my dark blue racing suit. The stall's sickly green paint was familiar, and it was strange yet wonderful to be wearing stretchy, smooth fabric again.

I stepped out into the bright fluorescents, tucked my clothes into my bag, and dug out my brush. I slowly pulled it through my hair, counting strokes as I did. One hundred strokes every day would keep your hair healthy and shiny. A tip I'd gotten from my aunt. I then started meticulously brushing my hair back into a ponytail. Wanting my crown to be perfectly smooth, I redid the entire thing three times—then realized I was stalling. *This is home. This is where you belong. Go!*

I threw my bag in a locker, clicked the lock closed, then had a quick, icy shower. Shivering, I headed towards the pool. At the corner in the passageway, just before the blue water came in sight, I balked. I ducked my head and stared at my feet on the familiar tiles, then veered left and tucked my towel into one of the many cubbyholes. I then made a one hundred and eighty degree turn and moved forward, carefully only looking at what was beneath my feet.

I cautiously took the ten or twelve steps that brought me to the edge of the fifty-metre pool. I'd swim a few laps first, then I'd search the whole pool.

I slid into the shallow end at the far right lane and pulled on my goggles. The sharp snap of the elastic echoed in my head.

As I began to swim the familiar strokes, my limbs fell into a rhythm I knew and loved. My muscles pulled and spliced the water, propelling me smoothly down the lane. I concentrated on swimming well, not fast. I still needed to be careful with my head. I could feel that. After four laps of freestyle I took a break and floated on my back, keeping my eyes on the entrance or the ceiling—anything to avoid scanning the waters beyond me. After a few minutes, I forced myself to do a few more laps. As I was finishing the third, I started preparing myself. I'd look at the entire pool once I was done this lap.

As I neared the bulkhead I flipped onto my stomach, then reached out to grasp its handle like it was a lifeline. My breath hissed in and out as I clung with both hands, my eyes closed. Finally, I opened my eyes and turned to face my fear. I slowly studied each swimming lane and forced my mind to register every person and item I saw. There wasn't anything there! At least, not anything that wasn't supposed to be. There were a few people swimming laps, and some children still playing in the kiddie pool, but the water before me was absolutely clear. I was so tempted to do a victory dance.

Wait. One more place to check. Bracing my hands on the deck, I hefted myself from the water. Shivering slightly, I glanced over at the deep end of the pool. My eyes scanned up and down the blue, searching for something ... that wasn't there. I grinned. All my worry had been for nothing. Now I could swim to my heart's content, or sit in the hot tub and let the water soak away my stress. I snapped my goggles on again and slipped back into the water, ducking beneath the surface. I watched the bubbles and movement in the water from the other swimmers in the shallow end. I specifically watched the empty water beneath them. I released some of the air in my lungs, sinking slowly, continuing to survey the clear blue depths. My eyes hadn't lied to me. I saw nothing. Ah, nothing!

That next instant, however, my world changed forever. Everything I'd known shifted and rolled like a sea tossed by the winds.

He appeared again.

One instant I was looking at clear blue water, the next he was there, floating in front of me as though he'd materialized out of nothing. A mosaic of dark blue scales, a tail twice as long as his torso, wavy dark hair. Small details coming to me even as I refused to see him.

He seemed shocked to see me. Confusion and then concern flashed across his features.

He *was* a merman. ...

I tried to pull in air, but choked. Torrents of bubbles exploded from my mouth. Water slid down my throat, catching as it entered my lungs.

I tore my gaze from his and swam away frantically—but not before I registered the hurt on his face. Kicking hard, I broke the surface, grabbed the wall, and heaved myself out of the water. I ripped my goggles off and practically ran towards the exit.

As I reached for my towel, though, I hesitated. What was I doing? Was I really such a coward? I'd worked so hard to get to this point. But was I actually seeing him or was my brain playing tricks on me again? It took a full three seconds, but I turned back and stared at the water at the far end of the lanes.

No. Not a trick.

My eyes found him in the water. He was staring at me, just as I was staring at him. Even at a distance I felt the power of his eyes. He was real. There was no possible way my brain could've created him. I saw that now.

Could I accept that merpeople existed? Was I ready to redefine all that I'd ever known about the world I lived in?

As I watched, his expression changed to something I couldn't define—respect?

Possibly. He was floating upright in the water, but suddenly he bent forward at the waist and dipped his head. It was a bow. He was bowing—to me. My mind reeled. As forcefully as I had previously not wanted this to be real, I now desperately wanted to know *everything*. Know where he came from and every other detail.

Who was he? How long had he been here? As the reality of what I was seeing—a *merman*, for crying out loud—hit me, my mind lurched. No one else had noticed him. I looked around the pool. Not a single other person was looking at him. If they could see him, they would've gawked. How could you not? Why was I the only one who could see him?

The merman straightened and a small smile appeared on his face. I smiled back, hesitant. I wanted to say hello or something, but logic returned. If I started talking to nothing, they'd send the men in white coats for me. I clenched my nails into my palms, took one last look at him, and turned to leave. My feet were heavy on the tiles. Each step away magnified the ache to turn around and race back. I wanted to ask him questions ... but could he talk? And if yes, would it be English? How could I find out without seeming crazy? *Diving practice.* I welcomed the thought. Practice would be an ideal time. The only other people in the pool would be preoccupied with what they were doing. If I whispered something occasionally, no one would notice.

Questions flowed through my mind as the day passed in a haze of colour and sound. My world had not just shifted; it had wholly changed. That night as I pulled on my cotton shirt and pj pants, I took stock of myself. I was confused and more than a little curious, but I was fine. I was okay and, well, *sane*. My head hit the pillow with finality as questions continued to swirl. Could I deal with my world no longer being what I thought it was? Yes. Yes, I could.

I knew I was dreaming, but I couldn't escape it or wake up. I recognized where I was—a field off one of the city's back roads, a place Theo and I frequented as children, exploring and playing. The sharp smell of grass hit me. The prickles and barbs of weeds caught at my clothes. Halfway down the field there was a flash of blue. My parents' SUV was crossing the field. The sound of another engine reached me before I saw it. The engine that would massacre so many that I loved. The steel-grey car careened towards my family and I was running.

-CHAPTER FOUR-
Greeting

My feet pounded the dirt, but I was too slow. I drew closer and closer, but the car was still too far away. Stumbling in my haste, I saw my mother's face in the passenger window. I saw her realize the car was going to hit them. She shrieked at my father, pointing. My father yanked the steering wheel, his muscles straining. My sister Meredith screamed and turned towards the back of the SUV. The car was a foot away. Theo crossed his arms in front of his face and pulled up his knees.

And then the two machines collided. A sickening metal crunch filled the air, and the side door where my sister sat caved in. A sob tore from my throat and I tripped, sprawling in the dirt and rough grass. I hauled myself up and kept running. I had to reach them. The force of the car propelled the SUV into the air, spinning it end over end. The entire front end was smashed in. I shrieked and shrieked. Hot tears poured down my face. The SUV kept spinning. It crashed towards me. Shards of glass rained down. Metal slammed into my body and face. ...

I thudded onto my mattress, then pushed myself up, gasping. I put a shaking hand to my mouth to quiet myself. My eyes ached with the grittiness of crying. I rocked back and forth as sobs wracked my body, holding my hand over my mouth tighter and tighter. I couldn't wake the house.

Slowly my weeping ebbed. Desperate to stop thinking, I scrabbled for my puzzle ring and started the mindless job of putting the pieces together again. *You're okay. You're okay.* Eventually exhaustion took over and I slept.

The rest of the weekend passed in a blur. I know that I walked and talked and ate—but if I'd been asked to recollect anything I said or did over those two days I would've failed miserably. I was completely preoccupied with my plan to meet the merman and all that would come after.

I started carrying around a notebook to write down questions as they came to me. I rewrote them in order of importance and then according to content, each one leading to more and more.

My mind chugged on. By the end of Saturday I was still coming up with questions and I'd made over a dozen lists. Sunday was worse. My aunt, uncle, and cousins went to church, which meant the house was unnaturally quiet. After what felt like a decade of weekends, it was Monday. I woke fifteen minutes before my alarm. My hands were shaking so badly, it took forever to put my hair in its usual ponytail. I couldn't think about anything other than what would happen once I got to the pool.

It took me three tries—and two near falls—to realize I was trying to put both feet into one leg of my blue jeans. I did, however, manage to pull on my black V-neck tee without mishap. I grabbed my swim bag and got into the car with my aunt. As we pulled away from the house I wasn't really seeing the street in front of us, and the closer we got to our destination the less my thoughts made sense. Questions and thoughts poured across the canvas of my consciousness in such disarray it was like I'd meant to paint a beautiful scene and ended up with an abstract. All my carefully arranged lists from the weekend fled.

I was completely out of my element. The bit of info I'd gotten over the weekend when I googled *merman* had been useless. If it wasn't a story about bloodthirsty sirens, it was sightings of a horrid little creature with a fish face and webbed hands, articles about some chick named Ethel, or info on how to buy a tail so I could swim around like a mermaid.

How did this merman feel, knowing that humans thought of him as nothing more than myth? Or did he even know that? If Heather found out about him she'd be morbidly curious about his anatomy, a veterinarian being her career goal.

Would he have any prejudices against humans? Would he be offended by curiosity? I had no idea what he was capable of. What if he was dangerous? Should I be worried about my safety? No. Other humans swam in the pool all the time and he'd never hurt any of them, so I had to be safe. And he had bowed to me. Did a bow mean the same thing to him that it did in our culture? In this day and age it was a little old-fashioned. It made me think of elegant balls, the London Season, long flowing dresses, titles, and the like. ... Who was he? I had to know.

When we arrived at the pool I barely gave my aunt a cursory goodbye, and it was all I could do not to run into the building.

Twenty seconds after entering the change room, I was walking down the hall to the pool. As I stepped out into the bright lights, I fought to rein in my excitement.

I searched the water. At first I didn't see him—but then a flash of movement drew my eyes. He dropped into the water from under the bulkhead. Ah, it made sense now. That's where he must've been yesterday. And why he'd seemed to appear so suddenly.

"Valerie, what are you doing here in your suit? Have the doctors given you the green light to start training again?" Coach Chase's voice lifted hopefully at the end of his question.

I cringed at his use of the D-word but jumped in before he noticed my reaction. "Ummmm, not yet—but there's no good reason I can't be in the pool. I'm just going to try swimming and see how I do with that."

"I guess I should've expected that. Go ahead. Let me know if you need anything, okay?" Coach Chase said over his shoulder, already turning back towards the deep end.

Watching the team warm up, my heart plummeted and I ripped my mind away from the fact that I still wasn't diving with them. But as my gaze shifted to the lane pool, my thoughts brightened slightly. I wasn't able to dive, but there was something else to keep me occupied.

I had spent so much time thinking about this moment, now that it was here, awkwardness hung between us. What on earth should I do? Should I approach him first? What did his culture dictate? I didn't want to offend him the first time I was brave enough to talk.

He was swimming close to where I was, far down in the shallow end of the lane pool. My senses were on alert, my muscles tense.

He stared at me with what seemed to be a sense of

hopefulness. As his dark eyes bored into mine, I slowly relaxed. If I was making a horrible mistake or some faux pas, surely his face would say so.

Very slowly and deliberately, so that I couldn't miss the gesture, his left hand raised with his first two fingers extended. He touched the top of his forehead and then moved his hand towards me, pointing. He brought his hand back, touched the left side of his chest, and again pointed at me slightly lower. Then his face broke into a beautiful smile.

He seemed to want to know me as much as I wanted to know him. I moved to the edge of the pool, taking a foam noodle from its box as I went. I slipped into the water next to him. Resting on my noodle, I soaked in all the details I'd refused to register the last time I'd seen him. His dark eyes that watched me so intently were wonderful. Intelligent and penetrating, they were the soothing colour of milk chocolate. Hair as black as the lane lines on the pool floor haloed his face. What hue would his hair be if it were dry? His face and jaw were angular and his brow was well defined, with dark eyebrows standing out in contrast to his fair skin. His ears were normal in size but set back slightly.

He was larger than an average human male. My eyes ran over his torso. His well-built muscles were long and lean like what a farm hand or a carpenter would have, as though physical labour was something he'd always done—an integral part of who he was.

He wore large blue-green cuffs of some type of skin around his wrists. Swirling designs had been carved in the skin, and bright white spots were spaced evenly throughout the swirls.

Then my eyes moved down to his defining feature. His tail. A zillion words battled in my head to try and describe it—strong and masculine were the most dominant ones. The tail stretched out long and flowing, twice as long as a human's legs would have been. At the end it split into two very thin membrane-like fins. The shifting hues of his scales were mesmerizing. At one angle the tail was a shining royal blue. In another light it shimmered turquoise. I could have looked at the shimmering colours for hours, but his human-like features drew me in.

His skin had a strange, slightly alluring hint of blue. The tint reminded me of when I bought new blue jeans. Sometimes, even when you washed them before wearing them, the dye from new denim seeped onto your hands. If my hands were like that right now, my skin would be close to his in colour.

But if you took away the blue in his skin he could pass as human from the torso up. Close up, his face was too sharp to be classically handsome, but there was something about it that drew me in—a kindness in his eyes, or a wisdom in the expressions that crossed his face, maybe. ... I sensed there was more to him than I could imagine.

I realized I'd been staring for longer than was polite and glanced down, embarrassed.

"Hello."

My head popped back up at the sound of his soft tenor voice. I was startled to find that even though he was fully submerged in the water I could hear him as clearly as if he were inches away from me. He smiled in encouragement when I hesitated for a split second.

"Hi." Thankfully my voice didn't squeak. I glanced back at the diving end of the pool. No one seemed to be paying attention to me, but better to be safe and only whisper.

"My name is Wyn Erelasai."

My head whipped back around again.

"What is your name?" he asked, smiling again. It lit up his whole face.

"Valerie." I took a deep breath. "Valerie Morgan." I tried to speak without moving my lips, so if someone happened to glance my way I wouldn't look like I was talking to myself.

I blushed and crossed my arms self-consciously as he studied me as intensely as I had just scrutinized him. I averted my gaze and my eyes rested on the cuffs around his wrists again. Each round white spot was the size of my thumbnail, and I felt my eyes widen in surprise. Could they be? I looked back at Wyn's face for confirmation.

He gave a slight nod. "Yes, they are pearls." He paused, then offered more information. "My father farms them, among other things."

"Really? Is your father here with you and I can't see him? Or is he in the ocean? Is that where you're originally from? Why are you in this pool? Why am I the only one who can see you? How long have you been here? Are there lots of merpeople or just you and your family? Should I use the word merpeople? Is there a different word to use? I want to know everything." The words fell out of my mouth so fast that my lips had trouble keeping up with my brain.

He grinned at my enthusiasm, then nodded towards Coach Chase and the others. "We have an audience."

I glanced back and saw Coach watching me, a concerned look crossing his face. I hadn't moved since I first got in the pool. I waved and started kicking down the length of the pool. I'd spoken my rush of questions out loud without thinking. I'd been careless. I'd have to be much more aware from now on.

As I kicked, Wyn swam below me on my left. He was so graceful, so different from what humans classified as beautiful, and yet he *was* beautiful. There was something so natural and elegant about the way he moved. Slow and rhythmic, his body and tail cut through the water as though one with it. I pointed my face towards the water, so my lips wouldn't be visible if Coach Chase happened to look up.

"I have so many questions. I want to learn everything. I don't know anything!" My whisper was soft but excited.

"Not *anything?*" Wyn's voice held a smile, but his gaze shifted and he moved away from me as if he wasn't entirely comfortable.

Hurt ran through me. "Please? Won't you talk to me? I ... well, I hoped ... but no ... If you don't want to, that's okay. I won't bother you again." I turned away from him and kicked towards the side of the pool so I could get out. I held my emotions in check. If tears were going to come (something I'd work hard to prevent), they would *not* come while I was within his sight.

"No, wait, please."

I turned back almost involuntarily.

"We can ... well ... we can talk." He was still looking down but he'd turned his body towards me. His body language made a connection in my brain. He reminded me of a girl from my biology class. She was extremely shy, and I was sure that was what was holding this beautiful merman back too.

He was shy. How hard it must have been to talk to me! Not only was I someone he didn't know, I was *human*. It must've taken as much courage for him to approach me as it took for me to come back to this pool.

I smiled, about to ask another question, when he spoke. "Before another word is said, the importance of our secret must be acknowledged. The human world cannot know about me. Experiments and many other horrors would result if that happened. Humans have the technology to not only find us, but to destroy us. Revealing this secret to anyone must not be done lightly. Only in a case of utmost urgency should the knowledge of our existence be given. The more who know of us, the greater the risk of evil coming after any and all mer. Have I your solemn promise to never reveal my existence to another human, Valerie Morgan?"

"Yes, you have my promise." My voice was sober and truthful. I would protect him.

"Have you my thanks." Wyn gave another small bow beneath the water and then continued. "Know you much am I sure. About myself most likely not. Asked you so many questions before. Want I to answer them, but which to respond to first? Choose you one and will I do my best to explain." He spoke quickly, as if wanting the words out before he lost his nerve. I worked backward through his comments. It was English but some of it was a little off.

Understanding dawned on his face. "Uh, well, want I to talk to you, but English is slightly different where come I from." He took a deep breath, as if to steel himself. "Simply put, the words 'you' and 'I' when used as the subject are always preceded by their corresponding verb. The rules are slightly more complicated than that, but ... I *can* speak the way you do, if you would like me to. It takes concentration, though. It might be close to you trying to constantly speak in an accent that is not your own. But I can do so."

"Oh no, please speak however is most comfortable for you. I'll just flip the verbs in my head." I smiled, encouraged that our conversation was continuing. I wanted him to be comfortable with me. I wanted him to feel like he could talk to me. If it took him time to answer to me, so be it. A shy merman, who would've thought?

"So that last sentence you said, it would have been 'But can I do so' speaking how you usually do. How are you able to tell what are questions and what are statements?"

He grinned. "Inflection."

I nodded and moved on to answering his request. What question did I want him to answer first?

"Is the pool your home? And if not, why are you here?"

"This pool is definitely not my home." I seemed to have hit upon the right question. He *wanted* to talk now. "My home is anywhere there are mer. The whole world of mer is called Lasera."

"La-sare-ah?" My mouth twisted through the new word.

He nodded. "Live I in the Elnias Province. It is much more beautiful and open, with many more colours to appease the eye. As for why am I here, well, am I a prisoner. Am I trapped here. My captors bring me food during the night. It has been a very long time since have I seen my home." His flowing voice grew unbearably sad at the end.

I still had to flip certain words in my head while I listened, but as Wyn's words seeped into my comprehension I yearned to reach out and comfort him. My own home had long since been lost to me.

But even as I considered offering my hand, I knew his shyness would prevent him from accepting it. Instead I tried to speak with feeling. "I'm sorry. Homes should never be taken from anyone." I stopped talking. His hurt was so deep there was nothing else to say. It seemed more appropriate to honour his loss with silence.

"Thank you." Wyn's eyes bored into mine, his gratitude evident. Kinship sparked between us as mutual feelings of shared pain became evident.

"Who are they? Your captors I mean."

"Do not I know. See I their faces, but know I not their names." Wyn's voice was resigned.

I did some more mental word flipping and then frowned at the uninformative answer. I opened my mouth to demand more details. Who could possibly want to keep him here? And for what purpose? What *right* did they have?

But I restrained myself. I didn't know if it was his shyness or just that the topic bothered him too much, but I sensed he wouldn't say more about his captors at the moment. *We're so coming back to this, though.*

Wyn interrupted my thoughts, surprising me with unasked-for information. "Watch I you. Are you very kind-hearted. Many times play you and watch your young cousins while they are here at the pool, so that your aunt can run errands."

"I ... well ... why?" Was I really interesting enough that someone would want to watch my life?

"Make you me curious. Your reactions are very often puzzling. Like I puzzles. Watching is all there is to do. Therefore watch I, day in and day out." He shrugged. "Are you one of the most interesting to watch out of many."

"You know so much about me I feel a little lost, because I know nothing about you. But I do *want* to know you." My cheeks burned. I wanted to get to know him, yes, but I also didn't want to seem desperate.

"Let's hear your next question." His smile said he had noticed my blush, but mortifying as that was, I couldn't bring myself to stop asking questions.

"You spoke of your father. How many merpeople are there? And er ... is that the right term? Mermaid, merman, merpeople? I don't mean to offend you or anything. ... I just don't know what's the right thing to say and what's the wrong thing."

"Understandable. Worry not about the differences in our cultures. We will just take it one step at a time." Wyn flicked his tail and drew closer to me. I smiled inwardly. He wanted to talk as much as I did—and it was even more difficult for him than it was for me.

"As to the correct term ... merpeople is fine, as is mermaid and merman. We use those same words as well, unless we are speaking our native language. Then it is Erna for mermaid and Erda for merman." Wyn's voice was softer and more fluid as he spoke the words from his true language.

"Native language?" With each answer he gave, my curiosity only increased.

"Erian. Our ancient language that goes back further than any memory recorded. Every infant is bilingual almost from birth, or within the first few years at least. The words have I given you for mermaid and merman are the Littera Erian words. There are two kinds of Erian, Littera and Syllaba. Littera is similar to English, but with Syllaba it takes three times as long to say anything. Each letter in English is at least two syllables long in Syllaba Erian, and often longer. E for example is ie-yeu. As a result, many of us alternate between English and

Littera Erian and rarely use Syllaba, except in ceremonies and some proceedings."

"Would you say something in Erian for me?" His voice had sounded so ethereal earlier that I yearned to hear more than a mere two words.

"What would have you me say?"

"*Anything.*"

Wyn's lips curled in amusement at my urgency, but I didn't care. "Lasar aie eneese. Mooneese fras toram."

The phrase flowed like music, with smooth, drawn-out vowels. It was softness put into sound. I couldn't help it. I grinned.

"What did you say?"

"'Watch you waves. Drink in deep.' It is a formal greeting, but can also be an intimate goodbye in my culture."

"What was the hand gesture you made earlier? It seemed similar."

Wyn nodded. "It is another greeting among my people, used mostly when introduced for the first time or when we speak the Farlan greeting. Touching my fingers to my mind and then pointing to your mind symbolizes an effort to understand and learn. Touching my fingers to my heart and then pointing to your heart symbolizes love and to always stay true to what you feel."

"Farlan greeting?"

"The Erian words just spoke I for you."

I thought about that as I turned to do another lap. English didn't really have informal and formal variations. A hundred years ago, there may have been more formality, but not now. It was also intriguing that merpeople had a greeting specifically designed to help you think about how to act. It was completely foreign to me, but fascinating.

I'd lost count of how many laps I'd done, but as I glanced up at the clock I gave a start.

"Practice is almost over." I couldn't believe it. How had so much time passed so quickly? Hopefully practice would go long today.

"Would still like you me to answer your question about how many in number we are?" The softness in Wyn's voice betrayed a desire to continue the conversation longer, possibly as strong as my own yearning to do so.

"Yes, please." My voice was eager, even to my own ears. I couldn't remember the last time I was eager for anything.

"Our population is upward of two million. The Royal Pacific Capital has at least one million and there are many other small communities and other provincial capitals. The community grew I up in was rather small with only approximately five hundred of us."

"*Only?* That's huge! I was thinking a maximum around a hundred. Oh, wow." My mind reeled as I thought about the complexity of so many merpeople. "So do you have a government, then? And a justice system and an economy and police ...?" My voice trailed off. There was just so *much*.

"Yes to all of those questions. We also have currency. In my own community, however, our economy is mostly barter-based. Trading what we have and make ourselves in exchange for other things we need."

"What—?"

Coach Chase's whistle blew. "That's it for today, team. Valerie, that means you too." The sound of my name broke into our conversation.

"Can I see you tomorrow?" I was almost panicked, realizing I only had seconds left with Wyn today.

"Of course. Look I forward to it." He glanced away, suddenly shy again as he expressed his feelings.

"Bye," I said. It seemed like such an anticlimactic word to use, especially when I had so much more to say, but I didn't have the time or words to describe the wonder I felt. Our conversation would be forever etched into my memory.

"Until tomorrow, Miss Morgan." Wyn gave a slight bow of his head. I was about to correct him and tell him I was simply Valerie, when Coach Chase intruded again.

"Valerie! What are you doing?"

-CHAPTER FIVE-
Reasons

I treaded water and looked up into Coach Chase's incredulous face.

"Since when does an athlete of mine just sit around doing nothing?"

Since she's having a conversation with an invisible merman.

"Being in recovery is no excuse. You keep up your strength, understood?" He sounded like a parent scolding a three-year-old, but I brushed off my irritation at his tone and answered civilly.

"Got it, Chase," I said, and pulled myself out of pool. For a fleeting instant I thought I saw Chase's gaze flick towards Wyn, but no, he turned back to the team. I must've imagined it.

I looked back before going into the change rooms and saw Wyn. His form and grace in the water still took my breath away. I couldn't wait to talk to him again.

The rest of my day passed uneventfully and was utterly boring after everything that had happened at the pool. I could not stop thinking about Wyn.

Not that I wanted to *stop* thinking about him. I just wanted time to go by faster, yet dwelling on Wyn's world and all the things I wanted to know slowed the clock's hands to a crawl.

"So you gonna study for the math final when you get home?" Zack asked as we walked out of school and across the parking lot to his Ford 4x4 truck. My aunt was still being ridiculous about me driving, so I was carpooling with Heather and Zack. We'd all been taking Heather's car to and from school, but she had to stay at school today to discuss more college applications with the school counsellor, so Zack had driven.

"Probably," I said. I was resigned to the fact that I still had many hours ahead of me before I could see Wyn again, but at least the lengthy school day was over.

"You wanna come to my place and we'll tackle it together? I'll make sure you're studying the right stuff. It'll be way quieter."

"Nah, I've got other stuff to do too," I said.

"Aw, come on. You know you'll have more fun with me. My mom's in Toronto on some corporate exec retreat and my dad won't be done helping some hothead sue his boss in Vancouver 'til Friday. We'll have the place to ourselves. I'll even throw in some of my famous mac and cheese." Zack's smile was conspiratorial.

"Very tempting, especially when I know how great your cooking skills are—but I have to throw a load of swimsuits in the wash, so I'll have a clean one for tomorrow. Thanks, though."

"A whole load of swimsuits? Wow. Next thing you know, you'll be at the pool during public swim too, going through more swimsuits than I can count." That was it. I didn't have to wait! *Public swim.* The only reason Coach Chase heard me talking to Wyn was because I'd let my guard down and spoken too fast and too loud. I'd be more careful now and no one would be the wiser. There'd be more people present to see me talking to myself, true, but I knew I could be stealthy about it.

"Don't tell me I've given you ideas." Zack's voice was disbelieving.

"I'm sorry, Zack, but I have to go."

"Really? But exams are looming. You're totally gonna procrastinate then need me to help you cram."

"Yeah, well, I need to be at the pool right now. I'll see you later, okay?" I threw the sentence over my shoulder as I turned around.

"Not like I could stop you."

I pretended not to hear Zack's last comment and hurried down the sidewalk to the bus stop. I called Jocelyn and tersely told her where I'd be, still annoyed about not being able to drive, but not wanting her or Zack to drive me either. Getting to the pool myself made Wyn more my secret, my something to know and get to.

After the long, boring bus ride I finally stood in front of the pool doors. I rushed into the change room and pulled on my still-damp suit, shivering at the chill as it snapped onto my skin. Yuck—but Wyn was totally worth the discomfort.

The pool was packed with teenagers, large families, and plenty of moms with screaming toddlers, but my eyes sought only him. When I finally found Wyn near the shallow end of the large pool, I was initially confused. He was floating just below the surface, quite close to two little girls and three small boys. All five kids looked to be around nine or ten; the two girls were on one floating mat, the boys on another. Wyn's expression was serious, and as I moved closer I even sensed some anger.

He was focusing so hard he didn't notice me as I sat on the edge of the pool. There were a number of other people around, swimming and talking, and I had to strain to hear what the kids were saying.

The harsh words of one of the boys carried over to me. He was making fun of one of the girls. It wasn't just the "I like you" type of teasing either. His words were cruel, and I hated the judgmental sneer on his face. He told her she was ugly, that her swimsuit was disgusting, and her mother was a "poor janitor."

"You're a loser." He snickered. "And you'll always be a loser."

The girl started crying and tried to swim away with the help of her friend, who put her arm around her and stuck her tongue out at the boys. As they turned away, I could tell they were valiantly trying to ignore their persecutors. *Good for you, girls!*

"Loser, loser," the ringleader started—and his rotten friends joined in.

"Loser, loser." They started following the girls.

I couldn't stand it anymore. I got to my feet, ready to tell the little jerks to leave the girls alone, but Wyn beat me to it.

He wasn't talking to the boys, but what he was doing was just as good if not better. His tail was beating fast beneath the surface, creating a current. No matter how hard the boys kicked they couldn't get their mat any closer. The girls got farther and farther away and the boys were forced to stop chanting because they couldn't risk the lifeguard hearing them.

Their confusion at being stationary was comical. They had stopped trying to reach the girls and were discussing what else to do. Splashing them was one suggestion, and getting off their mat and swimming over to the girls so they could pull them off into the water was another. Just as this idea was voiced, I saw Wyn's hand.

He had positioned himself beneath the boys and pushed up hard on their mat. They keeled over backward into the water, floundering and splashing. I laughed at their surprise and indignation. The ringleader blamed his friends for the fall into the water and told them to get lost and that he was going to go jump off the diving board. His friends followed him, looking dejected.

I looked back at the two little girls, happy to see them smiling and chattering away in their high soprano voices. I knew the boys probably attended the same school as them and that the bullying most likely happened often. In this particular instance, though, there had been an intervention and they had been left alone. Hopefully this would give both girls the courage to stand up for themselves the next time it happened.

I was touched that Wyn had defended the girls, especially when he was confined against his will to the place in which they played. He hadn't known I was watching, so he'd thought that no one would see his intervention. He hadn't offered help merely to be seen doing so, unlike shallow girls at my school who only aided causes to look good on college applications. Even though others might notice similar situations, few people act. Wyn did.

I slipped into the pool and swam to where the boys had abandoned their mat. I pulled myself up onto the red foam and chuckled at Wyn's shocked expression.

"Hi, again," I whispered.

"Hello, Miss Morgan. Am I surprised. Thought I that you

were only going to come to the pool in the morning for diving practice. Is not that what were you going to do?"

"Yes—but then I realized I had all this time during public swim that I was wasting. So, first off, I have a question."

"It would seem Miss Morgan that always have you a question." Wyn's smile was small, his teasing hesitant.

I smiled back, but pushed on. "Like that. Why do you call me Miss Morgan? I prefer Valerie. Miss Morgan is nice, but it feels like that's what you'd call me if we were in some fancy restaurant or at the opera. I know some people prefer Miss, Mrs., and such, but I'm not one of them. Is your culture much more formal than ours?"

"Well, would not say I so, no. Noticed I, however, that humans seem to use titles more often than we do. Much of the merpopulation is composed of scientists and those in pursuit of knowledge and a better understanding. Most of the time, individuals strive to specialize and have one area of expertise. Am I no exception. Consider I my speciality to be human culture and all there is to know about them, although this is not exactly common knowledge." Wyn's voice was as smooth as ever, but held a hint of excitement.

"An expert on humans? How so? Do you watch us or talk to many of us or ..." My voice trailed off, as a horrible idea entered my head. I didn't want to voice the thought, because it failed to meld with what I knew about Wyn's character so far. But I was still unsure. There was so much I didn't know. Could he and his people possibly have taken human samples to study?

"Or ...?" Wyn prompted.

"No one from your world has ever taken humans for study, have they? For experiments or anything?"

"No, no! Nothing like that. Definitely not. Our people have very strict laws about studies because so many of us are scientists. Our laws are much more stringent than yours, and it is extremely rare for anyone to disobey the law, because the punishments are so extreme. Our society has a very strong sense of life and no study is worth the risk of taking live samples."

For the first time since we had started talking, I grasped how different Wyn's voice was. I had noticed its smoothness before, but I hadn't registered that his words felt ... slow. Well, not slow exactly, more like *timed*. The cadences and nuances flowed and shifted fluently into one another.

I also realized *why* I had noticed it. This last explanation was spoken more quickly than any other time he had spoken. His voice had grown urgent, like he was worried. *Was* he worried? *Wyn worries about what I think of him?* The thought appealed to me. He didn't want me to think badly of him. I took a second to marvel at that before speaking again.

"I'm very glad to hear it. My best friend Heather wants to be a vet and she would've been appalled to hear about the mistreatment of any type of animal. But do merpeople consider humans to be animals? Or do you think of us more as equals?"

"That would depend on who talk you to, suppose I. We do not generally consider humans animals, although there is a high level of fear and mistrust toward humans throughout most of mersociety. Even within my own small community, only a small number of us place humans on an equal plane. But please, tell me more about yourself. Heather is your best friend and she is the girl with the blonde and pink hair, correct? How long have you been friends? Think I that there is also a large black-haired boy?"

"Yes, you nailed them."

He smiled, and I continued.

"It's been the three of us for a long time—ever since Zack moved here when we were about eight. ... But if you want to know more about me, you'll have to wait your turn. You already know way more about me than I do about you. What do you say to answering my questions first?" No way would I give up learning more about him just so he could hear about the mediocre day-to-day dreariness of my life. "Have our species always lived separately and apart? Was there ever contact between the two?"

"Well, in ancient times we had very open relationships with humans, but as centuries passed humans grew curious to the point of wanting to dissect some of us while we were still alive. That effectively ended our relationship with humans very quickly."

"Ugh. Would it be wrong to apologize for my race?"

Wyn laughed quietly. "It was long ago. Besides, still find I humans so interesting that disregarded I any negative feelings had I quite some time ago."

"Tell me how you feel you've become an expert, Wyn."

"Well, there was a man that met I many years ago now. A human who had retired and was relaxing on his own private island near New Zealand. For months, listened I beneath the surface as he passed hours and hours sitting in his boat making voice recordings. Apparently he wanted to write an autobiography. The longer listened I the more felt I that he would welcome the sharing of knowledge." Wyn's eyes said he was travelling back to that day.

"It took me a very long time to work up the courage to speak with him, a number of weeks, but eventually was I ready. That summer day was bright and beautiful. Had I listened for about an hour and when he finished his current chapter recording, flicked I my tail hard to push my torso and half my tail above the surface. The man jumped so high he almost fell out of the boat. Stayed I very still for a number of minutes while let I the man understand what he was seeing. He rubbed his eyes a number of times, muttering something about 'Too much Scotch.'" Wyn smiled at the memory.

"When said I hello, he had to recover a second time, as again he jumped quite high. It took me a full half-hour, but eventually was I able to convince him that was I real. From that point on learned I more than thought I possible. We spoke for hours upon hours for many months. Would sit I at the end of his boat with my tail in the water as we learned so much about each other.

"We talked about anything and everything: ethics, philosophy, logic, music, history, and societal differences. He would bring books and movies with a mini player for me to watch and would bring I him small things of our culture to see."

"What was his name? This man who taught you so much about us?"

"Initially he called himself President Siciur, but eventually he asked me to call him Darryl, and he called me Wyn." You could hear the respect in Wyn's tone as he spoke about this human man, like they'd had the relationship of a close uncle and nephew. I envied that and was about to voice my feelings, but stopped myself. I wasn't ready for that conversation yet, so I asked a more mundane question instead.

"Siciur. Is that S-e-a-t-u-r-e? And why did he call himself president?" What was he president of? If it was a country, I hoped I'd heard of it.

"His name is actually spelled S-i-c-i-u-r. Believe I that it has Italian roots, but am I not sure. As for being a president, he told me that he was the CEO of an oil company. Do not know I the name of the company because anytime he spoke about oil, was not I very interested. Most often simply changed I the subject." His smile told me that Wyn had spent much of his time teasing Darryl.

I happened to glance at the clock and almost fell off my mat in shock. It was after six! I was already late for dinner, and Jocelyn would be wondering where I was.

"I'm sorry but I've got to go. I'm late and I don't want to worry my aunt." I swam over to the side of the pool. "I'll be back tomorrow morning with more questions for you." I thought this was fairly obvious, but I didn't want to assume anything.

"Should have I expected otherwise?"

His teasing sent an unexpected surge of pleasure through me and caught me off guard. I shifted my weight, smiled back—and hurried off to the change rooms.

"What happened, Valerie? You were at the pool for a long time." Jocelyn's voice echoed with concern, when I walked through the door later.

"Sorry. I totally lost track of time."

My aunt always worried, part of her internal wiring.

"Are you all right? Being at the pool for so long, and not being able to dive. It must be hard."

"It is. But I still love the water. It's not all bad." I shrugged, not sure what else I could say. Jocelyn studied me. I tried to keep my expression smooth, but her eyebrows rose slightly in surprise. Then her face broke into such a smile, it left me wondering what the joke was.

"I'm glad to see you doing better, sweetheart. Come grab a plate."

I walked into the kitchen behind her, looking forward to what smelled like a hearty stew, but also dwelling on what she might have seen. What had I given away? Note to self: practise poker face in front of mirror.

As I brushed my teeth before bed that night, it hit me that what Wyn and I had wasn't enough. As much as I loved talking and visiting with him, he had to be free. He was a *prisoner*. We hadn't yet broached the subject of his captors again, but their intentions crouched over me like a monstrous shark. I couldn't sit idly by; I had to save him. It didn't matter how hard it was, or how long it took. I rinsed my mouth and strode back to my bedroom. I'd stay up a bit and get more info. I'd send emails to the biology department at the university, find books at the library, search page after page on the Internet. I'd find out more about Wyn and his biology. He *would not* stay a prisoner on my watch.

The next morning I practically raced to the pool. My whole body relaxed at the familiar smell of chlorine, but there was an underlying tension. Wyn was in the shallow end, waiting for me. This couldn't just be a gabfest. Whether or not he'd actually tell me more about his captors, I had to learn more about him to save him. I smiled and slid into the water, grabbing a small kick board to use for some exercises. I had to look like I was training because, as Coach Chase had proven yesterday, he was keeping an eye on me—occasionally at least.

Wyn returned my smile with a small one of his own. "Was your aunt worried when arrived you at home yesterday?"

"Yeah. I felt bad. She's super busy and really doesn't need me to add to her plate. Help me watch the clock, okay?" I realized my voice was at normal volume. I glanced at Coach Chase. His back was turned to me: good. I dropped my voice to a whisper. I wanted to ask about his captors again, or, heck, even just stare at him for minutes on end. But maybe I should work up to asking about his imprisonment. "So ..." I waffled around for a safe topic. "Tell me more about your father's pearl farms. How do they work exactly?"

Wyn explained the mechanics of how his father farmed the pearls and how his mother then refined them and made the best pearls into fine jewellery.

"Obviously, family is very important to you, but what are those families like? Is it very close like other mammals or more distant? Er ... are you mammals? Or cold-blooded?"

"Our familial units are close. We depend upon one another. Mer are mammals. We have live births in the same way dolphins or whales do."

We swam and chatted and I kept looking for an opening to ask about his captors. I learned there were only ten families in Wyn's community, and its ruling council was made up of the head of each family. Wyn's father was the head of the Erelasai family, thus on the ruling council. No elections occurred: just the oldest male or female who hadn't retired from each family filled the position. I wanted to ask how we could get him back to the ocean, but lost my nerve at the last second.

"When did the relationship between humans and merpeople end?" This part of the history of Wyn's people certainly drew me. Who wouldn't want to know everything about the previous relationship between his species and ours? And maybe it would give me an idea about how to help him.

"Some sixteen hundred years ago. My grandfather used to tell me stories as a child—although it has been decades since last I heard his stories. Wish I that could hear I them again."

Decades? "Wyn, how old are you?"

"My birthday is March sixteenth. Was I born in nineteen hundred and forty-eight. Am I sixty-five years old."

My mouth gaped; I closed and opened it again but no words came out. I probably looked like a fish but I couldn't begin to care. I was trying to process the fact that Wyn was *sixty-five.*

"You're what?" I shrieked, completely forgetting to whisper. I glanced around apprehensively. My teammates were preoccupied, but as I looked at Coach Chase, he turned back to the team. He'd been watching me. Crap.

Just then a whistle blew. Practice was over. I swam to the side of the pool.

"When will see I you again?" Wyn reached towards me, as though to take my arm and pull me back to him. "Valerie?" His gaze was searching, but he dropped his hand. "Age I at about a third of the rate that a human does. In human years am I much older than you—but in mer not. Are you bothered by that?"

"I don't know. It's super strange. Only a few years back I went to my grandfather's seventieth birthday. It sounds really old." I shrugged, then worked to brighten my expression. His eyes lit up as he saw my efforts.

"You'll see me again tomorrow," I said.

I was outside the pool, waiting for my aunt to pick me up for school, when Coach Chase stopped as he passed me on his way to the parking lot. "How are you doing, Valerie, really?"

My pulse quickened slightly. What had he seen?

"Frustrated. I want to dive. But otherwise I'm fine."

I waited to see if he'd explain why he was asking.

"Understandable—and good, I guess." Coach Chase stopped talking and his knees jerked, as though he'd been about to shift his feet but stopped himself.

I strived to keep my voice casual and pressed on. I wanted this conversation over. "Why do you ask?" There, that was okay. I didn't sound too worried or too bored.

"Well, I've noticed a few things lately."

I felt my face go pale. There was nothing I could do about the blood leaving my face, but I could control my expression. *Stay casual!* I shifted my features to convey what I hoped was only slight curiosity as I waited for Coach Chase to continue.

"I don't know much about head injuries or anything, but I've seen you talking to yourself more than once. It has me worried, is all. I guess I want to know that everything's okay with you." Coach Chase let out his breath in a short gust, waiting for my reply.

My mind chased around for an appropriate excuse. When I finally came up with one, I lifted one side of my mouth into what would hopefully pass as a smile. "I've been watching a lot of movies lately. Each morning at practice I try to repeat scenes from movies I've watched. I just need to keep working on my memory with the concussion, that's all." My answer was a second late, but maybe Coach Chase wouldn't notice.

"Hmm, I guess that makes sense." Chase nodded, then stared at me. Hard. "I just have one more question. What exactly did the merman do that made you scream in the middle of practice?"

I could've tried to control my reaction, I suppose, but the knowledge that someone else could see Wyn was way too much. I collapsed in a heap on the sidewalk, leaning against the rough brick of the building behind me. "You know?" My voice came out in a strangled whisper.

"Yes. But you didn't answer my question. What did he do to you?" Chase's stance was unyielding and he towered over me.

"He didn't do anything to me. He told me his age, and I freaked out because he's sixty-five. Seriously though, th t doesn't matter at all. Tell me how you can see him." I ard back at Chase's hard stare. He couldn't admit to seeing Wyn and expect me to take it in stride and then tell him all abo t o r conversations.

Chase sat down next to me, sighing. "Two months ago, my brother flew us all down to his place in California for my parents' thirtieth wedding anniversary. We went surfing I g t caught in a riptide." His right hand massaged his left han as if the movement was all that kept him talking. "My broth to d me later it was a freak accident, that it shouldn't ha e happened, and that he hadn't heard of anything similar occurring on that beginner beach before."

"So, what? A mer saved you?"

"Yes." Chase's gaze flickered like he was seeing water in front of him. "She pulled me from the currents and pushed me to the surface. I'll never forget her face. There was pity in her eyes, but also determination. I thought I was crazy and that my brain had found a way, any way, to explain how I managed to get to the surface. Then I saw him in the pool when I came back to work and knew I was insane."

Chase looked back at me with a grimace, then continued. "He was always there. But as far as I saw, he never hurt anyone. I struggled with going to see a psychiatrist or something, and had made up my mind to make an appointment when you came back for the first time after your accident. Your scream to watch out was telling enough, but then you ran from the pool after seeing him again. And then you started talking to him once you decided that you weren't insane, just like I did."

"Yeah, it was rough. Why didn't you tell me you could see him? I thought I was hallucinating. It would've been a whole lot easier if you'd told me I wasn't crazy."

"And just how would that conversation have gone?" Chase raised an eyebrow at me. "So you know that guy with a fin you've been seeing? I can see him too." He chuckled a little. "Yeah, not so easy, plus there's almost always other people around."

"True. So why say something now?"

"You seem really comfortable with him. Too comfortable. He doesn't know I can see him and I want to keep it that way. We know nothing about him or his intentions. For all we know, he could be getting close to you just so you help him back to the Pacific and then, once you're in the ocean, he'll get one of his kind to kill you because you know about them."

"Um, that's morbid. And more than a little creepy. What's your problem?"

"My problem is you trust him too much. You have no frame of reference for anything he tells you about himself or his kind. Maybe that mer that saved me only did so because she caused my accident in the first place and felt guilty."

"What? Why—?"

Just then my aunt's car pulled up. Chase stood and offered me a hand, pulling me up.

"Be careful. And don't do anything stupid." He strode off towards his car. I stayed frozen on the sidewalk, staring after him, until my aunt honked.

Chase didn't trust Wyn, didn't trust his "kind." But he could see mer! So didn't see that one coming.

After school it was just me and Heather in her car, and barely managed to acknowledge her. I was overloaded with thoughts of Wyn, and Chase knowing about Wyn, and Chase not wanting me to know Wyn. My head ached with the nagging complications. Zack would've been carpooling with us but he had a shift at the local bike shop where he repaired all types of bikes. With all the legal fees his dad collected and his mom's corporate salary, money was never an issue for him—but Zack loved the puzzle of figuring out what was wrong with a bike. I probably could've gone to the public swim to see Wyn again, but if I didn't study for the math final I was really in for it.

About halfway home, Heather cleared her throat.

"So, uh, Greg and I are an item."

"Wait, what? The guy who asked you to grad? When did this happen?"

"He asked me out at lunch, and I said yes."

"This is the same guy who's taking general studies here at TRU this fall and has absolutely no idea what he wants to do? You're going to SFU in September." Thompson Rivers is here in Kamloops, but Simon Fraser is in Vancouver, a three hour drive away.

She shrugged. "Yeah, I know—but he's so yummy with his dark hair and blue eyes. Very Supermanish."

I asked Heather to tell me the story of how he asked her out because I knew she wanted me to, but I listened with only half an ear. Heather would be an amazing veterinarian one day, and she was totally driven—but she gravitated to beefcake guys with zero mental acuity. Jerk Justin from when we were in grade eleven being exhibit A. Heather partially held to her Christian upbringing and had broken it off with the jerk a year ago, when he'd pressured her day after day to do more than she wanted to. I hoped with Greg it would be different; he did take calculus with Zack, and if I remembered right he was only involved with track, sports-wise, so maybe he wouldn't be too bad.

I thought I mumbled "hmm" and "aww" at the appropriate moments in Heather's narrative, but enthusiasm for anything still felt unnatural, except maybe when it came to Wyn. *Ah, Wyn.* He took up at least half my brain, making it doubly hard to concentrate on my friend's boyfriend stuff. Chase's opinions had given me pause, but hadn't changed my mind about Wyn at all. He was so kind. He'd helped those kids. He'd saved my life. I just couldn't accept that he was evil, solely because he wasn't human.

I made sure I said a cheery goodbye to Heather, and then forced Wyn out of my thoughts so I could apply myself to making sure I'd do tolerably well on my math final and other exams. I did homework the whole afternoon, and after dinner I finally tackled the math. Two hours later I slumped onto the lumpy comforter on my bed, too numbered out to plot any more graphs.

Staring out the window from my bed, I finally let myself think about Wyn again. His age, specifically. During our conversation about his age, he'd asked me *when* he would see me again, not *if*. He'd assumed that even if his age bothered me, I wouldn't be upset enough to never see him again. And I realized his assumption was correct. I would still go to the pool. I would always go. I was a swimmer. A diver. And yes, Wyn was there. My reason for going hadn't changed; it had simply multiplied. There were *reasons* for me to go.

As I got ready for bed, my mind stayed with him. Wyn's age was a shock, sure, but that didn't make him any less kind or fascinating. I wasn't going to give up getting to know him or about Lasera simply because I'd been shocked by something I'd learned, or because Chase was prejudiced.

I settled into my cool sheets, but five minutes later, just as I got to that blissful moment when your body relaxes and you know sleep is seconds away, my cellphone buzzed. Grrr, anybody who had my number knew I went to bed at nine forty-five, so who was calling me? If it was a wrong number I'd break something. The call display showed Zack's number.

"Yeah?"

"Sorry, Val. You weren't totally asleep yet, were you?" Zack's voice wasn't nearly sheepish enough for me.

"Lucky for you, no, I wasn't. What do you want?"

"Do you feel like a blast from the past? Let's meet at the park like the three of us used to and talk."

"Really? That's what you're calling about? Dude, I'm already in bed!"

"Will you take a bribe? There's an orange smoothie with extra yogurt in it for you. I already got it for you, so you have to come."

"Uhhhhn. You're so annoying." I slumped into my pillows. "Smoothie for a bribe, huh? So it's a strawberry-raspberry-banana-orange smoothie with black cherry yogurt?"

"Yup." Zack popped his lips on the *p*, and I could almost hear the cocky smile stretch across his face.

"Green Slurpee straw?"

"Yes. I even walked across the street to the gas station and got you a green Slurpee straw."

Dang. Thought I had him with that one.

"Your superstitions are weird. You know that, right?"

"Says you. The one time I took a straw from the dispenser at the smoothie shop I over-rotated my half-pike three times that day at practice. So it's gotta be the Slurpee straw. And I happen to know that tons of pro athletes have quirky habits and superstitions too."

"All right, all right. I give. But how about it? The park's only two blocks from your aunt and uncle's. You'll be home before the all-important curfew Coach sets for trainees, no problem. You can even stay in your pjs and throw on some flip-flops for all I care. Just come."

I closed my eyes. "Fine." I swiped my hand up and down my face to wake myself up. "I'll be there in ten." Ending the call I chucked my phone on the bed, sat up, and tried to decide if I'd actually go in my pjs or not.

Seven minutes later I walked onto the playground in jeans, my pyjama T-shirt, and the suggested flip-flops. The long summer hours had arrived; the last rays of sunlight were just disappearing behind the hills even though it was almost ten. The bright lights of the outdoor hockey arena next to the green space were coming on, and I heard the sounds of the we're-such-diehards-we-play-ball-hockey-every-night guys scuffling and yelling in their game.

Zack was sitting in one of the three swings our trio regularly occupied before any of us had cars. I held my hand out before saying a word, and only after I'd sat on my swing and taken a long drink of the smoothie-goodness did I look over at him.

"So you bribed me, and now we're at our old haunt. What's so important you dragged me out of bed?"

"Not so important. I just wanted to see you. I've missed this. We used to hang out here for so long that you and Heather were constantly getting in trouble for staying out too late. I'm just tired of all the future talk and the looming craziness. Colleges and scholarships and final exams and graduation ... I just wanted some time to chill." He stood up and began pushing me on the swing. "I couldn't find the tiny water gun I used to bring here to spray both you and Heather with. Too bad—you'd have already been shot a bunch by now."

I laughed. "You were so shocked the one night we retaliated and hid water balloons in our pockets and soaked you!" Our laughter echoed across the grass and he pushed me higher, my one hand clinging to the chain, the other tightly holding my smoothie. It was nice to laugh. "Ah!" I cried as Zack suddenly grabbed the swing chain and jerked my swing back. I dragged my feet through the gravel to bring myself to a stop. "Yeesh, you crazy man!"

Zack walked around the swing and stood in front of me, both hands holding the chains. His face was awfully close.

"I'm being serious here. Try not to faint."

"Kaaay ..." I raised an eyebrow.

"Will you go out with me?"

-CHAPTER SIX-
Distance

I dropped my smoothie, then fumbled to catch it. Zack reached for it too, and the lid popped off in our tangle of hands. A blob of orange slopped onto Zack's khaki pants.

"Ack! I'm so sorry!" I started wiping the mess off his thigh, then stopped abruptly. In the wake of Zack's out-of-the-blue question, touching him was suddenly awkward. I wiped my hand on the seat of my jeans and cleared my throat. "Um, are those super expensive? They look new. I'm really sorry if they are. You just totally surprised me."

"Yes, they're new—cost me half a paycheque." He tipped my chin up to look at him. "But I'd let you dump that whole smoothie on them if it meant you'd go out with me." His gaze was uncharacteristically serious. Coming from the guy who dry-cleaned almost everything and ironed his jeans, that was some sacrifice. Pulling my chin out of his hand, I shook my head.

"Is this really why you asked me here?"

"Yeah." Zack nodded, then took my hand and swiftly pulled me up to stand right in front of him. "I don't care that I had to bribe you to get you here, I couldn't wait another minute to ask you out. We've been best friends forever, but I've wanted us to be something more for a while now." His fingers brushed across my cheek, then tucked a piece of hair behind my ear.

I pulled my hand away and took a step back. "What kind of girlfriend would I be to you?"

"Sorry, what?"

"I'm still scarred by the bedroom details I overheard when your last girlfriend bragged about it in the gym locker room. You two were pretty hot and heavy. I don't wanna be your rebound girl."

"That was three months ago—and I was only dating her because I knew I couldn't get you. And we broke up because I wouldn't sleep with her."

"So all the bedroom details were—"

"A lie! I haven't slept with anyone. Last year, while Heather was with Justin. You and her had a ton of talks about sex, and they affected me. Your talks about when, the reasons why, and respect and all that. Plus, that phrase she used from her mom, 'Any guy will have sex with you. Wait for the one who'll marry you.'" Zack shifted his weight. "Harsh—but true too. It kinda blew me away."

I waited, hovering between believing him and dismissing him completely. I wanted to believe him.

"I want you to know, I *need* you to know, I respect you that way. I just want us to be together."

I was quiet for way too long as my brain jumped through all the whys and why nots.

"For five seconds I really thought we could, but I can't, Zack. I'm not even comfortable with myself yet. I just can't."

Zack sighed and sank into a swing. The disappointment in

his eyes and hard set to his jaw made me want to take back what I'd said. "I guess that's fair. Will you at least be my date for graduation? No pressure. We'll just have a good time."

"Yeah, okay. I guess I can do that. We'll double with Heather and Greg. They're actually going out now, not just going to grad together."

"Really? When did this happen?"

"He asked her out at lunch today ..." We walked towards my aunt and uncle's place together.

After a goodbye that was only a little strained, I went back up to my room and flopped back onto my bed. Zack wanted to date me. Weird. I'd had to tell him no, that much was certain. There was no possible way I could start any kind of relationship with Zack. If the three boyfriends I'd had previously were any indication, then dating meant drama, arguments, and inconsistencies—all things I so did not need right now. And yet in the back of my head was the nagging impression that with Zack it would be different. But then, where would Wyn fit in? I liked him, but was it ridiculous and impossible for our relationship—whatever it was—to continue? He was a *merman*. Then again, if Zack and I were dating he'd come to the pool with me more and I'd be forced to risk Zack seeing me talk to Wyn— or I'd have to stop talking to Wyn completely. I couldn't cut Wyn out like that.

Had I made the right choice, though? Should I have said yes to Zack? What if it was different with him? My stomach clenched. The last thing I wanted was to strain our friendship, but Wyn was too important to me now. Zack would have to deal.

"Am I glad that came you back this morning." Wyn greeted me as I slid into the pool beside him. "Was I worried that would not come you back until more days had passed. Knew I that your age span was different than my own. However, thought I not that it would upset you. Am I sorry." He was so repentant and worried that it was hard for me to remember why I'd been bothered. All I wanted to do was make him smile again.

"Thank you. I appreciate that. I'll just have to wrap my head around the fact that you're the same age as my grandfather— though you sure don't look it." I smiled, hoping he would laugh. I wasn't disappointed. His smooth laughter reverberated off the tiled pool walls and I giggled in response.

I *giggled*. I couldn't remember the last time I'd giggled about something. With Wyn, things were so different.

"My age may be the same as your grandfather in human years—but in mer years, am I hardly older than you."

I turned at the edge of the pool to do another lap, and saw Coach Chase working to teach Lydia to keep her mind on spotting. I couldn't understand how Chase could see Wyn every day and ignore him. It was crazy. I turned back to Wyn.

"Why am I the only one who can see you? The first time was after my concussion. Before that, I was here almost every day and I never saw you then." I'd asked this the first time we talked, but had been so distracted by his answers to my other questions that I didn't re-ask it.

"Have I been here for almost a year. But yes, was I never visible to you until after were you hurt. It was when hit you your head …" Wyn hesitated and didn't continue. He looked away, his shyness evident.

"What about it? How did that allow me to see you?" Confusion muddled my thinking.

I reluctantly thought back to that time. The memory of the pain made my head reel, but I persisted. I remembered the screaming when I was found on the side of the pool. I remembered seeing the hull of a wooden boat just before I hit my head, being surrounded by the water. ... And then I recalled a crucial detail. I'd been given air just as I was about to drown. ...

"It was you, wasn't it? You're the one who gave me mouth-to-mouth resuscitation." My body was motionless in the water as I floated with my kick board. Wyn had saved me. I owed him my life.

Wyn gave a slow nod.

"Thank you." My voice was thick. I had no doubt that I would have died had it not been for Wyn. I remembered the awful blackness encroaching on my soul. "Please." I swallowed away the emotion in my voice and tried to speak normally. "Please tell me what happened."

"Knew I who were you. Had seen I many of your diving practices and even some of your competitions that were held here. Heard I the crack as your head hit the wooden boat. Swam I over, anxious, watching and waiting. But no one came ... no one had noticed. Struggled I within my own mind for an infinite amount of time. Rushed I to the surface under the bulkhead and filled my lungs with air. Dove I back down to you. Darryl had taught me what to do, many years before, when asked I how humans drowned."

"Wait—why did you swim up under the bulkhead? I don't

understand." Why hadn't he gone straight to the surface above me? It didn't make sense.

Something flickered in Wyn's eyes. Uncertainty lingered on his features. I waited, unsure. Tension tightened Wyn's neck. Why would my simple question cause this reaction? Three long seconds later, Wyn seemed to come to a decision.

"When merpeople go above surface, anyone can see them. Needed I to fill my lungs in a place where would not be I seen. When my lungs were full hastened I back to you. Bubbles soon floated up to the surface. Was I so relieved to see the air coming from your lungs. Quickly began I to lift you to the surface, as gave I you the last of my air. Held I onto you until help came." Wyn fiddled with his arm cuff. "Struggled I to remember the type of person are you. Did not know I how would react you to seeing me. Because from that point on, would always you see me."

"How? I mean, what did you do that allowed me to see you?" All this was fascinating, and I wondered if the secret to saving him somehow lay in the details of how he'd saved *me*. I was desperate for any insight into how to get him out of this wretched pool and back into his ocean.

"It was my skin touching yours. We believe there is a chemical on our skin that reacts with yours and alters the sight of humans. If a merperson's skin touches a human's, that human will see through our camouflage. Was I surprised when were you able to see me so quickly. Had I no idea the change would happen so swiftly."

"What do you mean by camouflage? How can normal humans not see you when you're in the water?"

"Our genetic and chemical makeup is different from yours.

A merperson's body is made up of almost two-thirds fewer cells than your body. Our camouflage comes naturally; with so many less cells, to your eyes we become the same colour as the water."

"So your saving me caused my eyes to change ... you'll never be invisible to me again?" My whisper dropped another level at this question. I didn't know what he thought of this. Did Wyn like that I would always be able to see him, or did he consider it an invasion of his privacy?

"Yes, that is true." Wyn's voice was calm ... but I didn't know enough about him to read his tone accurately. I wanted to ask what he thought about me being able to see him, but couldn't bring myself to. Instead I focused on learning more about his species so I could make a plan.

"How could you breathe in air and be able to give it to me?"

"Merpeople have two breathing systems. One that can be used in the air and the other for beneath the surface. However, we must consciously decide to change from one system to the other. We can only survive a short time out of water. After two hours we begin to dry out. If we are not in the water after three hours, sickness incapacitates us. We die if we are completely out of the water for four or more hours."

"So you really are trapped in this pool, surrounded by humans who could expose you or touch you at any time. But you won't answer my questions about that, will you?"

His jaw hardened. "No, that is something will I not discuss with you. It is easier to not think about that part of my existence. Will I not endanger a woman."

What? So because I was female I couldn't know anything that might be dangerous? Bull.

"You refuse to tell me about why you're imprisoned? Who

your captors are? Anything?"

I clambered out of the pool and strode for the exit. It was too much. After all our conversations, he didn't trust me enough to help him. "Valerie ..." Wyn called, just loudly enough for me to hear. I ignored him and kept walking. He wouldn't be able to call me again without the others hearing.

Coach Chase's whistle blew. "That's it, kids."

I scowled, then tried to hide my anger from my teammates as they'd be coming in to the change room with me.

"Valerie, are you okay?" Coach Chase caught up with me. "You got out of the water pretty quickly." He glanced around and said in a lower tone, "There's no danger?"

"I think I need to take it easier the next few days. ... I was close to seriously pulling something just then. I can't risk it. And no, definitely no danger." The lie came easily, fed by my anger. Wyn was trapped and refused to tell me anything about it simply because of some notion that he had to protect me, the *woman*.

"Well, you're the best judge of what your body can handle. Just take it easy, come back when you're ready, and *be safe*. All right?"

"Thanks, Coach."

How could Wyn say that? I fumed as I changed, and then left the building to wait for a bus. All through the bus ride to school my anger simmered. Heather knew something was wrong, and my school friends and classmates in my biology class seemed to sense it too. Heather was smart enough not to ask, however, and the others followed her lead.

Zack caught up with me in the hall after Bio though, and wasn't as smart.

"Seems like a storm cloud's hovering over you. What's got you all grumpy? Should I put on a dress like Snow White's and make you a pie?" Zack threw an arm over my shoulder, laughing.

"Piss off. I'm not in the mood." I shoved his arm off.

"Whoa. I get you're mad. I was just trying to get a smile. There's no need to bite my head off."

I clenched my teeth. "Sorry. I'm pissed at Wyn, not you."

"Who's Wyn?"

Oh crap. Oh crap, crap, crap.

"Just a guy at the pool who's getting on my nerves." I barely managed not to stutter. I *could not* have Zack curious about Wyn.

"Who is he? What'd he do?"

"Some idiot who made a sexist remark and it's still grating, that's all." My anger was fleeing fast in the face of protecting Wyn. No one could know about him. "Just drop it, 'kay?"

"'All right, fine, I guess. So how do you want to get to grad? I could maybe get my dad's Jag."

"Sure, sounds great." I plastered enthusiasm on my face, even as I fretted about making sure Zack didn't come back to the subject of Wyn.

That afternoon I walked into the house to hear my six-year-old cousin, Sasha, screaming and lashing out at her eight-year-old brother, Michael. Apparently, Michael had been playing with his rocket ship, but he'd tripped and fallen on Sasha's dollhouse, breaking it into three pieces. My aunt was kneeling and holding Sasha back in her tirade towards Michael.

He bent down and gently lifted the pieces of the dollhouse, his face devastated. "Sasha, I'm sorry. Mom, can you fix it?"

"I'll see what I can do, sweetheart." Jocelyn carefully took the pieces from Michael and headed for her sewing room.

"I'm still mad at you," Sasha said determinedly.

"Okay. Tell me when we're friends again?" Michael's sweet, humble reply touched Sasha as much as it did me.

Sasha hemmed and hawed a little bit and put her hands behind her back as she thought.

"You said sorry," she finally whispered. "I don't wanna stay mad. We're friends again. Let's go help Mom fix it." Michael reached for her hand and they both ran up the stairs laughing.

Not only had my slip with Zack faded my anger towards Wyn, but the scene between my cousins piled on the guilt. Sasha hadn't run away. She'd seen Michael's reaction to her anger and hurt. I however hadn't stayed long enough to see Wyn's reaction. I'd simply run. I sighed, looking at the clock. It was early afternoon; I still had time to take the bus and go see Wyn.

Just over an hour later I stood in the change room hall just out of sight of the water. Seeing him again flared my anger at his lack of trust, but I had to give him a chance to explain.

I slowly walked to the edge of the pool. Wyn was swimming in the shallow end. *He looks so lost.* I sat on the side of the pool and dipped my feet in. Wyn saw me immediately despite there being so many other people around. He swam over, but hesitated as he drew close.

"Hello," I whispered. I'd rehearsed this. "I won't say I'm not angry, because I am—but it wasn't fair of me not to let you give an explanation." I waited. I wouldn't say anymore.

"Valerie ... honestly, do I not know. Trust I you. And yet there is so much danger. Accept my apology, for truly would never intentionally hurt I you, but will not I put you at risk." I saw the truth in Wyn's eyes—eyes that always said so much. I had an inkling that Wyn would never lie, *could* never lie. His eyes would continually reveal his emotions.

I gripped the pool deck. "I accept your apology, but I can't just sit around and keep chatting with you. You're a captive. I won't push you to tell me more until you're ready, but don't expect me not to try and save your life when you saved mine."

"Owe you me nothing."

I stared at my feet as they made circles in the water. We didn't agree about that. "Plus, calling me 'woman' in that context really didn't help." I looked back at Wyn.

Wyn's eyes widened. "Am I sorry. Had I no idea. In my culture, to call a female a woman is a term of respect. It is a natural part of our conversation."

My heart softened. "Something that happened with my cousins earlier showed me how unreasonable I was being, so I came back." I shrugged, not sure what else to say.

"Valerie, why do you live with your aunt and uncle and cousins? What happened to your father and mother?"

It was inevitable he'd ask this at some point, but I hated that he had. Everything in the dark corner of my mind fought to get out. I was breaking, cracking at the edges, as Wyn waited for my reply.

I jumped to my feet, almost slipping on the slick pool deck, then turned and ran, barely registering the look of shock and hurt on Wyn's face. This exit was different from the last, though. I wasn't running in anger now; it was desperation.

I *couldn't* think about this. The wound on my head throbbed. Changing took mere seconds because I was still dry. I could only focus on one thing ... getting away.

The second I was dressed I threw headphones on, selected a loud, obnoxious album, and blasted it. The music didn't block out all thought, but it helped.

The bus ride to Mac Park took an eternity. I needed to be able to drive again. My hands moved continuously while my body swayed with the movement of the bus. I undid and redid my ring again and again.

Once outside, I reached the familiar rose garden before my brain even registered where my feet were taking me. I hesitated. *I can't sit still.* I wheeled around and made my way to the circular path that looped around the island.

My feet pounded the pavement, and a sledgehammer attacked the wall in my mind. Fear overtook me as it became harder and harder to keep my mind blank. Each step I took was a hammer blow. I tried to force a blank space to the forefront of my brain, working to keep the images behind the wall.

I timed my blank spaces with the steps I took. Take a step, take another step, wipe the mind blank. Step, step, blank. Step, step, blank.

Step, step, blank—but no matter how hard I fought, I couldn't avoid the fact that if I'd agreed to therapy when Josh and Andrew suggested it months ago, maybe I would've had ways to deal with the thoughts attacking me now—but I couldn't talk about the dark corner with a stranger.

Faces slid past me. Time leapt about in strange ways. I counted my steps. Three thousand steps and the sledgehammer cracked my wall. Five thousand, three hundred, and twenty-seven steps, and I'd made one circuit of the park.

My breath quickened. I dug my fingernails into my palms.

More faces shifted past me. One face held concern and I could see lips forming the words "Are you okay?" but I'd already passed. I was losing the fight. The crack in my wall was a gaping hole now.

I screamed and broke into a run, desperate to escape the images trickling through the hole. I pushed and pushed, running faster and faster, my backpack thumping against me with each jolt. My blood beat in my head, growing louder than the heavy sound of my stride. I heaved for air. My arms pumped harder and harder, spurring on even more speed.

And then I was face down in the grass. I didn't know if I'd tripped or collapsed. I tasted dew. My eyes closed. I gulped air. My limbs felt disconnected from my body, and my muscles trembled. I clutched at the ground, and dug down to the soil, the dirt and grit coming away in my hands.

Then the tears started, for the first time since it happened. I felt each drop fall. Sobs shook my body.

It had been a Thursday. And our family tradition was a weekly jaunt every Thursday night to the local ice cream shop, where we'd each get a two-dollar ice cream cone. Dad always got fudge ripple. Mom loved pralines and cream. Meredith alternated between the three different fruit sorbets, while Joshua got mint chocolate chip without fail. Theo and I switched each week, one of us getting rocky road and the other cookies and cream, each of us sharing half with the other.

It was the beginning of my grade eleven year. That Thursday it was just Mom, Dad, Meredith, and Theo. Josh was in Vancouver, working to finish his practicum early so he could move right on to a residency at a hospital down there. I was at the pool. I'd just finished Provincials the past weekend, and Coach Chase wanted me to work out a few of my mistakes right away.

The police report said it was a drunk driver. Some idiot, pissed out of his head before six o'clock. He'd run a red light and broadsided my parents' SUV, smashing them across the intersection and into a lamppost on the other side of the street.

I hated hospitals. Had loathed them since I was ten, when my Grandpa Leroy died of cancer. We'd been close and it was hard on me—but nothing compared to walking those disturbing hallways again because my family was gone.

My mother and my older sister, Meredith, were killed on impact. My father died later at the scene.

I trembled as memories paraded across my brain.

Coach Chase was with me. My aunt and uncle were on their way back from the lake. I sat in a hard plastic chair in the hall, my head in my hands, tears flowing swiftly. Coach Chase had been talking with a doctor; he sat down beside me. I glanced up at him and asked my most pressing question. "Where's Theo?"

"He's still alive. But the internal injuries are ... severe. They just brought him back from surgery. The doctors say he's conscious and asking for you, but there's nothing more they can do but wait."

"So ... I can see him ... but only to say goodbye?"

Coach Chase nodded and helped me get shakily to my feet.

I walked swiftly, halting at the fork in the hallway. Coach Chase stepped ahead of me and led the way, matching my urgent pace. If Theo was still alive I couldn't waste another minute. I wanted to be with him every second he had left.

In the ICU, I was overwhelmed by the amount of machines hooked up to my brother. *Oh, Theo.* My partner-in-arms. My friend. We'd constantly pulled pranks on our older siblings together. I'd teased him about being shorter than me. He'd embarrassed me anytime one of my boyfriends came over—

"Val," Theo whispered. His voice was raspy and caught on the *v*.

"Hey, Theo." I hated how small he looked, trapped in the bed by tubes and wires. He lifted his hand, and I rushed over and clasped it tightly.

"They said ..." Theo drew in a long breath and it scraped at my heart. "Only I made it to the hospital."

I nodded mutely, and swallowed twice before I could respond. "Yeah. Just you." Theo had a small scratch on his right cheek, but the rest of his features were unmarred. I gazed at his face hungrily, willing myself to etch it into my mind forever.

"Stay close to Josh, okay?" Theo said with a determined look, then licked his cracked lips. "Don't retreat—" He stopped talking abruptly when a fit of coughing attacked him.

I clutched his hand tighter. "I ... I don't know if I can." I covered my mouth as a sob escaped without my permission. My head fell and my eyes closed. It had to be a dream. He was fifteen! He couldn't die!

"Look at me." Theo's voice cracked, but it was stronger than before. I opened my eyes and focused on him. "Promise me you'll live. Let yourself be happy."

I nodded again, still unable to speak.

"You gotta live ... for me." Theo dragged in another ragged breath. Part of me thought I should tell him not to talk because it was probably painful, but I couldn't do it. I needed every word he was giving me. "Go to school," he said. "Dive. Get married. Have four kids." He chuckled and I smiled despite myself.

Another harsh cough cut off Theo's laugh. His whole body shook as he hacked. He took a gasping breath, then gripped my hand with surprising strength.

"I promise, Theo." I squeezed his hand back with both of mine to reaffirm my words. "I promise I'll live."

Theo smiled and relaxed into the pillows behind him.

"Love you," he said, and his grip loosened.

"I love you, too."

He stared at me and I saw a laugh in his eyes.

"Flirt," he whispered.

I could barely see him through the blur of tears as I teased him back.

"Midget," I said.

His eyes closed. I pressed my lips to his forehead, and as I moved away his hand fell from mine. Theo, my amazing younger brother, had lived for three long hours before succumbing to his injuries.

Tears continued to flow down my cheeks and my hands gouged the earth as I relived the last moments of Theo's life. And now that I'd finally let the images through, more pressed into my mind.

I'd screamed and beat the floor with my fists. I'd broken three lamps in our house and punched a hole in the wall. But I didn't cry.

During the funerals I'd sat deadened beside Josh. Surprised that my eyes refused to cry the sobs my soul ached with, I woodenly accepted the good wishes and sympathies of those who'd come.

Eventually it was decided that I would stay with Jocelyn and Andrew instead of moving to Vancouver with Josh. They told me I'd probably want to finish high school here. I nodded and agreed with everything. I didn't care.

Josh, my newly appointed legal guardian, stayed in Kamloops only long enough to arrange everything. He'd wanted my word that I'd call him often, but we talked maybe once a month and our phone conversations barely lasted a half-hour. He lived for school and nothing else.

My problems with Josh aside, my mind began seriously dwelling on the promise I'd made to Theo. Had I been living? No, I hadn't. I groaned into the grass and curled into myself. Pain tore through me. I'd broken my vow to him. Not only that but I'd had a complete breakdown simply because Wyn brought up my family. That was wrong and I knew it.

Everyone else in my life tiptoed around it. Wyn had merely been curious. He hadn't known. His innocent question had thrown light into the dark pain I kept carefully locked away.

I'd been forced to think about things I'd been unable to deal with until now. Wyn didn't know anything about my family, and I suddenly realized I desperately wanted him to.

Hearing people refer to my family in the past tense had been the worst, but I could do this. For Wyn. He mattered that much to me. I wanted him to know my family, especially Theo, as well as I knew them.

Wyn hadn't dispelled the darkness from my mind, but even the tiniest candle could brighten a dark room. *My own personal light in the darkness.* I liked thinking of Wyn as light. It fit.

-CHAPTER SEVEN-
Changed

I'd been lying in the grass for a long time. I shakily got to my feet. Surprisingly, my body wasn't half as tired as I thought it would be. If my body had matched my mental exhaustion I'd be lying in this random field for days.

I walked to the bus stop, unhurried. I knew I'd be late for dinner, but it was unavoidable. Part of me wished I could've warned Jocelyn early so she wouldn't worry, though. I shot her a quick text to prevent any further stress. The shift in my thoughts was shocking. I'd spent so long bottling up every emotion—devoted so much of my time to *not* thinking—that I felt out of sorts. Now my mind had so much room! The sheer expanse daunted me. It was liberating to slowly let go of my fear of what certain phrases or situations might trigger. I'd relived the worst in my mind. I'd survived.

On the bus I started doing my puzzle ring out of habit—but then I stilled my hands, slipped the ring back on my finger, and allowed a memory to trickle into my brain. One of the few times my parents could force Josh to come home from school was Christmas—and one particular Christmas vacation, Theo came to me with a mischievous gleam in his eyes.

"Come on," Theo whispered, and then yanked me up the stairs.

"If I've timed this right," he said, glancing at the bathroom door, "we should hear a scream right about now." He crouched beside the door and pulled me down beside him.

"What is it this time? Frogs or slugs?" I whispered.

"Neither." Theo grinned in his goofy way I loved.

"I'm fifteen, so I really shouldn't be encouraging this anymore." I started to stand, but Theo gave me a look.

"He won't be hurt and it's nothing permanent. Plus, you know Josh needs to chill out. If we don't help him forget medical school, sometimes, he'll turn into a freak," Theo said, barely loud enough for me to hear.

"He's already a freak. Who goes to school year-round and is into his second year of medical school at twenty-two?"

Theo jerked a thumb towards the door and opened his mouth to say something else—but then the shower turned on and a scream ripped through the door.

"AHHHGGH! THEEEOOO!" There was a slipping and sliding sound. Theo and I could barely hold in our laughter. "What did you do? Why is the water red?" Josh roared.

"That's our cue," Theo yelled, and then jumped up, pulling me behind him as we raced down the stairs.

"What was that?" I asked, when I'd stopped giggling and caught my breath.

"Kool-Aid in the shower head," Theo managed to say through his laughter. "*Red* Kool-Aid."

"He'll look very Christmassy, won't he?" I said. It was all we could do to stay standing, we were laughing so hard.

Theo and I had pulled prank after prank, but he also knew how to make me laugh for the pure fun of it. We'd spent many Saturday afternoons in his room, comics strewn around us. We read and reread all the superhero stories Theo loved so many times. He'd loved the drawings and art and seeing his heroes defeat the villains. When he was younger, Mother had tried to teach him to draw his own comics, but wasn't patient enough. Remembering that small detail, I carefully let other images of Mother pass through me. Stolen afternoons with lemonade and a hundred colours of paint. She'd been planning a joint show, featuring her art and mine.

Painting. That was the first thing I'd do when I got to the house, I decided, suddenly impatient to be home.

The second I walked through the door, I slipped over to the stairs.

"Valerie, is that you?" Jocelyn called from the dining room, and then came to the entryway. "We're just finishing dinner now. Would you like me to warm you up a plate?"

"Thanks, but I'm okay for now. I'll be in the attic loft if you need me."

Surprise flitted across Jocelyn's face, and she lifted an eyebrow.

I smiled a little at her expression.

"Yeah, I'm going to be painting." I turned and continued up the stairs.

Her voice followed me. "Take all the time you need. I'll put together a plate for you to eat later."

The loft's door creaked and the smell of dust and mustiness greeted me. This was where most of my family's things had been stored. My eyes were drawn to the northwest corner. Drop

cloths covered two large easels. I pulled both covers off,
sneezing at the dust. My mother's last projects rested before
me. I stroked the edge of the canvas. One painting had been the
start of a lively carnival, the other a solemn mountain scene.

I searched the boxes closest to the easels, and found the two
I was looking for in moments. From the first one, I pulled out a
blank canvas and a palette. I set the canvas on one of the easels,
shifting my mother's mountain painting to lean against a wall.
From the second box I pulled containers of brushes and paint.

Hesitantly, I began mixing the paints on the palette. As the
hues mixed and the vibrancy of the colours reached me, I
became more animated. I found my favourite brush. The
bristles smoothed over the canvas, and shapes began to form of
their own accord. When I realized what my fingers wanted to
paint, I excitedly embraced it.

A little over an hour later, I heard a soft knock.

"Can I come in?" I turned and saw little Sasha peeking
around the door.

"Of course." I smiled and turned back to my painting,
adding a few more brush strokes.

"What are you doing in the attic?" Sasha moved towards me,
still hesitant.

I laughed and placed my palette and brush on a small box.
"So curious!"

I took her hand and pulled her in front of me so she could
see the painting better, then knelt down and wrapped my arms
around her waist.

"I'm painting, little munchkin. See?"

"Yup. But the munchkin would like to know what the
painting is of."

"Oh, she would, would she? It's a coral reef beneath the sea. This light blue is where the sun's shining down through the water. These pinks and reds are the start of the coral and the choppy part here is going to be the waves, where the sea touches the sky." I pointed to each element as I explained.

"That sounds beautiful—and it looks really pretty so far."

"Thank—"

A loud grumbling interrupted my thank-you. My hand went to my stomach as Sasha and I both giggled.

"How about you come help me warm up my dinner? We can play a game of Candy Land while I eat."

"Yeah!" Sasha burst from the room and rushed down the stairs.

Later I was downstairs, my head in the pantry searching for munchies while I studied, when I heard my aunt and uncle talking in the den. All my cousins were asleep.

"Josh emailed me saying she thinks she's seeing mermaids." My uncle's low voice carried.

"She's hallucinating?" my aunt asked, her voice full of concern.

"According to Josh. He thinks she hasn't grieved properly, and that if these imaginary visions persist we need to get her into therapy right away."

I slipped out of the pantry and tiptoed to the stairs, dodging the cracked door to the den. So I had to get it together, play the part, or I'd end up on some leather couch talking to a stranger about how my imagination conjured Wyn to help me deal with my family's death. My uncle had messed up my family enough. I wasn't about to let him dictate any more of my life.

Struggling to put what I'd overheard out of my head, I

distracted myself by pulling out the box of things I'd collected in my research about Wyn. I'd printed off every article that seemed to have even a hint of slightly true information about mermaids. None of them agreed about their biology, some called them sirens, others were convinced they were part seal and something called selkies, but regardless, I had to know everything.

The emails I'd sent out to professors of biology departments at the three most local universities were dead ends. Two hadn't even responded, and the other one sent me a perfunctory note saying he didn't have time to answer research questions and to try the library. I'd already read every book I could get my hands on about aquatic mammals, and whenever my homework wasn't too overdue I was doing more research on the Internet. I'd compiled tons of lists of renowned marine biologists and other university biology professors and looked them over now, to send a few more requests. I needed more info than I had, and the only way I saw to get it was to talk to people who knew animals and knew the ocean. The research and lack of anything concrete was daunting, but Wyn needed me, and I would help. Once I'd sent so many emails that the letters blurred on the computer screen, I went to sleep.

When I woke the next morning I pulled on my blue jeans and reached for one of the plain T-shirts scattered across my floor, but then I glanced at my closet. A turquoise satin caught my eye. The shade was so similar to the sea I'd started to paint last night that I ran my fingers over the silky fabric and put it on. I loved the thought of bringing the sea with me to go visit Wyn. I couldn't believe it was only *yesterday* that Wyn had asked after my family. A jolt of pain flared through my heart at the thought of them, but I took three deep breaths to lock the panic that wanted to take hold.

I felt like I'd lived for months upon months since Wyn had asked. Everything had shifted. I wasn't who I'd been. I never would be. But I could move forward now, and I was filled with gratitude for Wyn and his role in helping me begin to face the tragedy. Maybe I could start talking about what had happened and how it affected me. No more running, no more cowering. Yes, it would take me time to conquer my fear of hospitals and to truly let myself grieve, but it wouldn't take forever. There was hope.

I'd finally convinced my aunt to let me drive and it was an amazing relief to drive my yellow Felicity again. I had so much more freedom! Long bus trips and depending on others for rides had gone on long enough.

At the pool I didn't exactly stall in the change room, but I did take a little longer putting on my swimsuit than usual. I had no idea what kind of reception awaited me. Wyn's emotions and reactions were still foreign to me, and it wasn't like I'd reacted well to different situations the last little while, either. I sighed. Knowing I'd become someone who ran from anything I couldn't handle was depressing.

I shook my head. *No more.* I'd dealt with thinking I was insane, I'd faced my anger over Wyn being protective and not trusting me, and I'd confronted the fact that I hadn't kept my promise to Theo. I'd run each of those times, but I had also come back.

It had taken a lot for me to get to this point. I hoped Wyn would forgive me, and that he would understand.

"Hey, Coach," I said, then scanned the pool, eager to see Wyn but also slightly afraid of what I might see in his eyes.

When my gaze found Wyn, I watched in surprised delight as his face broadened into a wide, welcoming smile. I slipped into the water, grabbing a kick board as I went, and immediately began to propel myself down a lane.

"I want to tell you everything but I also want to keep moving as I do," I explained, as he glided below me. "It feels like it will be easier. Please don't interrupt or ask questions until I'm done. Now that I've started talking I want to keep going."

Wyn nodded solemnly.

I told him everything about the accident that killed my parents and two siblings, and how I'd had to say goodbye to my little brother. Wyn's eyes widened in shock during the telling, and he looked as though he wanted to reach out to me.

"Theo was only fifteen when he died." I closed my eyes, fighting tears, and struggled to maintain a steady pace, knowing Coach Chase would be watching for anything amiss. I really didn't need another conversation with him about Wyn.

"My older brother, Josh, was in Vancouver doing his medical practicum when it happened. When he was notified about the crash he took the first plane to Kamloops. Thankfully, he took over then, and I didn't have to do anything more." My legs trembled, but I kept on kicking and moving.

Wyn swam below me as I talked, and with a jolt I felt his finger and then his hand touch my arm beneath the water. His touch was soothing, comforting. It gave me the courage to keep talking, to actually finish this.

"I live with my aunt and uncle because I can't live with Josh. He lives in Surrey now and works too much—this way I can graduate with my friends. It sounds logical enough, but the real truth is that Josh doesn't want me living with him. My own brother can't be bothered." My words were fast and clipped.

Wyn's face hardened, and his brows drew together. He opened his mouth to say something.

I shook my head. "Please, I have to keep going."

Wyn nodded and I let the words fall from my mouth again. "Before he died, Theo made me promise to keep living, to not retreat into myself like I usually did when I couldn't handle a problem. I didn't keep that promise. The first time I laughed in this past year was only a few days ago, with you." A small smile appeared on Wyn's face and I felt even more connected to him. His hand rested more firmly on my arm. "At the funerals, it was like pieces of me died too. A part of my heart was locked up and buried in each of the coffins with them." I stopped swimming and my feet crashed to the floor of the pool. I clutched Wyn's hand and gave it a tight squeeze. He squeezed back, and that pressure alone seemed to buoy me up.

I let go of his hand, cleared my throat, and started swimming again. "Everyone in my life simply knew not to mention my family." I stared into Wyn's deep brown eyes. "You didn't. Your innocent question forced me to face what I hadn't confronted in over a year. A part of me wishes you'd never brought it up, but another part realizes how much better this is."

The understanding compassion in Wyn's eyes gave me courage, I continued. "It was so much work to keep all the bad memories away. ..." My voice cracked a little. "But worse ... it also meant I couldn't let myself remember the good." I slowly pulled a memory through my wall, the pain of it washing over me, but a smile escaped me despite the ache.

"Theo and I were best friends, total pranksters."

"Am I sorry. Pranksters?"

"Oh—like people who play practical jokes. We'd loved pulling pranks on Josh and Meredith, even on my parents. One time I came home from school and Theo was in the kitchen with an open box of Oreo cookies next to him, and a cookie in each hand. Meredith, Josh, and I all happened to walk into the kitchen at the same time."

Wyn looked confused, like he didn't know what to expect. I rushed on. "I grabbed a few Oreos out of the box and got a glass of milk. Theo nudged me, telling me something was up, so I kept the cookies in my hand, and let Meredith and Josh taste them first."

"Josh popped a whole one into his mouth just as Meredith bit off half of one. I had taken a drink of milk. Seeing the looks on Meredith and Josh's faces made me spurt liquid out of my mouth and nose, as Theo and I both burst into laughter. Josh sprayed chunks of cookie everywhere and Meredith spit hers in the sink, gagging."

Wyn laughed with me. It was strange to laugh and swim, but it was exhilarating, too. My arms were getting tired and I knew practice was almost over. I wished for more time.

"What was wrong with the cookies?" Wyn asked.

"I'm getting to that." I grinned. "Josh screamed, 'What the heck is in these cookies?' and then Theo said, 'Oh nothing,' but he couldn't stop giggling. 'Just toothpaste. What? Don't like chocolate mint, Josh?' Josh was furious. He chased Theo around the room, yelling that he was dead meat. I laughed so hard I had to hold onto the counter to catch my breath.

"Then Meredith asked me, 'Did you know?' and I said I'd guessed and showed her the three uneaten Oreos in my hand."

I chuckled again, glad to realize that I hadn't forgotten such a funny and happy memory. Wyn touched my arm again. I'd been talking for a long time, but I realized I was done for now.

"Am I so glad you told me. Your family sounds amazing and wonderful. Am I so glad that you have good memories. When are you ready, would I love to hear more." Wyn's quiet voice held the kindness I'd come to expect and yet it still sunk deep into me.

I wanted to reach into the water and return his touch, to let him know how much his words meant to me, but while swimming it was awkward and would draw attention to me. Looking into his eyes I saw our shared pain. Wyn had been separated from his family for too long; he was still trapped. This wasn't enough! I wanted to be able to speak to Wyn normally. I wanted to sit on the side of the pool and talk at a regular volume, for hours on end. And if need be, yell at him to get him to understand that I *would* save his life.

But how? I stopped swimming at the end of the pool, pulled myself out of the water and sat on the side. The loss of Wyn's hand on my arm was distracting, but then he gripped my calf and I could concentrate again. I studied the water, the bleachers, and the cement walls, hoping something would jump out at me from the concrete. The longer I stared and the longer I thought, the more it seemed there was no solution.

Wyn's expression grew concerned—and that was when my eyes happened to stop on the door to the parking lot on the far wall by the lifeguard office. An idea formed and I smiled in anticipation.

"Wyn, I want to talk to you, just you, in a normal way. I don't want to have to whisper, and I want you to be able to come above the surface if you want to." Wyn started to shake his head before I even had the words out. "No—listen. If I knocked at that door late at night, say one in the morning, would you be able to open it for me? Er, do they have an alarm set on their doors at night? Do you know?"

"No, there is no alarm. When they bring my food they simply open the door with a key and come in. They do not have to turn off an alarm."

"Excellent! I'll come tonight then."

"Will not be you tired staying up so late? And what if get you caught?" Wyn's whisper was forced and his hand flinched as though he wanted to reach out and stop me from coming to him in the night.

"I'll be okay. I'll go to bed early and set an alarm. I'm not worried about getting caught. If it means more time with you, it's worth it." I glanced at the clock. "Practice is over. Instead of coming during public swim today, I'll have a nap and visit tonight."

A shrill whistle cut into the last word.

"That's it, team. Let's go!" Coach Chase's voice bounced off the walls.

"See you tonight, Wyn!" I whispered and headed toward the change rooms.

"Valerie, wait!" Wyn called, but I kept walking. His worries were baseless, and maybe I could finally get him to trust me and tell me more about his imprisonment. Kamloops was a sleepy city. Who would be up at one in the morning? No one. I wouldn't get caught.

Biology couldn't go by fast enough, especially because we were studying insects. If we'd been studying fish or sea mammals, maybe I could've got some useful information. My growing excitement kept me surprisingly alert, however. I sat at one table with Heather and Greg. One of Heather's study-aholic friends sat behind us. They all had their careers mapped out for the next twenty years and all blended together in my head—but I think this one was Beth. She and Greg were discussing a change to the transit system as Beth skimmed her colour-coded notes.

"From now on, when you get a transfer from whatever bus you're on, the transfer will say a time on it. Each transfer is good for an hour and a half, and you can go on as many different buses as you like. They're also adding three new bus routes."

I turned around. "Timed transfers? Really? That's so much better! I wouldn't have to pay for more than one fare to the pool anymore, except ..." I grinned and looked at Heather. "I don't need the bus anymore! I can't believe I forgot to tell you. I'm allowed to drive again—and that means I'll be able to dive again soon, too!"

Heather blinked twice, seemingly stunned. I admit I expected her to be more excited for me. I glanced around. Beth and Greg were gaping.

"Close your mouth, Greg. You're drooling," I said, laughing a little.

Heather looked even more surprised—but then she cleared her throat and broke into a wide smile. "That's awesome! You'll have to let us know when your next meet is."

Greg and Beth nodded with equal enthusiasm, though both still looked a bit dazed.

Beaming away, I finally realized what had them so shocked. I hadn't been excited about something or laughed with them in over a year. In fact, I couldn't even recall the last time I'd chimed in on a conversation. And all of a sudden I'd done both things at once.

"I'll definitely do that. I don't think there are any meets until Nationals in Toronto, but if there are, you guys will be the first to know." It was still strange to talk and visit so normally again, but I pushed back hard on the sadness clenching my stomach. I couldn't dive, so I could try to live for Theo. Living meant talking and participating.

Beth and Heather chatted about grad dresses and the Grand March and how Beth wasn't sure how to get her father's tux to match her dress.

She turned to me. "How are you matching your father's clothes—?"

"*Shh*," Heather said sharply. Beth broke off abruptly, a look of horror on her face.

I shrugged, knowing what they were worried about.

"It's okay. I mean, it's really hard that my dad—" I cleared my throat. "I was thinking of having my aunt escort me for the Grand March. Possibly even all six of my cousins. That will make quite the splash, eh?" I laughed at the thought of little Sasha there with me. She'd probably pull me along, taking charge as usual.

Beth's laughter joined mine, and Heather's eyes lit up as she giggled along with us. Heather knew I had changed, and I knew that she knew. I had to escape quickly after class in order to avoid her questions.

I didn't have an easy explanation for the shift—especially since I couldn't tell her I was secretly visiting a merman every day. Part of me wanted to, but I'd promised Wyn I wouldn't. When the bell rang, I rushed out the door, giving a small wave to Heather. She could've caught up to me easily, but thankfully our teacher stopped her to ask something about an assignment she'd handed in.

I zipped away after school too, not talking to anyone. Most of my cousins were playing outside when I got home. I hoped it would stay that way, so that I could sleep before dinner. Pulling the blankets over my head, I settled in to nap.

I woke with a small start when a door slammed in the hallway outside my bedroom and one of my cousins yelled unintelligibly. I rolled over to look at the clock. Four forty-five. I wouldn't fall asleep as easily tonight if I tried to go back to sleep now. I'd get up and see if I had any results from my research emails.

I stumbled out of bed and checked my inbox. Zero responses. Really? Was it so hard to help out a high school student? I grabbed a diving technique book from my floor and started to stomp down the stairs, but the sun was streaming in the windows and it calmed me. I knew just where I wanted to be. I opened the book on the rec room's carpeted floor, stretched out like a cat in a large square of sun, and reminded myself that I wouldn't give up on Wyn. I'd get the info somehow, someway. I put headphones in and turned on the music I used for diving practice. I'd finished half a chapter when I realized that I was humming along. I smiled at myself. Me *humming!*

"Valerie?" I lifted my head and saw Sasha standing beside me. She knelt down and gave me a hug. "I'm glad you're not sad anymore." Her sweet bell of a laugh rang through me and then she ran off to play.

I was stunned. Had I really changed so much that even Sasha noticed? I barely saw my cousins. Maybe she was just an exceptionally observant kid.

The phone blared, making me jump. A second later my aunt yelled from the kitchen. "Valerie, the phone's for you. It's Coach Chase."

"Got it." I called back, picking up the rec room's handset. *Please, please, please.* This had to be the news I so desperately wanted.

"Coach?"

"Hi, Valerie. I'll get right to it. Josh phoned. Your doctors gave him the okay for you to dive again. He asked me to pass on the news, said you'd want to hear it from me—"

"YES!" My yell of triumph cut Coach Chase off. "Sorry, Coach. Is there anything else, or can I hang up and go tell everyone now?"

"No, that's it. Welcome back. I'll see you in the deep end tomorrow."

"Thanks!" As I hung up the phone, I couldn't help but break into a very cheesy victory dance. I pumped my arms and jumped up and down in circles.

"I get to dive again! I get to dive again! I get to dive again!"

My aunt appeared in the rec room and pulled me into a hug. "That's wonderful news. I'm so happy you can do something you love so much again!"

"Thanks, Aunt Jocelyn—now I absolutely *have* to call Heather!"

Jocelyn chuckled as I frantically dialed Heather. When Heather finally picked up after what felt like an eternity of rings I couldn't get the words out fast enough. "HeatherIgettodiveagain!"

I spent the next hour calling all my friends and teammates to share the good news. At dinner, I could barely sit still and my little cousins whispered and laughed at my absurd excitement. The second I'd eaten my last bite I excused myself, thanked my aunt, and bolted to my room so I could watch all my old competition videos.

The alarm on my cellphone went off at eight o'clock and I jumped up and started shutting everything down, getting ready for my nap. I was so hyped up it would be a miracle if I fell asleep—but I needed to get some rest if I was going to wake up in just four hours to see Wyn, and then dive five hours after that.

My cheeks hurt with the intensity of my grin. I was going to see Wyn. I could tell him my news in person! It was the perfect way to start the night where I could actually talk to him face to face *above* the surface.

I made myself go through an evening cool down, putting on my pjs slowly, brushing and flossing my teeth, washing my face, brushing the knots out of my hair. This helped some, and my brain was somewhat calmer as I slipped back into my bedroom.

I pulled down my window shade. The sunset was still more

than an hour away, and I definitely wouldn't fall asleep with light pouring into my room.

The darkness wasn't perfect but it helped, and I must've dozed off faster than I thought I would, because after what seemed like only five minutes of lying still I jolted awake to the sound of my radio alarm. The blue digital numbers said 12:45. Perfect.

I slipped off my sheet and tiptoed to my dresser. After letting my pjs drop silently to the floor, I pulled on a comfortable pair of faded jeans and a competition diving circuit T-shirt. I pulled my purse off the bedpost, slung my swim bag over my shoulder, and opened my bedroom door a crack.

I surveyed the hall. My aunt and uncle hardly ever stayed up late, but it was better to be safe than sorry. I opened the door wider, listening hard. Soft telltale snores drifted down the hall from the master bedroom. Aunt Jocelyn always went to bed first and Uncle Andrew's snores told me they were both in bed.

Sidling out of my room, I eased my bedroom door shut behind me and stole down the stairs and out the front door. I was going to see Wyn.

Zack arrived from his shift at the bike shop to find his mother home unexpectedly. After a fifty-minute lecture from her on how he was wasting his life at that "stupid" shop, and the ills of not applying his intelligence to a more suitable life vocation, he was furious and couldn't fall asleep. Hours of tossing and twisting later, he got out of bed and went for a drive. It wasn't as good as biking, but it was the next best thing. Driving the nearly empty streets cleared his head and helped him forget about all his parents' pressures and expectations.

He pulled into the park where he'd asked Valerie out—just another thing that wasn't going how he wanted—and was about to head over to the swings when headlights swept over the grass and playground. Another car was driving by on the cross street. Its bright yellow paint caught his eye. Valerie's car. But where would she be going at one o'clock in the morning with diving practice only a few hours away? Zack started his truck and went home. He'd definitely ask her about it tomorrow.

-CHAPTER EIGHT-
Ajana

Pulling through an intersection on my way to the pool, I had to frantically swerve into the lane next to me as a silver vehicle nearly sideswiped me doing an illegal turn. Stupid Volvo driver with his shiny car, probably drunk. *Stop. They're gone. Focus on the good memories.* ... I flexed my hands and refocused on the road. I headed for the back side of the pool, parked Felicity, and walked up to the door, clutching my swim bag to my chest. I raised my hand and knocked, combating the urge to look behind me.

The door creaked open and there was Wyn. Inside, I stood very still. Only a few utility lights were on, and the low light played off Wyn's blue-hued skin in a strange and new way. I watched as he made his way back to the water. He wasn't as graceful on land, but it amazed me how easily he was able to manoeuvre around, supporting his full weight on his arms. I followed him to the water's edge, rolled up my pant legs, and plopped my feet into the warm water.

Wyn slipped back into the pool silently, then turned towards me, his face like stone. "Should not have you come. It is too dangerous. What if were you seen?" Wyn raked his hand through his dripping hair. "Can I not let this happen anymore. It is too much risk! All so can you simply visit me. It is wrong for me to allow such recklessness." Wyn frowned and looked away. "This should not—"

"Wyn."

Wyn's eyes swept back to mine, searching. I met his stare. He wasn't going to stop me.

"So I'm reckless, am I? Nothing bad happened when I came here tonight—and even if it had, I wouldn't have cared. I hate trying to talk to you while swimming. It's awkward and we're constantly at risk of being seen. This is so much better." I leaned forward. "That's assuming you still want to see me?"

Wyn looked shocked. "Want I to see you, of course."

I struggled not to grin. "Good. I want to see you too—which means some small risks aren't going to stop me. Even you can't stop me. You're stuck in this pool. You can forbid me, but I'll come anyway." I fought a smile, knowing I shouldn't laugh at Wyn's kind, albeit ridiculous concerns. "You can refuse to answer the door, but that would be poor repayment for the trouble I take to get here. So now that that's settled, I have something I'm bursting to tell you." I had to stop myself from clapping my hands with excitement like a kid.

Wyn looked at me quizzically.

"I can dive again!" A laugh of joy escaped me and echoed across the water. "I can't wait to feel my body fall into the water. I want to keep learning all the different twists and turns, there's still so much!"

"Valerie, that is excellent. Am I so happy for you. Falasa."

"Falasa?" I said.

"Is a Littera Erian word, meaning both congratulations and

good luck." Wyn's smile brightened his whole face. "This means we will have less time to talk, but will I enjoy watching you dive again." His voice grew teasing. "And now can I critique you as well."

"Critique me, hey? Hmm. And what would a merman know about diving?" I raised an eyebrow.

"Plenty. Went I cliff diving many times with my brother. We pull ourselves up with our hands and enjoy throwing ourselves from heights just as much as humans do."

"Huh. Who would've thought?" I leaned forward, placing my elbows on my knees and my chin in my hands. "Tell me more about your world and your family, Wyn." I gasped as he spun around and flipped his tail, splashing water on my face, splatters hitting my shirt and pants. Then the mischievous look on his face made me laugh. My shirt stuck to my skin, and I shivered a bit. All of a sudden, Wyn surged above the water and pulled himself up on the pool deck. He sat next to me, his tail dangling in the pool, laughing hard at my surprise.

"Well, guess have I no other choice." Wyn rolled his eyes, but then shot me a sober look. "Please be careful though! Do not take risks simply to see me, or rather do not take unnecessary risks. Please." Wyn's eyes bored into mine. "It would be better if only took I the risks and consequences. Protecting you and the secret of the existence of mer is more important than our conversations or my wants."

"You think that. I disagree. Your life isn't a sacrifice to offer up to protect the secret of the mer."

He shook his head in resignation, and the stillness of the empty pool settled around us like the warmth of the sun.

"Want I to share what has happened to me."

I gasped and Wyn looked a little taken aback. I held my breath. Would he finally tell me? Did he trust me enough?

"Honoured was I that chose you to share so much with me about your family. But it is ... difficult. Many parts of it are strange and still know I so little." Wyn's shoulders rose in the smallest of shrugs. My body was taut and I let out all my breath in a rush.

"It happened while my brother, Faorin, and I were hunting. Was I collecting pearls about half a league from my brother. While collecting we are always in sight of one another. Close by me was a deep ravine. Out of this ravine, five mermen swarmed me. Fought I hard and called for Faorin. Cut I one of them with my knife and incapacitated another by smashing his face with my tail. By this time, though, the other three had their arms around me. One of them gripped my throat and choked me. Before blacked I out, struggled I hard to see what had happened to Faorin. Two more mermen were attacking him and all could see I was him floating in the water. Whether he is dead or alive, do not I know."

The pain in Wyn's voice was an ache that tightened my stomach.

Wyn's head dropped into his hands, and he gripped his hair so hard his knuckles turned white. "Should have I fought harder. My brother may be dead, all because was I incapable. There—"

"Wyn, look at me." Wyn's eyes rose to meet mine and I spoke with all the force I could. "You did everything you could. Seven against two is hardly a fair fight."

Wyn nodded and took a deep breath. "After that woke I up here. A man comes once a week in the middle of the night and leaves enough food for me to eat—barely edible refuse, trout or salmon from one of your markets. Merpeople can survive eating only once a week, but it has been a long time now without sufficient nourishment." He flicked his tail, disturbing the pool's calm surface with large, long ripples, and studied his scales. "The chemicals in the water ... they are worse for me than the hunger."

I clasped my hand over my mouth. How could I have been so blind to his suffering? I'd been so focused on getting him out of the pool, I hadn't seen what it was doing to him *now*. I had no words, no adequate way to express my sorrow and outrage, so I did the next best thing I could. I took his hand, lacing my fingers through his.

He stared down at our touching palms and a shuddering sigh went through him. "Know I my jailer's face," he continued, "but have I never seen him during the day. Have I no idea why they kidnapped me, or why they left me alive. It seems like a lot of trouble to go to, keeping me prisoner. Why not just kill me?" Wyn slapped his tail against the surface of the water.

I tightened my grip on his hand. "You don't know the half of it," I said. "You said you were unconscious when they brought you here?"

Wyn nodded.

"This pool is a good three hours from the coast, at least. They've brought you all the way to Kamloops." I shook my head. "That's quite a feat—bringing a merman this far inland without being seen."

"Studied I human geography, but not in any great detail. This is so perplexing." Wyn's brow creased, and he glanced at the wall behind my shoulder. "It is two in the morning," he said, withdrawing his hand from mine. "Time for you to go. Your team will be here in four hours, and if are you joining them will need you some sleep."

"Humpf. You would have to be a responsible merman, wouldn't you?" I crossed my arms and glowered exaggeratedly.

Wyn grinned. "What if I don't want to go yet? And how can you tell time, by the way?"

"Want or not, need you to go or will be you too tired for practice. And despite your obstinacy, will not I be the cause of your diving suffering." Wyn gave me another smile, then turned and looked towards the east windows. "As for telling the time, in every city or village there is a time keeper. We have camouflaged sundials close to the surface and large clocks with gears of coral and rock in the middle of the village. The clocks are usually in a crevice that can be hidden away should any humans trespass. It is a great honour to be the time keeper and ensure the clock is in good repair and accurate to the sundial." Wyn's eyes skirted across the dark shapes out the window, as though he were trying to see past all the equipment and outdoor track. "Miss I my home and the sky." Wyn frowned and brushed the scales on his tail.

I couldn't imagine not seeing the sky for months and months, and I was stunned that being trapped here for a year hadn't completely broken him. "I'm sorry." I followed his gaze towards the high windows and realized that even from this angle you still couldn't see the sky through them.

Wyn shrugged. "There is nothing can you do. And now it is time for you to leave. Need you sleep."

"Fine. I'll go—but I won't like it."

He laughed and I pulled my legs out of the water and slipped my flip-flops on.

"That is fine. Do not have you to like it. But if have I to be the responsible one in this relationship, so be it." Wyn smiled and I stopped dead. *Relationship?*

"Even though do not like I it, because know I that will you be coming tomorrow night, bring a swimsuit. Have I something special planned."

"Um, okay," I managed to say, despite my reeling thoughts. "See you later." I left in a daze.

I had trouble opening my car door. Wyn had said relationship. Did that word mean the same thing to him as it did to me? Was it even possible for a merman and a human girl to have a romantic relationship? And was I fooling myself pretending I hadn't seen him in a romantic way all along?

Nerves and happy anticipation buzzed through my body as I fell asleep. If Wyn didn't clarify what he'd meant tomorrow night, I'd ask him about it.

"If I come close to the pool, are you going to splash me again?" I asked the next night, raising an eyebrow.

"Not today." Wyn smiled. "Come. Want I to swim with you tonight."

I tried to keep my hands from trembling as I pulled off my T-shirt and shorts. *Relax, Valerie! There's no need to be nervous.* I slipped into the deep water, then moved away from the wall and treaded water as I looked at Wyn. What did he want me to do?

"Swim all around me in whatever pattern and way like you. Maybe should hang on you to the bulkhead for a minute. Need I to ask you something before we begin."

I swam the few short strokes to the bulkhead. Wyn wasn't looking at me; his gaze rested on the water surface just beyond me.

"This is awkward for me. Normally with my own people they would understand right away what wanted I. Because are you human, however, will not you understand if began I." Wyn took a deep breath and raised his eyes to my face. His features calmed. "Valerie, we have something called Ajana. Most merpeople will have only one in their lifetime. Ajana are friends but more—and sometimes romantic, though not always so. Did not I realize how hard this would be to explain." Wyn frowned and swished his hands through the water. Then he began again. "It is a connection between two. The start of a story, a journey, an outward declaration that the other matters to you."

"So kind of like *Anne of Green Gables*? Where Anne asks Diana to be her bosom friend?"

"Do not I know that reference. When spoke I of our relationship last night, hoped I to be able to call you something more than friend today." Wyn's cheerful smile was replaced by a fervent stare and a hint of worry in the lines around his mouth. "Being Ajana sounds different than being bosom friends. More important, more binding. Will I always be there for you. No matter what. Want I this for us. Worry I that this will seem too strange to you, that it will not be something want you. Am I wrong to ask this? Will you be my Ajana?"

I hesitated, shivering at both the cool water and the implications. Was this something I wanted? It was obviously a heavy commitment in his culture. I knew I cared about him. He'd changed my life and helped me face my demons. But did I

care enough? Would that caring hurt me later? Looking at his
face, my heart squeezed tight. He mattered to me. I wanted
this.

"I'd be honoured, Wyn. What do I need to do?"

"Nothing." Wyn's smile was larger than I'd yet seen. "Just
swim and listen."

I let go of the bulkhead and swam into the centre of the pool,
Wyn at my side. I was treading water and Wyn was staring at
me. His stare didn't make me uncomfortable. It pulled me in.
So softly I didn't even realize it was happening at first, Wyn
began singing.

It was the most beautiful, haunting music I had ever heard.
The melody seemed to be the embodiment of Wyn. The sounds
and notes were not in a language I knew, yet they stirred me all
the same. As Wyn's eyes continued to gaze into mine, his music
all around us, I instinctively knew that through this medium
Wyn could fully open up to me.

As I listened the song changed. While the melody still floated
in my mind, Wyn began to weave a harmony with his voice.
These notes were lighter and somehow more feminine. My
breath quickened as I grasped who he was singing about.

Me.

Wyn slipped beneath the water, but his song did not stop. I
could hear him ever more clearly. His voice grew in strength
and power, and then he surfaced and his music peaked. My
hand reached for his even as he extended his hand toward
mine. With a breath we were beneath the water.

While Wyn pulled me through breathless circles and spirals,
I heard the melody merge with the harmony of his song. The
next moment we were above surface again and I was gasping

for breath. And then under we went once more, Wyn's song building and the water frothy with the bubbles from our speed. When Wyn brought me to the surface next, his song was changed. The music grew slower and calmer, a graceful pairing of melody and harmony falling towards a natural end.

Wyn's voice faded and the silence between us was as beautiful as his song. He turned my hand over so our palms were touching, and then he took my other hand. I followed his lead when he took a deep breath, and he pulled me under the water. Then Wyn sang the first words I understood.

Sing down our moon,
That its tide might tie us.
Ajana are we,
Until the white light fails.

The last note disappeared into the water and Wyn leaned towards me, closing his eyes. I closed my eyes in reaction and his forehead touched mine.

"Now and forever, we are Ajana."

Suddenly Wyn's hands were on my waist and we were shooting through the water. We broke the surface and Wyn threw me high in the air, following beneath me with a great leap. My breath caught, and then Wyn's hands reached to meet me and pull me safely back down as we plunged into the water.

I was breathless when he pulled me to the side of the pool, and his eyes never left mine. And then he was lifting me to sit on the side of the pool, and with a swish of his tail, he was up on the deck beside me.

He took my hand once more, his touch gentle, and placed it

on his tail. His scales were like silk beneath my fingers—and yet there was a hardness and strength to them. They were steel wrapped in a thin layer of the smoothest satin.

I couldn't tear my eyes from him, and as he held my hand upon his tail he hummed the last few notes of our song. The faint sounds faded away and Wyn leaned forward, again resting his forehead on mine.

"My Ajana." He pulled back and shook his head, as if marvelling. "What a pair we are."

I could only smile.

"Come. Should you go home now."

"But I—"

"We will speak tomorrow." Wyn slipped back into the water and I stood to go.

My hand was on the door when Wyn called to me.

"Oh, and Valerie? Happy early birthday." He broke into a small, knowing smile and then disappeared beneath the ripples in the water.

I felt my eyebrows raise and my mouth open. *How did he know?* I turned the knob and left the pool, with a huge sigh. For the first time in almost a year, I was truly happy and—

"Valerie?" Zack's voice, loud and abrasive and completely out of place in the peaceful night, shattered my reverie. "What the heck are you doing at the pool this time of night?" All the warm joy flooding through me dripped away as he came out of the shadows beyond my car, a glower on his face.

"I, uh ... had to do some stuff." I wracked my brain for a good reason, any reason I might be at the pool at two in the morning. "I could ask you the same thing. How'd you know I was here?"

"Well, I ..." Now Zack looked uncomfortable. He sighed. "I

had a fight with my mom last night and took off for a drive. I saw your car and was going to ask you about it, but I forgot. And tonight I couldn't sleep, so I went driving again—and saw you again, so I followed you."

"What? That's like total stalking behaviour!" I crossed my arms and glared. "Leave. Now. I don't want you here."

Zack started pacing, his steps agitated and jerky. "I've spent the last hour trying to figure out what in the world you'd be doing here. You've got practice in just a few hours, so it wasn't to dive, but why else would you come to the pool?" His hands clenched and he stopped abruptly, staring at me. "You're meeting someone, aren't you? Who? And why on earth at the pool so late at night?"

"That's something we'd all like to know," said a deep voice, and both Zack and I jumped. A huge man stepped out from behind the trees and bushes beside the pool. His legs were as thick as my torso, his arms Hulk-like. A layer of cement dust covered his T-shirt and ripped jeans. I took a few steps back and bumped into Felicity. "There are cameras. Talk to him as much as you want, but try anything—" Hulk-guy's big beefy finger pointed at me with a jerk. "Anything at all and the fish dies. You got it?"

"Don't threaten her," Zack said, stepping forward and putting himself between Hulk-guy and me. Faster than I could see, there was a thud and then Zack was on the ground, blood pouring from his nose.

"Like I said, don't try nothing." The guy turned and stalked off towards the other parking lot. I grabbed Zack's shoulder.

"Are you okay? What were you thinking? That guy's thicker than a bulldozer."

"What was *I* thinking?" Zack groaned. "What were *you* thinking? What was all that about?"

I stalled and dug around in my purse for a couple tissues, which I handed to Zack to stem the blood. "Is it broken?"

"No, just hurts like the devil." He flung his hair back and stood, glaring at me and pinching his nose. "Whoever you're meeting ith not worth thith. That guy ith beyond dangerouth."

It was hard to take lisping Zack seriously. "Enough. You're fine, and I'm leaving. Don't follow me again. Way too creepy. Seriously." I got into Felicity and watched Zack walk towards his truck far across the lot from my car.

Monster-guy said I could keep talking to Wyn, and I would. I had to see him. But as for not doing anything else? Like hell. As much as I craved seeing Wyn, this situation was plain wrong. I pulled out of the parking lot, not looking back.

Zack waited until he saw Valerie pull out of the lot; then he got out of his truck and made his way to the back of the building. Mystery guy had to be told how much danger he was putting Valerie in.

His nose had stopped bleeding so he threw the bloody tissues in the garbage, then stepped up to the door he'd seen Valerie knock on and rapped softly.

After a minute or two and no answer, Zack shifted his feet. Maybe the guy had left? He lifted his fist to try one more time, just as the door opened. But no one was there.

"Come in."

Zack looked down—and stumbled back. What the—?

He rubbed his eyes, shook his head, stared again ...

No, he really was seeing what he thought he was. A blueish hand at waist level propped the door open, and the arm and torso attached to that hand had a tail! The guy glaring out at him was a merman. Despite the fact that the merman's head barely reached Zack's navel and a tail stretched out behind him, the hardness and sheer power of the merman's presence overwhelmed Zack.

"You are here about Valerie?" the man said coldly.

Zack could only nod.

The merman shifted backwards. "So come in. And shut the door."

Shaking a little and cursing himself for probably being an idiot, Zack did as the merman asked.

-CHAPTER NINE-
Diving

Zack couldn't reconcile what he was seeing with what he knew. Mermaids and unicorns and little elves making shoes were all myths and stories. And yet a myth was before him. Strong and lithe, the guy was the most intimidating creature Zack had ever seen. He watched as the merman lifted himself up by his arms and pushed back into the pool. Then he was gone. Gone! Zack had seen him dive into the water, but now there was nothing. He took a couple quick steps closer to the pool. The merman had to still be there. Apparently you just couldn't see him in the water. That's when the realization hit.

"You're Wyn, aren't you?"

Zack scanned the still water, looking for a ripple, a sign, anything.

"You're Wyn and you're letting her sneak out here in the middle of the night to see you?" Zack clenched his hands into fists. He paced next to the pool. "I've got no idea what's going on—but that big guy who knows about you threatened Valerie tonight, and he practically broke my nose. Maybe you've got her under a spell or something, but I will not let you hurt her." He stopped pacing and looked back at the water. "Do you hear me, fish?" he screamed.

The pool surged and frothed; Zack was soaked and the merman was in front of him. The merman yanked Zack up by his collar until he was inches from his face.

"Do not make the mistake of assuming only care you, human, about Valerie. She is kind, she is strong, and she comes of her own free will." The merman released Zack's shirt and Zack fell back, landing heavily on his butt. "Yes, am I Wyn. No, will I not ever hurt her." He glared at Zack, eyes burning.

Zack tried to work out the merman's words.

The merman huffed impatiently and waved his hand. "Speak I differently than you. I ... Will ... Not ... Hurt ... Her."

Zack nodded. The merman could be lying, but what could he do about it? He slid back farther from Wyn, shivering.

"So if you don't want to hurt her, why do you let her come? That guy's huge—and violent." Zack licked his lips. "The only reason he hasn't hurt her already is because he said he doesn't care if she talks to you. She just better not try anything else."

"That is what he said?" Wyn asked, and Zack nodded. Wyn's face grew stern. "Have I told her not to come!" he roared. "She does not listen. There is nothing can I do. Will not leave I her outside to keep knocking on the door late at night. Even refused I to tell her anything about my imprisonment. She would have none of it."

"That does sounds like Valerie," Zack admitted. "But now what?"

"Do not harm her, but do whatever you can to prevent Valerie getting here. Would I not risk her life. Not for anything."

"Okay." Zack got shakily to his feet. "I'm just going to leave now." He inched towards the door, and before he'd even put his hand on the knob, the merman had disappeared back into the water.

The next morning I woke before my alarm went off to a rousing chorus of "Happy Birthday." My aunt walked into my room holding a tray laden with breakfast. Andrew and my cousins were there too, Michael and Lisa both rubbing their eyes. "The kids almost didn't want to give you breakfast in bed because of your diving practice, but Sasha insisted," my aunt explained after I raised an eyebrow. My clock read 5:30.

"Happy birthday, Valerie! I have a present for you before you go to practice." Sasha held out her hand. I sat up and let her drop the little gift into my palm. It was a key chain, and hanging from the silver ring was a delicate water droplet of a brilliant blue.

I had to smile and held out my arms. Sasha jumped into my hug.

"I thought you could put it on your swim bag. It took two whole weeks of allowance, but it was too pretty not to get it for you," Sasha said very seriously.

"It's beautiful, sweetheart. Thank you."

"There's actually one more gift for you this morning," my aunt said. "We'll talk about doing a party or dinner later, but I thought now would be the best time to give you this." She handed me a simple white envelope. "It's from your parents."

My hands shook as I opened the envelope. Inside was a thick stack of papers, detailing a bank account.

"You know your parents gave Josh and Meredith ten thousand dollars each when they turned eighteen. When they were settling your parents' affairs, the lawyers from your dad's firm found this money set aside for you. So happy birthday from your parents too." I was speechless and the familiar ache in my chest opened wide and throbbed at the mention of my family, but as I looked at Sasha's smiling little face I couldn't help but give a small laugh.

"Can we go back to bed now?" Michael whined.

"Yes, of course. Thank you!" I was relieved to have the serious moment lightened. "You wanna help me eat this?" I asked the giggling Sasha. She answered by taking one of my sausages and tucking into the breakfast feast.

It was hard getting through diving practice that day, as I had no opportunity to speak with Wyn because Coach Chase was pushing us so hard. It was definitely a tough first practice back, but I understood his urgency. Provincials were coming up fast. Just over a month away. I caught Wyn's eye a few times as he swam in the deep waters beneath the diving board. His answering smile inspired me to work even harder to perfect my diving.

Zack accosted me at lunch, as I was putting my textbooks away in my locker. "I'm taking you out for a birthday dessert. Come on." He latched onto my arm. "I'm definitely not gonna let you get out of it." I smiled and let him drag me to his truck and we drove the few blocks to Menchie's.

"Wow. Not even the run of the mill DQ stuff. We're going fancy and getting some frozen yogurt then?"

"You bet!" Zack opened the door for me and we both picked our flavours and started piling on toppings.

Zack made a weird tower of raspberries, Cap'n Crunchberries, and sour gummy worms on top of his carrot cake frozen yogurt, with extra pourable Reese's peanut butter for good measure. *And he called my Slurpee straw superstition weird.* (My flavour combo was way better: key lime yogurt with peaches, blueberries, coconut, and caramel sauce.) Zack seemed fine as he talked about some drama in his Chem class, while we enjoyed our desserts, but his body language was off. He clenched the spoon too tight, his shoulders seemed hunched, and a weird vein was almost popping in his neck.

"... I couldn't believe it when the guy turned around holding his Bunsen burner and waving it like it was a torch—"

"What's wrong?" I could've skirted around it, but that vein was seriously freaking me out.

Zack put down his spoon slowly, and the slowness was even more worrying.

"I talked to Wyn last night."

Oh hell, no. *Don't react, don't react!*

"I thought so. You bite down on your tongue like that whenever you don't want someone to know what you're feeling."

Zack's brow pulled down into a hard ridge. "What"—he ground his teeth and lowered his voice—"in the *hell* do you think you're doing?"

"I don't want to talk about it," I said, taking another bite of yogurt. Speaking around my mouthful I pointed at him with my spoon. "This isn't the time or place. Seriously."

"Not good enough," Zack whispered harshly. "That monster of a guy practically broke my nose, and speaking of monsters, you have no idea what Wyn is capable of. Why do you talk to him? Why do you sneak out and go see him at night?"

"He is not a monster. Don't call him that!" I pressed my fingertips into my forehead, staring down at my bowl. "He saved my life." I looked back at Zack and saw his blatant shock. I shook my head and leaned my forearms against the table. "The accident. I was drowning. He didn't let me die."

"So ..." Zack placed his hand on the table like he was reaching for a lifeline after having wandered into a live volcano. He opened his mouth again to say something more. Nothing came out.

"So I'm aware there's danger, and risks, but he's stuck and I have to do something. ... Yeah."

I picked up my spoon again, but the once great flavours were tasteless in my mouth. I had no idea what the heck was gonna happen now.

"What did he say to you?" I asked, trying for nonchalance and failing.

"Um ..." Zack picked up his spoon again too. "That he wouldn't hurt you. And that I should do everything I can to stop you sneaking up there."

I shot Zack a look. So Wyn was now enlisting help in keeping me from trying to save him? "Wyn is kind, he's good, he cares about me, and won't hurt me. I will not abandon him." I was done my yogurt. I stood and threw the empty container in the trash. "End of discussion. We have nothing more to say about him." I went out the door and waited by Zack's truck for him to unlock it.

Twice on the way back to school Zack opened his mouth, like he was going to say something about Wyn again. Finally, I snapped. "Would you just back off? There's this huge secret of the entire existence of merpeople on my shoulders and apparently because you couldn't leave me alone, now you know too. I have to protect him and his world. Wyn would sacrifice his freedom and his life to protect this secret, so the less we talk about it the better."

"Fine." Zack huffed out a breath. "So I almost got blamed for the moron who tried to start a fire in Chem ..." He continued with his earlier story, with only a little strain. I slouched back into the old bench seat of his truck. This secret, this knowledge, was exhausting. I had to get Wyn out of the pool and back in the ocean where he belonged sooner rather than later.

Later, after the last bell at school, Heather grabbed me.

"You, Beth, and I are going dress shopping." She pulled me away from the hall that led to my car, tugging me towards her car instead.

"But—"

"No. You haven't been shopping with me in ages and it's barely more than a month till grad. None of us are wearing the last gowns on the racks or—horror of horrors—a semi-formal from our closets. This is grad. Grade twelve. We're all getting killer dresses, period."

I recognized the tone and stopped resisting. There was no stopping Heather when she was like this. At least I would be spared the draining experience of explaining Wyn.

"Plus I'll take you out for dinner and dessert for your birthday afterwards. It'll be great." Heather's smile was conspiratorial, and I let her lead me away.

An hour and a half later we were in our third dress shop. I'd tried on at least twenty different dresses, but still hadn't found one that I liked. Blue, orange, pink, red, black lace, purple— none of them were what I wanted or could see myself wearing. It didn't help that all I could really focus on was Zack's discovery of Wyn and what that would mean. At the first store we hit, Beth had found her dress, a baby pink mermaid style that she loved. I had to hide a smile every time she talked about her dress with the mermaid skirt. I didn't need a mermaid skirt because I had my own merman!

I came out from the changing room wearing a lime green dress, even though one look in the mirror had already told me it was a big no. I'd been informed, however, that Heather needed to see *every* dress I tried on.

Beth was taking pictures of Heather in a canary yellow gown with brown lace accents that was stunning on her.

"I like this one best so far, and it makes my curves look awesome, but I'm not about to give up the search yet." She fluffed up the skirt and then saw me standing behind her. "I like that on you, Val, but I can tell you don't."

"Too many sequins and it falls around my hips weird."

"But the heart-shaped neckline is great on you." She eyed me critically in the mirror. "Let's find another one like it, but maybe in sky blue."

The words, "heart-shaped neckline" brought back a memory so quickly I was a little whiplashed.

I'd been thirteen and Mom, Meredith, and I were dress shopping for Meredith's grad. Mer had been going with the same guy for about a year, and she was excited about them going to the big formal dance together.

"That heart-shaped neckline is beautiful on you, Meredith. I think we've found the dress, don't you?" Mom had said.

"Yeah, isn't it gorgeous?" Mer turned and twisted, admiring the dress in the mirror. "I didn't like the colour on the rack, thought it was a little strange, but, wow, I love it!" She gave my mom a hug and for a minute, with their similar colouring and chestnut hair, they blended into each other.

"And what do you think?" Meredith asked me when they pulled apart.

"I love it, too," I'd said. "The burnt orange is stunning and really makes your brown hair stand out."

Mom stood up and pulled us against her.

"My girls," she said, sighing happily. "Sometime soon—or soonish, like in the next decade or so—we'll be going shopping for wedding dresses. We'll have so much fun! When either one of you get engaged, we'll make a trip of it and hit the most stylish shops in Vancouver. It'll be a real girls' weekend." She laughed and we both hugged her tighter. Mom's laugh had always made anything fun.

As the memory slipped away, a couple tears sped down my cheeks. I wiped at them hurriedly. I didn't want them dropping onto the dress that wasn't mine.

Heather turned and looked at me.

"What's wrong?"

"Nothing, I ... well, I just had a memory of shopping with Mom and Mer for her grad dress." I shrugged and clenched my fingers into my bare arms to hold back more tears.

Heather swished over to me and yanked me into a tight hug.

"We won't talk more about it, so there's no more crying, but it's nice to hear you mention them." She pushed me back towards the changing room. "Get out of that dress while I find you a blue one."

Minutes later Heather was lacing me into sky blue satin and chattering about how she'd have to bug Greg to get the boutonnière and corsage soon.

"So you and Greg, then, how serious is it?"

Heather's hands slowed on my laces a little bit. "He's kind

and I like him a lot—but I guess it depends on how he treats me in the next while and what happens at grad. I don't want to be pressured again, and I don't want a guy who'll get totally wasted at any and every opportunity. So yeah, maybe he's boyfriend material, and maybe we'll do the long distance thing, come September. I'm not sure. For now, I just know he'll look gorgeous in a tux." Heather laughed and I giggled along with her.

"There," she said and the bottom of my corset tightened with a jerk. "Don't look in the mirror in here. Go out to the big three-way. You're gonna love this one."

I gasped as soon as I saw the dress, even before I stepped onto the little platform in the middle of the mirrors. This was it. This was the dress. I loved the neckline, but it was the taffeta material that sold me. It made the sky blue colour shimmer like water. The gathers and folds in the skirt mimicked waves and I had to spin in the dress. A huge laugh burst from me. Yes, I had found my dress, a gown that reminded me of Wyn and the water that always surrounded us. I couldn't be happier.

Heather and I reserved our dresses with the clerk (she ended up choosing the canary yellow, after all) and told her we'd be back to place the order within the week.

The three of us went to a Korean grill place for dinner, and it was wonderful to just sit and talk and eat with them. I hardly knew Beth, but Heather filled in any gaps and kept me laughing throughout the night. On the way home, Heather pulled into a Dairy Queen, insisted we dine inside, and treated me to an ice cream sundae. The cold treat reminded me of my dessert with Zack earlier—and the nightmare discussion we'd had—but I tried hard to put aside worries about Zack and trying to save

Wyn.

"Because no birthday is complete without ice cream and chocolate," Heather said, then pulled a sparkler from her purse and stuck it in my ice cream. After she lit it, she and Beth embarrassed me completely by singing "Happy Birthday" so loudly the whole restaurant could hear. I blushed, but laughed too. The sparkler melted half my ice cream away while they sang and it spilled all over the table—but the unmelted parts were delicious.

When they finally dropped me off at home I was relieved, as it had been a long day between fending off Zack's questions and doing a lot of socializing that I still wasn't quite used to—but it had been a good day, too.

Later, as I settled under my covers to watch an old musical on my laptop, Josh called.

"Happy Birthday, Valerie! I'm on my way to a night shift but I wanted to call."

"Thanks. I appreciate it."

"Did you have a good birthday? What are you doing right now?"

"Yup, it was nice actually. Got breakfast in bed really early this morning before practice. Went dress shopping this afternoon with some friends and then out for dinner. And now I'm in bed watching a movie before I crash."

"Wow. Really? That's what you're doing the night of your eighteenth birthday?"

I rolled my eyes. "I have practice tomorrow, Josh."

"Right. Anyway, listen, I want to come up and take you out for a celebration dinner, too. Would a week from Saturday work?"

"Sure, sounds fine."

"Great! I've got to run now, so I'll let you get some sleep. Happy birthday again."

"Thanks. Have a good night."

"'Night."

Soon after I hung up with Josh I turned off my computer and snuggled into my blankets, happy to daydream about Wyn as I hugged my pillow. I fell asleep hearing his voice in my mind and remembering what his tail felt like beneath my fingers.

Just a couple hours later my alarm went off, and I snuck out of the house again, carefully watching the whole time I drove for any sign of Zack's truck. I also looked through the bushes at the pool for the Hulk-ish guy. I had no idea what I'd do if Zack had been following or I'd found the mammoth of a human, but it felt safer somehow to look around before knocking on the back door of the pool.

"Look you happy today," Wyn said, once he'd let me in and we were both sitting poolside.

"I am." The truth of the words surprised me. "It's been a good birthday—which leads me to a very important question. How'd you know it was my birthday?"

"A number of months ago, before your accident, Heather asked what wanted you to do for your birthday. Told you her nothing. She said 'So I'm just supposed to act like May eighteenth is a normal day?' Therefore knew I when your birthday was."

"Becoming Ajana yesterday was a birthday present for me?"

"Yes. The ceremony takes place on the first night of the full moon. Wanted I to make our ceremony as close as possible to what would happen in the ocean, which is why did not wait I for your actual birthday. Had I to have you as my Ajana. Mean you too much to me. Tell me about your celebration."

I complied and enjoyed telling him. When I started to get chilly with just my legs in the water, he tugged me in and we swam together. First, he pulled me through the water so fast everything blurred and I laughed and laughed—and then I swam next to him to warm my arms and legs. All too soon it was time to leave, but seeing Wyn had made a wonderful birthday amazing.

The next morning I was getting ready for school (on the one day in ages Chase had cancelled diving practice because of some sort of meeting), and throwing shirts and pants all over my floor. The regular jeans I wore all the time were dirty, and I couldn't find my second pair. I was about to go and toss the laundry room in search of them when I saw a flash of colour beneath my black dressy pants. I pulled out my coral-coloured skinny jeans. The last time I'd worn them had been before ...

I closed my eyes and took a deep breath.

Before my family had died. I took another deep breath and ran my hands over the material. They really were a gorgeous colour. I pulled them on, and liked the look of them in my mirror. I put an oversized three-quarter-sleeve shirt on over top. The shirt had geometric shapes in blues and greens on a white background. I'd only worn it maybe once in the last year. I pulled out the stud earrings I normally wore and dug around in my jewellery box. I put in some dangly silver earrings and pulled my hair into an easy side messy bun instead of my normal ponytail. Checking out the whole outfit in my full-length, I was surprised. It was more colour than I'd worn in a long time and yet I liked it. The designs on the shirt made me think of brush strokes from when I painted with my mom, and the bright orangey-pink of my jeans reminded me of the reef I was painting on my canvas upstairs. I kicked some of the clothes on the floor out of my way, found my purse, and rushed out the door.

My dives continued to progress. I had a list of eleven, and Coach Chase had a very specific strategy for this competition for me. I needed to keep working and practise my basics, because messing up an easy required dive was a good way to lose.

I was showing Wyn some of my dives while we were together one night. I was working on controlling my somersault, as Chase had made a point of telling me that learning to control the somersault was key to having a good twister dive.

As I popped up in the water, Wyn swam over to me.

"Your approach was good," he said, "although the last few dives your head alignment on entry was off, but your hands were excellent. Maybe try focusing on your head?"

"Thanks," I said. It was wonderful to practise with Wyn. He knew what he was talking about, and diving always made me feel amazing. It was hard and took focus, but I was always rewarded with seeing his face when I finished. I tried a somersault again, focusing on my head alignment when I entered the water. There was no smack of any body part and I knew it was a great rip entry. When I popped up from the water, I saw Wyn's huge smile and had to laugh in response. Diving with a merman. Crazy.

I soon eliminated my nightly visits to Wyn. I knew Coach Chase was beginning to notice how tired I was. With Wyn's encouragement and assertion that I needed sleep to be at my best, I only saw him during public swims three days a week. Coach Chase had us doing afternoon gym resistance training, so I couldn't get to public swim as often as I wanted to.

Wyn and I were occasionally able to sneak in snippets of conversation when no one was looking during these public swims, but it was never enough. It wasn't only his world my mind craved to hear more about, but him as well. He loved his studies and his art. Studying humans was his main hobby. His parents had encouraged this, but also enforced caution and stressed the importance of never being seen. I listened intently when he told me about all the songs he loved to sing. His sister Aina was an accomplished composer in their community, and I couldn't wait to hear him sing some of her melodies just from the few bars he'd hum for me occasionally. I regretted each time I had to leave the water, but soon all this hard training would be over and I'd be able to spend more time with Wyn again.

Zack hadn't confronted me about Wyn since our frozen yogurt trip. Maybe it was because he could tell I wasn't as tired and was focusing more on my diving. Whatever the reason, I was grateful. I carefully avoided the subject of the guy with a tail trapped in the pool, and so did he.

Few things broke the routine of the following days: training, school, eat, sleep, work, and Wyn. I was therefore surprised when I got a text message from Josh saying he'd pick me up the next evening at six. I'd forgotten about our dinner plans. A part of me wanted to see him, but another part of me didn't feel close to him at all. Would we even have anything to talk about?

I was a little hesitant as I climbed into Josh's red clunker of a car the next night.

"Hey, Val." He gave me a little one armed hug.

"Hey." Small talk started slowly and felt perfunctory at first, but as we visited I began to relax.

We arrived at a moderately fancy restaurant and Josh ordered prime rib while I ordered a seafood salad.

As we ate, Josh asked about my diving, and I told him all about my training and how Provincials were less than two weeks away.

"It's finally my year to win because the girl who kept beating me has moved up from juniors. I just have to keep my confidence up and dive the way I know how. Wyn says I'll have no problem, because—"

I felt the colour drain from my face even before Josh spoke.

"Who's Wyn?"

"Uh, a friend." I shrugged. *Keep cool*, I told myself. "He watches me dive and stuff."

"Really? The only guy I've ever heard you talk about is Zack. When did you meet Wyn?"

"A couple months ago."

"Will I get to meet him?"

"Um, probably not. He's pretty private. He doesn't even have a phone." I tried to keep my voice level so Josh wouldn't hear my fear. I could *not* expose Wyn's whole world. Not again, Zack was more than enough to deal with.

"Yeah, right. Everyone has a phone."

"Seriously! His parents aren't ... uh ... around, and he lives on his own and can't afford one right now."

"Well, maybe I'll meet him in person, then. Surely you're not going to tell me he's unable to walk?" Josh's eyes narrowed with his sarcasm.

You'd be surprised.

"Uhhh, how about next time we hang out I'll phone you from my cell and you can talk to him, okay?"

"Is he your boyfriend?"

I glared. "That's none of your business, Josh."

"Just be careful."

"Back off, Josh. You're not Dad!"

"That's right, I'm not—but I highly doubt you take the trouble to confide in Aunt Jocelyn or Uncle Andrew, so I'm trying to be interested, to know what's going on with you."

"Interested?" I sucked in a breath. "You wanna talk about me? You left. You and I have spoken on the phone maybe twice a month for the past year. You don't know me."

"Keep your voice down." The words were a slap. "You're making a scene. And I've been here for you. You know that."

My muscles tightened. "No, you haven't. You ran before their graves were cold. You turned your back and threw yourself into your job. How many hours a week do you work, Josh?" I spoke louder and louder. "Oh, wait—I wouldn't know that number because you're too preoccupied with your job to drive three hours to visit your sister." I was on my feet now. "You wanna be my brother? Try actually caring once in a while and talking to me about something more than superficial chit-chat." I turned and stalked off.

The ride home was silent. Josh tried to start a conversation more than once, but I wasn't about to listen or allow that. Once we reached the house, I got out and slammed my door. Let him think about how he'd abandoned me and left me to my own devices when I really needed someone.

My anger lasted a couple of days. But with Wyn, I only got away with avoiding the subject of why I was upset for one day. I told him what had happened and just listening to his calm voice talk about my argument, I knew I'd overreacted. Wyn had a way of making me see what I ignored or blinded myself to out of anger. When Josh called me only four days after our dinner and I told him I was sorry for overreacting, it actually wasn't a half bad talk. Apparently he was doing really well and had assisted on a pretty complex surgery the day before.

Before I knew it, it was the last practice before Provincials. I pulled into the parking lot to see a bright banner above the front door. "Come see the new renovations soon!" Thankfully, Coach said their reno schedule wouldn't interrupt our practice times—and with us out of town for the competition this weekend, it wasn't going to be a concern for long.

In an unbelievably short amount of time, practice was over. I'd made hardly any mistakes and felt confident. Before I knew it, evening arrived and I was off to see Wyn. It would be the last time I saw him before I left with my team in two days. I had decided to make a single exception to my no-late-nights-with-Wyn rule, as I had a surprise to show him. I gingerly pulled the canvas out of the trunk of my car, and held it behind my back as Wyn let me in.

"I'm not going to stay long, but I had to say goodbye, and I wanted you to see something."

Wyn sat perched on the pool edge, his tail swishing in the water.

With an unnecessary and corny flourish, I pulled the canvas out from behind my back. It was an ocean scene with a reef and merpeople. I'd painted the mer in such a way that you never saw a face and just hinted at the enormity of the world that might be there. The bright colours of the reef were a sharp contrast to the deep colours of the water and the tails of the merpeople.

"I've only been working on it occasionally." I tucked a piece of hair behind my ear. "Which is why it took me so long to finish it." I knelt next to Wyn with the painting propped against my knees. "My mom and I used to paint together. I loved it. But since her death I hadn't picked up a brush. I started painting this right after you told me about your world. I wanted to capture everything you said." I watched Wyn study my painting. My hands were trembling slightly. It had been a long time since someone had looked at one of my paintings. "It may not be the best, but I think it's what I want to say. When others see it they'll think it makes your world seem magical and impossible, even though I know the truth. I wanted—"

"Stop," Wyn said. "It is beautiful, Valerie. Just right. The beams of sunlight coming down through the water remind me of home. Like I that you did not put any of the faces of the merpeople in view. It adds mystery. The coral in the many colours and long swirls of current are painted in a way that makes me think of the water and how it moves and shifts."

"I'm so glad you like it." I returned his smile in full force. "Every time I got nervous or worried about Provs, I'd paint and it calmed me. You gave me that, Wyn. It means so much to me. I wanted to show you how much, and so I put that into every stroke. It's a thank-you."

"This painting is the highest compliment have you ever given me." Wyn touched a finger to my cheek. "Leave you in two days. Need you sleep. Thank I you for this. But go. Will not have

I you not at your best because of me."

I nodded, letting go of my determination to stay longer for once. The moment was too perfect to ruin it with squabbles about how long I should or shouldn't stay. I stood.

"Wish me luck."

"Good luck," Wyn said.

"I'll think of you just before I dive, then it'll be kind of like you're there with me."

"Will I be there with you then in thought. Now go, Ajana."

I turned and strode out the door.

Without any more practice sessions, I had time to focus on saving Wyn. So the next night before bed, I sat at my computer with my box of research beside me. The Olympics were back in reach, and yet instead of constantly thinking about my next dive, my head was filled by Wyn. The knowledge that the chemicals were so damaging was horrifying. I was watching a video about soap healing animals from oil, when there was a knock on my door.

"Come in."

"We need to talk," Andrew said, as he walked into my room.

"I'm busy. Can it wait?" My hand clenched on the computer mouse. There hadn't been any fallout from Josh's email saying I was hallucinating—yet. Was my uncle here to force me to talk to him about it?

"You're watching a video of a duck. How busy could you be?"

I bit my tongue. "It's for an assignment," I mustered with as much calm as possible. "And because of the competition this weekend I won't have any other time to do it." I had to protect Wyn. I had to protect Wyn.

"Your aunt and I are concerned, as is Josh. Finish this

homework tonight, but as soon as you get back from your competition, expect a long conversation."

I really didn't want to have any conversations with this guy who'd messed up my family for so many years, but there was only so much I could do about it. Hopefully, it had nothing to do with Wyn, and I could say whatever he wanted to hear to get the conversation over.

"All right. I gotta finish this, though."

Andrew nodded and left without another word, a resigned but concerned look on his face. Instead of going back to the video, I started writing a list of reasons and excuses I could give my uncle during our upcoming talk. I had to convince him I was sane. Wyn depended on me to do that.

Saturday came. I piled onto the bus with my teammates. After a few hours of watching grass, trees, towns, and farms flash past, we arrived in Vancouver. I ate dinner, checked into my hotel room with two other girls, and then it was lights out. Snuggling into the starchy hotel sheets, my thoughts turned to the upcoming competition.

I'm here. And it's my year!

My stomach lurched with feelings: anticipation and excitement, nervousness, the thrill of competing, and the worry about losing focus. I visualized each of my dives over and over, but after the third run-through it hit me. This was the first time I'd be competing in Provincials without my family there.

I pushed myself up and put a shaking hand to my mouth. How could I do this without them? Why even bother to? My chest tightened and my throat ached, but I couldn't cry and disturb my roommates.

Think about Theo, I told myself. *Think about Theo.* I tried to concentrate on his strength and courage facing death and his wishes for me. My mind turned to Wyn. I stopped shaking and sank back into my pillow. *Wyn cares about me. He knows what's happened to me. He is my light. Keep it together.* Repeating this to myself over and over again, exhaustion finally took over and I slept.

I'd never been on a stage for a play, but I imagined this might be the same feeling. Bright fluorescents illuminated the length of the pool. I was standing on the board, with every eye in the audience on me. The water was glass. I raised my arms. Counted. One bounce. Two bounce. Three bounce. I closed my eyes. *Wyn.* And then I was in the air, turning and twisting. I felt the smooth slip as I entered the water almost perfectly vertical. YES!

This dive was a forward one-and-a-half somersault with one twist. I'd had only slightly more splash than my previous best. Nailing it meant I wouldn't be cut after the semi-finals and I'd be in the finals. There were still quite a few dives to do, but I couldn't stop beaming.

Usually time seemed to slow between events at Provincials, but not this year. Maybe it was because my mind was full of Wyn, or maybe because it was finally *my* year. I was pumped up with adrenaline at the thought of finally getting gold.

Regardless, time whooshed by after my last set of dives, and then I was on the board again for the finals. I'd already done well with all my other dives in the final set; I only had one left to do, a forward one-and-a-half somersault dive in pike. Its degree of difficulty wasn't that high, although it was one of the required dives, and I was thankful Coach always had us concentrate on the fundamentals.

Again I thought of Wyn just as I finished my bounces, and then I had a tight grip on my legs as I spun in the air. There was a rush in my ears as I entered the water and bubbles exploded around me.

With water dripping down my legs and a towel wrapped around me I heard the scores called out.

"Eight five. Eight nine. Eight two ..." The high scores kept coming. Excitement hummed through me. They were excellent marks and put me in first with only one competitor left to dive. Sitting next to Coach I felt a tap on my shoulder. I turned and there was Heather.

"Ahh!" I cried and hugged her hard. "What are you doing here?"

"I couldn't not be here!" Heather's huge smile was infectious "This is your senior year Provincials. I left insanely early this morning to get here."

It was a perfect surprise and I clutched her hand tightly as the last girl stepped up to dive. I held my breath and watched her execute her dive. It was a difficult one, and from what I saw she over-rotated slightly; I grabbed Chase's arm with a little gasp.

The marks were called and all three of us were on our feet, cheering. I'd won.

"Congratulations!" Chase pulled me into a hug, and then stepped back to look at me. "You deserve it. That last dive was one of the best I've ever seen from you."

"Thanks, Coach," I said, and then Heather was pulling me

around to face her, and Coach left to go support some of my other teammates in their events.

"Your last dive was amazing. You totally had a perfect rip!" Heather gave me another hug, then pulled back. "Wait. That's the word, right? For when you enter the water with almost no splash? That's a *rip*."

"Yes, that's a rip." I laughed. "I can't believe you're here. I can't believe I won. Oh, my gosh—I won!" I couldn't stop smiling.

"Your aunt wanted to come too, but she wasn't up for making the trip to Vancouver with all the kids by herself, and your uncle's working. And Zack wishes he could be here, but his parents are in town at the same time for once and made him stay home to visit."

"I'm just glad you're here," I said, laughing.

"So are you excited to go home and tell Wyn about this?" Heather said.

And just like that all my excitement left me, pooling at my feet like the water dripping down my legs.

"What?" I said, trying hard not to stare at Heather and seem nonchalant.

"Oh, come on, Val. Josh and I talk." Heather shifted her weight. "We've been talking for over a year. You refused to talk about anything in depth with him, and he felt like he wasn't getting the whole story from your aunt, so he asked her for my number. I kept him up to date on how you were doing. Why haven't you told me about this Wyn guy?"

"Seriously? What is wrong with you?" I pulled off my towel and started vigorously drying myself off. "So the two of you, what, made a pact to watch me? You spy on me and report back to him? Nice." I snatched up my duffel bag and stomped off to the change room, Heather following closely.

"You shut us all out." Heather's voice was pointed, and I hunched against it. "I care about you and so does Josh. We just talked about—"

"Enough." I shoved my way into a shower stall and let the hot water pour over me. How could they? I so didn't want to deal with this right now, and yet I knew Heather was outside the stall, waiting to have it out. *What would Wyn do in this situation?* And that's when the anger wilted and a pit heavier than my resistance weights settled in my stomach. Heather knew about Wyn. I'd latched onto the fact that her and Josh had been talking about me behind my back, but Wyn was the priority. I had to know what Heather knew, how much she had guessed. Threats to the secret seemed to be coming at me from all sides. What was I going to do?

I finished showering, dressed quickly, and walked out of the stall towards the mirror, drying my hair.

"Say I didn't give you a whole lot of crap about you going behind my back," I said to Heather while looking at her in the mirror. "Why did you mention Wyn like that?"

"Josh called me a little while ago concerned about a guy named Wyn that you'd met. I said I didn't know him, and we were both worried that you'd never mentioned him." Heather shrugged. "It was just a shock to me that I didn't know about this guy who is apparently important you. You're my best friend. I guess I didn't need to spring it on you here at the competition but it, well, hurt that I didn't know about him."

I shook my head trying to make it seem trivial. Wyn's world depended on me shifting Heather's interest away from him.

"We're friends." I started combing my hair. "I see him at the pool. He swims competitively and goes to a high school across town." I hated lying to Heather—she usually knew when I was—but hopefully she wouldn't push this. Not here. Not now.

"So he's only a swimming friend?"

"Yeah." I started packing up my stuff and putting it into my duffel bag. "I think Josh might've been overly concerned because I freaked out when he asked if Wyn was my boyfriend. He's never pried into my boyfriends before and I hated it." This had to work. It had to be a good enough reason. *Please, please, please just drop the subject, Heather.*

"Guess that makes sense," Heather said. "Are you okay if I still talk to Josh occasionally? I don't say anything bad about you."

"I guess. Just talk to me more and tell me what you'll be talking to him about, okay?"

I resisted the urge to heave a sigh of relief. Wyn's secret was still safe. Heather followed me back out to the pool for the medal ceremony, and I forced the worry from my mind and tried to enjoy getting my medal.

I wore my gold medal on the bus ride home, and the high from winning returned. Although I felt slightly ridiculous at my giddy amount of enthusiasm, I couldn't wait to see Wyn and tell him how I'd won. Public swim was out, though. I'd never be able to whisper the news.

"Come into the kitchen, please, Valerie," I heard Andrew call, even as I was still taking my shoes off in the entryway after being dropped off on the Sunday night.

I walked in and both Josh and Andrew were sitting at the small breakfast nook table. I took a step back.

"Josh?"

"Hey. Congrats on the competition." He nodded at my medal.

"Thanks. Why are you here? Don't you have work?" I asked, even though I knew exactly why he was here. They were so doing an intervention in case I was insane. But I wasn't about to give in and let them put me away. I mentally rehearsed the lines I'd come up with. I'd only managed to think of a pitiful three ideas, but it was better than nothing.

"Sit." Andrew pointed at the chair across the table from him and Josh. "Your aunt will join us shortly, after she finishes bedtime with your cousins."

"You seem to be all ready for me and waiting. How'd you know I'd get in right now?" Like really, were they sitting in the kitchen like this for an hour waiting for me?

"Your coach texted me as you pulled into town."

What the hell? Coach *knew* about Wyn. Why was he helping these two force me into therapy or into taking anti-psychotic drugs or something?

"Josh got here this afternoon. We wanted to talk to you together and you did agree to this conversation before you left."

I agreed to a conversation, yes. If I'd known it was going to be a two against one interrogation type thing I would've said, "screw that." I plopped into the chair Andrew had pointed at.

"What?" I said, with all the respect I could wring out of my voice. I still hated my uncle for what he did to my dad, but if I was to make them believe that I hadn't seen a merman I needed to keep my focus steady.

"We're all concerned. We feel you haven't been handling your grief well and want you to go to therapy," Andrew explained.

"It's been over a year, and we want to help you. Plus, seeing a merman hallucination could be a manifestation of the fact that you haven't coped with this," Josh added. His face held only concern, and I couldn't fault him for that, but dang, he'd just used one of the reasons I'd come up with. Here's hoping my lying had improved.

I nodded in what I hoped looked like agreement. "Thinking about it afterwards, that sounds pretty plausible. I've never seen the mermaid guy again. But do you guys seriously want me talking about everything that happened with some stranger? I can't." And that was perfectly true. I couldn't imagine spending hour upon hour dodging questions and talking around Wyn to someone who was probably an expert at telling if people were lying. Exhausting.

"Yes." Andrew stared at me, and I forced myself not to squirm.

"But aren't I doing better?" I pleaded. "I'm painting again. I'm hanging out with my friends more, and doing well at school. I even went grad dress shopping with Heather."

"That doesn't mean you don't need therapy. You won't talk to any of us, and you need to talk to someone," Josh said, taking my hand across the table. "How much do you know about this Wyn guy?"

All the muscles in my legs and back tightened, but I forced the hand Josh was holding to stay relaxed. "A fair amount. Ummmm ... why?"

"Because I think he may have slipped a hallucinogen into your drink or something, and that's why you saw a mermaid."

My mouth popped open.

"I am *not* on drugs." I ripped my hand away from him, crossing my arms tightly over my chest. "I know you never did drugs in high school, so what makes you think I'd be so stupid?"

"How do you know I never did drugs? And a hallucinogen is the only thing that makes sense. I asked to see your medical records this afternoon, and there's nothing about your injury that would cause this."

"Mer told me you never did drugs." An ache tore through my heart at her name. "She said you were proud of the fact and told her so." Josh had seen my medical file. That eliminated the whole concussion excuse. I hadn't even thought of drugs to explain a hallucination. Freak. Maybe I should've said I'd been on an acid trip. Too late now. I'd been so angry at the accusation that I hadn't stopped to think about it.

"Is this Wyn guy a dealer? Did he slip you something?" Andrew demanded.

"You flipped out at me when I asked about him. Is it because you know he's a dealer and are getting drugs from him?" Josh said.

I wanted to sigh and press my fingers into my hair and massage out the tension. Instead I relaxed my shoulders and unfolded my arms. Trying for calm. Trying to convince them.

"Wyn is a good guy. He's a competitive swimmer. He'd never do drugs. I've never tried anything and don't plan to. The merman? It must've just been my imagination going into overdrive. I've never seen it again. I'd stopped painting, and I think my brain needed an outlet. If I agree to see the school counsellor, Susan, for at least one session, is that good enough?"

Zack had talked about Susan the counsellor before. He'd seen her tons of times because his parents wanted him to completely plan out his career and post-secondary school years in advance. He called her Seven because her face was so expressionless, like the cyborg in that *Star Trek* show he liked to watch. He told me she was smart and organized but didn't push on the emotional, like how he felt about his parents being gone all the time and stuff. If I could go see her and not a dig-into-your-feelings kind of psychologist, so much the better.

Just then my aunt walked in and sat down next to me.

"How are things going in here? Sorry it took me so long. Tristan was giving me some guff."

"Valerie says she'll go see the school counsellor," Andrew told her.

"Really? That's wonderful." Aunt Jocelyn looked at me. "I know they wanted to talk to you about hallucinogens, because that was the only thing your uncle and Josh thought made sense. But you haven't taken any drugs, have you?"

"No, I haven't." I stared back at her. At least this I could be honest about.

She nodded. "I believe you, and I think you're a lot more like your mother than you realize. She used to see the fantastical all around her and then paint it. She also had a ton of imaginary friends while we were growing up. So you're not worried about these things you're seeing?"

"No. And that's a comfort. About Mom." I gulped down the lump of pain that formed in my throat at talking about my mother. I turned to Josh. "And I'm sorry again about how I reacted to you asking about Wyn. I blew up. I know. It was just really unexpected."

"I know." Josh took my hand again. "Someone pointed out to me that I was being pretty hypocritical, wanting you to open up but not making an effort to get to know who you are now." He smiled. "You'll see the counsellor?"

I nodded. That was it? They believed me? Whooof. That was a relief-and-a-half. Wyn was still safe.

"Okay. Enough. Enough." My aunt bustled up and across the kitchen. "Now let's see that medal and share some of my really good chocolate I hide from the kids." Aunt Jocelyn pulled down a brightly coloured box from the cupboard above the fridge, and I told them all about the competition. I finally pled exhaustion twenty minutes later and escaped to my room. It was now past ten, but I still set my alarm to see Wyn. No way I wasn't going.

I snuck out without mishap, only feeling a little tired. My excitement at seeing Wyn again amped me up, and I finally had more time to focus. First we'd stop the chemicals harming him and then get him free. Maybe he'd have some ideas about how to hinder the toxins hurting him.

I turned my key to start Felicity, but she groaned with a thud and wouldn't turn over. I tried again and all I heard was a faint click from under the hood. Of all the—! I slammed my hand into the steering wheel a bunch of times. Why did Felicity have to fail me now? I tried a whole bunch more times, but gave up after fifteen minutes of trying to get the engine to start. Yanking my purse onto my shoulder I stalked down the sidewalk and pulled out my phone to call a cab. I refused to let a little frozen car defeat me. I would see Wyn. The yellow cab finally pulled up half a block from my aunt and uncle's place twenty minutes later. The night was creeping on and I was losing my time with Wyn. Even though I didn't have practice again till Tuesday, I still had school and had to get some sleep.

When I finally got to the pool I ran in through the door, tearing my shirt off as I went, and saw Wyn slip back into the water after opening the door for me. I had to forget about all the crap: therapy, clunker cars, and so many people knowing or thinking they knew about Wyn.

"Wyn!"

His head popped up out of the deep end. I stepped out of my shorts and leapt into the air. "I WON!" I drew my knees up into a cannonball and pounded into the water. The wave I made crashed over Wyn's head. I surfaced and my laughter laced with his.

"Wonderful!" He grabbed my hips and threw me high. I gasped as the air whipped past my face and I dropped back into his arms. All the worry seeped out of me. I could handle all the stuff thrown at me. I was with Wyn.

"I did it. I actually did it. Not only did I get first, but I'm going to Worlds! I can't believe it."

"Of course did you. Can I believe it." His face radiated with his smile, and we swam together to the side of the pool. I pulled myself up and leaned back on my elbows, my legs dangling in the water. Wyn propped his head on his arms at the pool edge.

"Tell me everything," he said, and I loved his laughing tone.

My words flowed fast and fell on top of one another, and Wyn kept smiling and listening. I knew my excitement was also his own.

"It was so amazing. I wish you could've seen it."

"Am I happy for you. Deserve you this." Wyn paused, then reached out and gently ran his fingers along my cheek. "But why is there a shadow of tears and worry upon your face?"

I startled and sat up. "How did you know that?" I could tell him about the tears, but had to keep my worry about Heather, Josh, my aunt and uncle, Zack, and everything else out of my face.

"Forget you that my eyes are more powerful than a human's. What could have had such an effect upon you at your happiest time?"

"I ..." I gulped air and tried again. "I missed my family. I was visualizing my event before going to sleep and thought of my family in the crowd, and it hit me really hard because they wouldn't be there." I turned away from Wyn, unable to look at him as it struck me again, the hard ache of their absence. Then the water swished and Wyn's arms were around me. I leaned into him, my back against his chest. Soft tears spilled down my cheeks, in part for my family, and in part for the stress of keeping his secret. I couldn't betray him, but it was so hard.

"Do not worry. All is well. Are you safe. Are you okay." Wyn stroked my hair. "They still love you. And they are watching over you because they have gone on."

I pulled away and looked at Wyn's face. "You really believe that? That there's a life after this one?"

"Yes." Wyn's voice was quiet but filled with conviction.

It was comforting to know that Wyn believed as my parents had, despite the fact that I was still undecided myself. I settled back into his arms again and felt my tears still and my body relax as we both watched the water.

"I wish death would've just left us alone."

Wyn's arms tightened and he shifted behind me.

I sat forward and turned to face him. "What?"

"Have not I been fully honest with you."

"What do you mean?" The tone of his voice and the slump of his body was a slap to the chest, like a bad dive. Whatever could he have to say that would make his face so stricken?

-CHAPTER TEN-
Plans

"Am I dying."

No. No. It wasn't possible. He was Wyn. He was strength and fortitude personified. He was my light. He couldn't be dying.

"The—" Wyn cleared his throat. "The chemicals they put in the water to keep it clean are destroying my cells and my ability to heal. Under normal circumstances my body would fight the effects of these chemicals the same way your body would repel a disease. The high concentration, however, and the continued exposure is not something my body can continue to stop."

"But you can't ... no." I shook my head. "You can't be dying, Wyn."

"Look at me, Valerie." Wyn stared into my eyes, his jaw set and hard. And then I did. I really looked. Seeing the minute details my eyes hadn't noticed.

If I hadn't seen Wyn and spent time with him almost every day for the past three months, I might not have noticed the changes. His eyes were sunken and had dark circles. His scales lacked their original lustre and their once-bright hue had faded.

The skin on his arms and torso was taut and thin, like a person who'd been on a diet a little too long. I stared and fought to accept what I was seeing. I turned my head away, trying not to let him see the tears welling in my eyes. I was as helpless as when my family died. Death was still haunting me, laughing. As suddenly as it had come, however, the shock and pain of Wyn's revelation turned to anger. I glared at him.

"What do you mean by keeping this a secret?" I yanked my legs from the water and started pacing. "We're Ajana. You say you care about me, and yet you don't tell me this?" My whole body was shaking, and pacing wasn't enough. There was too much anger in me. I sprinted to the edge of the lane pool and dove with all my strength, then swam fast and hard. My lungs were heaving when I heard Wyn's voice next to me.

"Valerie." His voice cut through the rush of the water and the pulsing of blood in my head. I clutched the side of the pool and let my breath drag through me, fighting sobs.

"Why?" I stared at him and saw the despair in his eyes.

"Am I sorry. Should I have told you. But it hurts that am I the one who has put that look on your face." Wyn grasped the top of my hand as I held tight to the pool, my knuckles straining. "Did not I want to cause you more pain."

No. No. This wasn't happening. I turned and clung to Wyn. Why? Why did he have to die?

He's not dead yet. The thought hit me hard and I fixed on it. We had time. We had notice. I wouldn't stand idly by when I could do something to save him. All my research to get him out of the pool would be for nothing if he died now. *I must save him. But how? What can I do? Even if I could slow it down, that would be something—*

Suddenly it was like someone turned out the lights. I couldn't see the pool anymore. I could still feel Wyn's hand in my own, but other images filled my vision. Wyn sat at the side of the pool. Water was pouring over him and his tail, and a steady river of white flowed into my hand. As my palm filled with the grainy substance, I threw it in the water. I could smell the strong scent of it. I blinked and swayed slightly. What was that?

Salt. Salt. *Salt.*

"Wouldbeinginsaltwaterhelpyou?" I couldn't get the words out fast enough.

"Pardon?"

"Would being in salt water help you?"

"Do not I have enough time to let the salt heal me, or stop me from dying. Need I weeks in the water of my birth, not hours."

"All right, but would salt slow it down at least?" I dropped Wyn's hand and pulled myself out of the water, then stood and looked down at him. "Would it give us more time before you started to get dangerously sick?"

"Do not I know. It could help."

I started pacing again. "Then that's what we'll do every night. For as long as we can."

"Valerie, are you being impractical. How would we get salt water here, free of chemicals? And don't I want you spending that much time here every night doing something that may only possibly help me. Won't I let you do this."

"You won't *let me?*" I knelt down and looked him right in the face. "Listen carefully, Wyn Erelasai. There is nothing that I need your permission to do. I will help you and I will save you. I don't know how yet, or when, but I'll figure it out. I refuse to lose anyone else. And if I have to bring the salt water and sit here all night for you to actually use it, then I will."

"Stubbornness is quite strong in you it seems."

I huffed and sat back. "I might've been called that a time or two, yes—but it's a good quality. And I've never been so adamant or rigid in my life." I touched my fingertips to Wyn's cheek. "I won't ..." My voice caught. "I won't let you die, Wyn. With everything that is in me, I will free you."

Wyn sighed and gently moved my hand from his face to hold it next to him.

"Wish I that you would not, but can I see that it is pointless to argue. If plan you to come every night then insist I that you leave again as soon as possible. Must you sleep, need you energy. So go now. Despite the fact that have I no wish to, know I that we will speak of this tomorrow." Wyn squeezed my hand. "Till then, Ajana."

"Tomorrow," I said and left.

Once outside, I collapsed on a bench and let myself succumb to the fear pulsing through me. Tears poured down my face, and I gripped the hard metal bench so long and so hard that my hands hurt and I let go in pain. I held my hand over my mouth, struggling to stifle the sobs escaping me.

Another time I had cried this hard came back to me.

Christmas was close and Grandpa had only been dead a couple of months. I'd been playing in the snow, but my dad found me weeping behind one of the big firs in our yard. It would be our first Christmas without Grandpa, and it had hit me that he wouldn't be there, making jokes and teaching Theo more pranks. He wouldn't sneak in while Meredith, Mom, and I were making pies and tarts and steal some. Mom wouldn't scold him, and he wouldn't laugh and say, "My girls wouldn't begrudge me a couple of fortifying tarts now, would they?"

As I cried I felt large strong arms wrap around me and pull me close against his puffy, warm, down-filled jacket.

"I know. I know," Dad whispered, and wiped some of the tears off my cheeks, the wool of his gloves scratchy on my face. "My father died before you were born and you were really close to Mom's father. But he still loves you." My dad's eyes were teary but he smiled, and his smile gave me strength.

"You know what we're taught in Sunday school and what your mom and I believe—that life continues after you die, and that right now both your grandfathers are watching over you." Dad kissed my forehead. "It's okay to cry and be sad, but it's also good to know when to stop, too. You know that Grandpa lost his wife in a car accident when you were only three, but he was still happy and loving and showed you so many fun things. We had a chance to say goodbye before the cancer took him, and I'm grateful for that, and so is your mom. She wasn't able to say goodbye to her mother, and that was much harder."

I nodded, still sniffling, and he straightened my toque and retied my scarf.

He continued. "We're gonna have a great holiday. Your mom and I, your brothers and your sister, plus tons of aunts, uncles, and cousins will all be here—and I'm always here to talk. Remember that. Now let's go back in the house and have some hot chocolate, hmm?"

I nodded and followed him into the house. He'd always known what to say and how to help, and even though letting in a memory about him made my heart ache, I wanted to be strong like he'd been.

Alone in the dark outside the pool, I straightened up a little. I still felt like I had many more tears in me, but my eyes were dry. I got out my phone and called another cab. While riding to my aunt and uncle's, my mind worked furiously. Despite my overwhelming emotions, a small fire of hope burned in my chest. This time I could do something! This wasn't cancer or a car crash. My mind whirled through all of my research and different plans and possibilities. I snuck back up to my room and when my head hit my pillow I fell asleep with images of pools, salt, and the ocean still occupying my thoughts.

It wasn't until I saw Coach at my next practice a few days later that I remembered the text. He'd texted Andrew about when we were in town so they could do their little intervention. I grabbed his arm.

"We need to talk, Coach. Privately."

He turned to the team. "Do a normal warm-up. I'll be back in five." He pulled his arm from my grasp and led the way to a back office.

"What's the problem?"

"You texted Andrew! I'm not crazy and you know it, yet you still helped stage their little intervention. What the hell is that?"

"That's me being a responsible adult. I've seen you. You've been using that freak as some kind of psychologist, talking to him all the time. I see him watch you while you dive. It's not healthy! Of course I helped them. You need to talk about your grief to a *human*. I still think he's dangerous and that you should leave it alone."

"He's not a freak, he's not dangerous, and no, I won't leave him alone. He needs me, and if you took even one second to talk to him you'd realize he won't hurt me."

Chase crossed his arms tightly, and his voice lowered. "My only concern is you and your future. I've seen you become a phenomenal athlete. You have your whole future and life ahead of you. I'm not interested in anything about a guy who's half fish. You shouldn't get involved."

"He's a freaking merman! Why *aren't* you interested?"

"Because he's in this pool surrounded by humans for a reason. Whoever put him here is not someone anybody should mess with. Stop taking needless risks."

"You and I disagree on what's 'needless.' He needs me and I'm not going to ignore him and pretend he doesn't exist like you do."

"It's dangerous!"

"Fine! I get it. You don't want me helping him. Are we done?" I stalked out of the office without another word and threw myself into the pool, swimming my warm-up laps hard.

At my uncle's insistence I had made an appointment with Seven the counsellor for that afternoon. Her real name was Susan Miller, but she'd always be Seven to me after all the times Zack had talked about her. I was so glad I only had to see her the once. After my blow-up with Chase that morning, I wasn't sure how much more I could handle.

I walked into the worn brown office and sat in one of the greyish chairs at the edge of the room. Seven was a nondescript woman: plain brown hair and eyes, nothing interesting about her face, and she wore a navy blue pantsuit with a simple white shirt.

"Well, Valerie, what brings you in to see me today?"

"My uncle wanted me to come in and talk about what happened ..." I gulped. "What happened to my parents."

"Oh, that is hard. I'm here to listen."

Hard? That was the understatement of the century. But if I kept the conversation on the car crash and my diving accident, maybe we'd never have to talk about hallucinations. If my uncle hadn't called ahead, maybe she didn't even know about it.

I talked for an hour. I told her about the crash and how I sometimes felt guilty that I wasn't with them. I talked about saying goodbye to Theo and how I'd thrown myself into my diving and distanced myself from everyone. I hated for Josh and especially Andrew to be right, but saying it all out loud did help. I still cried a butt-load and used up half of Seven's tissue box. (How in the heck was there still water in me?) But she never asked about hallucinations or mermaids. I let out a huge sigh at the end of our talk. I'm sure she thought it was because of my family, but really it was because Wyn was still safe.

Whenever my brain was free over the next few days, I was thinking about Wyn. How to get salt water to the pool. How to save him. How to get him to the ocean. I brought a container of salt each time I went to see him at night. I used the hose on the side of the pool and poured fresh water over him while he rubbed salt into his tail. I tried not to let Wyn see my horror when scales fell away at his rubbing.

With finals creeping up on me, I started to study a lot more in the afternoons, but I managed to go to the occasional public swim to simply enjoy swimming with Wyn so close by. Leaving the pool after one of these swims, I walked towards the exit and rummaged in my purse for my keys. The next second I smacked into something hard—and then I was on the floor, my head spinning. I looked up, raising a hand to my head.

"Watch it!" someone snarled.

"Sorry." The word fell out of my mouth reflexively. And then I looked up. It was Wyn's captor, the one who'd punched out Zack! He pulled on my arm and hauled me up. To anyone watching it must've looked like he was helping me stand, but his grip and closeness was menacing and disturbing.

"Try anything and the fish is dead," his scratchy voice whispered in my ear. "We know about the salt massages. He won't be here for much longer. Talk only." And then he strode off towards the administration offices.

I looked around me, shocked that the world was still moving and people were still going about their business. I clutched my arms to my chest to try and stop the trembling. They were watching me. I wasn't going to stop seeing Wyn—and I wasn't going to stop trying to help him. That was not an option. But what did he mean Wyn won't be here? They were moving him? Where? I had to get Wyn out of that pool! As I drove home, I tried to shake off the slimy feeling the creep had left on me.

Doug had threatened the girl, just like he was supposed to. Neil said he wanted her scared. Panicked. They were being paid a lot of money to keep the fish guy alive and out of reach of the ocean, but Neil had another plan. The other tank being built was taking too long, too many setbacks. Doug liked the money, but more was always better. He put some chew in his mouth and sauntered back to his truck. Neil had it all figured out; Doug just had to do his part and they'd be richer than kings.

Later that afternoon I was surprised by a small epiphany. I knew how Wyn could soak in salt water.

I ran out to Felicity that night, excited about the answer I'd found, only to find she wouldn't start again. Seriously? What the heck was wrong with the stupid car? It wasn't like it was winter and she needed to be plugged in. I called a taxi and stalked to the place I'd waited the last time Felicity hadn't started. I waited and waited, solving my puzzle ring a whole bunch of times just for something to do. After half an hour I called the taxi company again and asked where the car was. Initially they'd told me it would only be fifteen minutes until the car arrived.

"I'm sorry. We got a call to cancel the taxi to that location," a generic female voice said.

"What?"

"Twenty minutes ago, a call came in cancelling the taxi to that address. Is that incorrect?"

What in the ...? Not what. *Who.* There's no way Felicity wouldn't start two separate times when I took such good care of her. Zack must've done something and then called and cancelled the taxi tonight. Which meant he was watching.

I punched Zack's number and waited for him to pick up. My muscles zinged with tension. This was so not happening.

"Valerie? Why are you calling so late?"

"Cut the crap, Zack. I know what you sound like when I wake you up, and this is not it. What are you doing messing with my car? Cancelling my taxi? You've been watching me, haven't you, Creepy McStalkerson?"

"I'm trying to stop you from getting hurt or *killed*. Wyn doesn't want you to risk your life going to see him any more than I do."

"He needs me!"

"You said yourself he'd sacrifice his life and his freedom to protect his family. Do you really think I'm not gonna risk you being pissed at me to stop you? It's too dangerous."

"Wyn is dying. The chemicals in the pool are killing him. I'm not about to let the merman who saved my life die, while I sit around studying for finals!" I hung up and ran back to the house.

So I needed some other way to get to the pool, something that couldn't be sabotaged. I'd deal with Zack tomorrow. Buses didn't run this time of night. There were bikes in the garage, but that would take a really long time. *Wait a minute.* I crept into the garage and saw what I sought buried behind four bikes. Grandpa Leroy had been Aunt Jocelyn's dad too. And I remembered that he used to ride a motorized scooter all the time between all our houses. I shifted the bikes out of the way and pulled out the scooter. It was dusty and covered in cobwebs, but it looked like it might still run. I opened the gas tank and heard hardly any sloshing when I shook the scooter. Gas? I looked around the garage and my eyes fell on the red gas can on a high shelf above the lawn mower. There wasn't much in it, but it would be enough to get me to one of the open gas stations on the highway. I strapped on the little red helmet that matched the scooter and then pushed the scooter to the end of the drive. I started it up, and surprisingly it wasn't that loud. I rode away, triumphant. I was still going to see Wyn.

When I walked through the pool door later that night, I gave Wyn only a cursory hello. I was still super pissed at Zack but there was work to do. I unloaded the inflatable pool and foot pump I'd brought in my backpack and set them up next to the freshwater hose beneath the stands. My aunt had filled the pool for my cousins that afternoon, and I knew I could use it tonight and go buy one of my own from the dollar store the next day.

I had to get this done and fast, because Wyn needed as much time as possible in the salt water. I pumped the pedal as fast as I could, switching feet every couple of minutes or so. Once there was a small amount of air in the pool I turned on the hose and let it run, knowing it would take a while to fill the pool up. The slowness of the process weighed on me. Even as my feet kept moving I felt helpless, despite the work I was doing. This was all I could do—and it might not even help. Wyn would still die. "How much time do you have?"

"What do you mean?" he asked.

"I mean if this doesn't work, how long do you have before the chlorine kills you?" My voice hitched on the word *kill* but I kept on. We had time. Saving Wyn was all that mattered.

"About six months, maybe. If this helps me, a possible two or three months more." Wyn's brow creased. "Do not distress yourself or ignore all those other things that are important in your life. Would I not have this take over your life, not for me."

I pressed my lips together in a hard line. "Enough, Wyn, enough. I'm still studying, still training, and still sleeping, but I have to help when you're dying!" I turned my back on him. The small pool's edges had enough air to be stable. I yanked out the pump hose and pushed in the stopper, then turned and opened my bag with unnecessary force to get the salt.

"My diving is important to me and I love doing it, but it's not all that I am." I opened the box of salt and poured it into the now half-full pool. "If I don't do everything in my power to help you, I'm no better than someone who sits on the beach watching a person drown." I set the box down and churned the salt into the water with my hands. "You can't help yourself, and no one is coming to rescue you. You've already been here over a year. If someone *was* coming, they'd have been here. There are no other options. You need my help." I paused from my stirring and looked back at Wyn. "You don't want to die, do you?"

"No! Of course not. It is just ..." Wyn's hands rose as though he needed to reiterate some point, but when he looked at me he lowered his arms and sighed. "Cannot abide I the thought that am I putting you in danger purely for my sake. And there is danger; have I no idea who my captors are or how ruthless they might be."

"And I can't abide the thought of doing nothing when your life is at stake!" I yelled—then my shoulders slumped and my anger left as swiftly as it had swelled. "We're talking in circles, Wyn. I'm going to try to save your life no matter what you say, but it would be much easier with your co-operation. Arguing is pointless." I smiled. "At least on this subject."

I pulled my hands out of the water and saw Wyn smile in resignation, although the crease never fully left his brow.

"Come on. The pool's three-quarters full. Let's see if this helps." Wyn heaved himself up, walked on his hands across the floor to me, then with an awkward flip, propelled himself into the salt water. Water pushed over the edge of the pool and half of Wyn's tail and most of his chest were above the waterline, but the expression on his face was more than telling.

"Ahhh." His sigh of relief was a balm to my raw nerves.

I looked around and saw a bin of children's toys. I hurried over, grabbed a bucket, and started pouring the salt water over the parts of Wyn not in the pool. Wyn splashed the water onto his chest and face and then rubbed his arms with his hands. Each time I poured a bucket, I tried to aim the water so it would fall back into the pool so we could reuse it. Eventually I handed the bucket over to Wyn and fetched my laptop.

"You can pour just as well as I can," I said as I dragged a chair over and plopped myself on it. "I'll do some research instead of just sitting around talking while you soak in the salt."

"Do not you have to stay."

"Yeah, I do." I turned on my Wi-Fi hotspot on my cellphone to access the Internet on my laptop. "I gotta make sure my aunt's stuff is back before they wake up. They use that pool almost every day. I'll buy my own tomorrow though."

"But why do not go you home and sleep for a few hours and then come back?"

My eyes were already roaming over the results displayed after I typed my first inquiry into the search engine. "Because that would be a waste of time and gas—and I can nap during the afternoon. It's better for me to do this research around you, so I can ask you questions if I need to." *Plus the scooter might not be up for it.* "You once told me that your tail can only be out of water for a short time. How long is that, exactly?" I asked as I kept searching on the laptop.

"Any longer than four hours and death comes—but even at three hours the sickness could be fatal." Wyn's mouth turned down again at giving me such information, but I ignored this and clicked onto the next link that might help, sighing. (So much for putting him in a truck and just pouring water over him as often as possible like they did in *Free Willy*.)

A few short hours later, Wyn helped pour the salt water out of the inflatable pool and into the large drain beneath the hose. Then I kneaded the air out of the inflatable pool's edges so I could fold it back into the same shape my aunt stored it in.

As I rode the ridiculous-looking scooter home, I dwelled on how I'd fund this escape. The ten thousand dollars from my parents might take care of the expenses of rescuing Wyn, but there was so much more I needed to pull this off besides money. Wyn needed to be transported in a tank. The trip would take at least three hours, but getting to ocean access could take another hour with traffic in the smaller cities around Vancouver. It would be better for Wyn if he had the protection of being invisible in the water. So on top of a tank I also had to have enough gas to get to the coast and to buy a truck and trailer on which to load the tank. We had just under four months to buy everything we needed and figure out all the logistics before the highway pass over the mountains would be too cold and dangerous to traverse with Wyn. It was so little time, but it would have to be enough.

Safely home, I opened the front door quietly and started towards the stairs.

"Where have you been?" The harsh voice came from the dark living room and I jumped, stifling a scream. Andrew flicked on a lamp and stood up from an armchair, levelling an icy gaze at me.

"I ... um ..."

"Zack called me over two hours ago. Were you drinking? I don't want some cops bringing you home at some awful hour because you didn't pass their Breathalyzer."

In a flash my sheepishness melted into white-hot anger. I could kill Zack. I hated Andrew.

"How dare you?" My whisper was deadly. "First drugs and now this? My entire family was killed by a drunk driver and you have the gall to ask me that? I wouldn't touch the stuff. Ever."

"Just the same." Andrew strode over to me in three quick steps. "What were you doing?"

I would not tell this man anything. "My mom told me what you did as a teenager." My anger was like waves crashing into my brain. "You were wasted every night, and after you drove drunk one Saturday, everyone in the car you hit miraculously walked away and all you ended up with was community service. You could've killed them all." Andrew's face paled and my breath hissed out between my teeth. "Don't you ever lecture me about drinking. You've done enough to me and my family. I won't let you bully me."

"What on earth is that supposed to mean?" Andrew looked like it was all he could do not to yell and wake up his kids.

I clenched my teeth. I would not talk about this with him.

"Fine," Andrew snapped. "So what were you doing, then?"

"Research with a friend from the pool. This is the only time we can get together."

"You've got to be kidding." Andrew shook his head.

My eyes bored into Andrew's. I had nothing else to say. And in that moment he seemed to know that I would tell him nothing else.

"Will you check in at least? Every night when you get home, whatever time that might be? If only for your aunt's sake? I won't have her staying up worrying about you till all hours of the night."

Some of the tension seeped out of me.

"Fine. I'll check in. Can I go to bed now?"

Andrew nodded and I went up the stairs, stopping short of stomping up every step.

The next day I stormed into the school, my eyes raking around me to find him. I saw Zack taking some books out of his locker down the hall. Then I was next to him, yanking him around to face me, my hand clutching his arm so hard I thought I'd break my fingers. "Who the hell do you think you are? You told Andrew? What are you, four?" Half a dozen heads turned towards us. I lowered my voice. "You had absolutely no right to do that."

"I had every right." Zack pulled his arm from my grasp and shoved his finger in my face. "What you're doing is dangerous, that guy could kill you. You're one of my best friends; do you think I'm not up at night worried you might be dead because you risked too much to meet Wyn?"

"I'm telling you again. He. Is. Dying. I can't leave him." My eyes narrowed.

"No one is worth your life." Zack grabbed my shoulders and gave a little shake. "I won't let you die!"

I shoved Zack off me. "You ever pull anything like that again and we're through. Done."

"Fine." Zack huffed and glared at me. He put his hands in his pockets with an air of resignation. "I won't tell your uncle again and I won't stop you from getting to the pool, but you have to promise me you'll be careful. And text every night when you're home, no matter how late."

"Fine."

I turned to go, but Zack's hand on my shoulder again—though gently this time—stopped me. "I'm ... sorry. Are we still okay? Can I still pick you up for grad in a few weeks?"

Grad. In like three weeks. Already. I suddenly wanted to break down and weep. That meant finals were closer too, because they were the week after grad.

"I'll let you know," I hedged. "I need some time. Just leave me alone for a bit, 'kay?"

"Sure," Zack said, but he looked hurt.

I stalked off to class. Wyn needed me. Why was everything else crashing in on my limited time?

A few days later we still couldn't tell if the salt was helping Wyn, but I'd established a fragile routine. I'd wake a few minutes before midnight and Wyn would soak until about three a.m., and then I'd go home and sleep a few hours, go to diving practice, go to school, nap in my bedroom in the afternoon (my aunt thought I was working on homework), study for an hour after dinner, and then leave for the pool at midnight and get Wyn in the salt water all over again.

Over the next week Heather texted me repeatedly about grad and plans for hair and makeup and anything else she felt we needed to do together. I made a point of confiding about a lot of trivial things like school work and finals so she'd have something to tell Josh. But she and all the other girls in my classes were talking about the dance and dates and dresses so incessantly I had to work hard not to snap at them to shut up.

My brain was filled with sizes of aquarium tanks, gas mileage, down payments for trucks, and finding out where someone could deliver a tank to me. Dresses and hair didn't really matter in the face of Wyn dying.

This had been going on for two weeks when Heather pulled me aside in the hall after biology class on Friday.

"What's up with you lately? Grad is a week from tomorrow and finals are the week after that, but you're dead tired, like you've been pulling all-nighters to study. That's not like you. And you're even more behind in your homework than usual."

"Uh, nothing much. I'm just working on some research stuff. Don't you have another class you need to get to?"

"I'll be late." Heather shifted her books from one arm to the other. "Does this have anything to do with Wyn? He's what? Keeping you up all hours of the night and keeping you from studying for finals? That's not good. I don't want someone that selfish hanging around you, whether or not he's your friend."

"Whoa, whoa, slow down. It's nothing like that at all." I worked to make my voice reassuring. "I've been up late studying and prepping for Worlds. I want to do well and reach my goals. Yes, maybe I should scale back a bit—but it's not Wyn's fault."

I pressed my lips to keep from cringing at Heather's face. She didn't believe me. How to divert her?

"You know what?" I said. "The reason I'm doing so much better now, why I feel like I can face things, is because of Wyn." Could I distract her with anger and half-truths? If she was upset with me for saying Wyn helped me more, maybe I could steer the conversation in another direction. "Are you jealous that he knew how to help me better than you?"

"You did not just say that." Heather's eyes widened in shock and I saw anger in the set of her chin. *Success!* "I have only ever been there for you. And yeah, I messed up by talking to Josh but that doesn't mean I didn't do everything I could to help you. Are you saying this guy was a better friend? I can't believe you."

"Sorry. Sorry. Wrong thing to say." I linked my arm with hers and talked in soothing tones. "You both helped me in different ways. You gave me space and time to heal, which I needed. You and Zack are still my best friends. Wyn helped me see how much I needed you both. He's a nice guy, but he's not you and he's not Zack. I really don't want to argue about this. Can we forget I said anything?"

"Fine, but cool the drama then, will ya? You and me are going to be friends until we're ninety, so let's stop with the accusations. Deal?"

"Deal. Now tell me about the boutonnière you ordered while we go to class, before we're seriously late." The halls had cleared and there were barely any stragglers left.

"Oh, it's so perfect. Greg's wearing a yellow cummerbund, so I wanted some really sharp dark colours in his boutonnière as a complement."

I only half-listened as Heather elaborated. When grad was over, there was no way she'd be as easy to distract. I had to get Wyn back into the Pacific, the sooner the better.

I was getting more and more frustrated with how to take Wyn to the ocean. I'd started trying to make lists of what I needed, and comparing prices and places to buy the items, but they were pitiful lists indeed. One night after dinner I'd shoved my research away and was focusing on memorizing some definitions for the biology final, when the doorbell rang. I went downstairs to answer it. My aunt and uncle, plus all the kids, had gone to a science fair that Michael was participating in. I'd begged off because of my finals and promised Michael he could tell me all about it later. The result was a completely quiet house, an unusual occurrence and welcome relief.

Zack was standing on the doorstep.

"Hey, Zack. What's up?"

"Not much. It's been like almost three weeks. Have I given you enough time yet? I just wanna hang out again." His voice was sheepish, his face hopeful. Yes, he'd been a creep telling Andrew, but I couldn't really blame him for worrying and freaking out about not wanting me to die, when I was constantly doing the same thing about Wyn.

"Sure." I stepped back. "Come on in."

"What's with the lack of background noise?" He raised an eyebrow.

"I'm the only one home. They all went to a science fair. I was trying to get some studying in."

As we went up the stairs, I took in Zack's strained expression but held off asking what was bothering him. I knew he'd tell me when he was ready—besides, my life didn't have room for any more problems at the moment.

I sat on my bed while Zack took a seat in my desk chair. I watched him take three full breaths before he spoke.

"I know I messed up, and you asked for time, but not talking to you or hanging out with you for the past three weeks has killed me. I miss you. And the only reason I called your uncle is because I care about you. I don't want you hurt or in trouble with that really scary guy." Zack crossed and then uncrossed his arms. "But I need you to know that I lied to you."

I gave him a sharp look. Where was he going with this? Was he going to sabotage me again? Or worse, tell my uncle everything?

"I told you I'd wait for your okay to ask you out again," he said, wiping his palms on his pant legs, "but I can't wait."

Crap. Really? Now? I worked to keep my face smooth.

"I asked you to say when you're ready for a boyfriend, but that's not good enough. I've held these feelings in for over a year, since well before the car crash. And not being around you only solidified it all. I've seen how much you've changed in the last months, how positive you are again. It doesn't have to be huge or big. We can take things really slow. I just want us to start being more than friends. I need to be your boyfriend."

I frowned and dug my teeth into my bottom lip. The visit was nothing about Wyn, true, but I found that small comfort. It had barely been a few months since we'd last had this conversation. Talk about worse than rotten timing. I'd already told him I wasn't in any place to think about dating. "You 'need' to be my boyfriend? What about what I need? I already told you I couldn't consider being a girlfriend to anyone for a while. I'm not ready for any kind of commitment, right now."

"I realize that, but—"

"You know what, Zack? Can't means can't," I snapped, my voice taut and harsh. "I'm not in any kind of position to evaluate my social life right now. I'm just finally getting my head above water." I folded my arms tight against me and glared at the floor, fighting the impulse to jump to my feet and yell at Zack to get out. I did not need this right now. I was recuperating, barely, from losing my family. I had finals. I had diving. Wyn needed me ...

"Valerie, please." I looked up and he was moving to sit beside me. "Please let me convince you." And then he kissed me.

-CHAPTER ELEVEN-
Confrontations

I tore away and stood up. "What the hell, Zack? What part of no don't you get?"

"I'm sorry. I guess I shouldn't have kissed you." He stood too, looking away from me. But then he whipped back around, his mouth set. "No, actually, I'm not. I'm not going to apologize for kissing you. I told you that I want to convince you we should be together." He stepped closer to me and placed his hands on my shoulders. "I've liked you for almost two years, and I haven't done anything about it. I'm insanely jealous of any guy who even looks at you, and I like you even more now that you're yourself again. Can you really blame me?"

"Yeah, I can, actually. A no is a no."

"It's Wyn, isn't it?" Zack's voice was pointed in accusation. His hands dropped from my shoulders.

"Of course Wyn has something to do with it. For the seventy-sixth time. *He's dying!* When I've figured out how to help him and get him back to the ocean, then maybe I can consider a social life, but not a second before."

"Are you kidding me? You've known Wyn how long? A few

months? If that? And you're continually risking your life for him?" Zack paced the short length of my room. "I've seen how tired you are. Obviously you're not getting the sleep you need. You have finals, you have your diving, how can you not see that he isn't good for you?"

I tried to ignore his glare and not let it irk me, and sat down heavily on the bed. It was too much. Emotionally I was spent. How much was I going to have to deal with?

"Has he kissed you?"

"Oh. My. Gosh. Seriously? You're supposed to be my best friend. You know you're just adding to my problems and not helping with anything, right? I have to help him!"

"He has no one else? Where are all his mer people? Why does it have to be you, when you're already pushed to the limit with everything you have in your life right now?" Zack was yelling.

"Exactly right—there is no one else. And it's not like you've jumped up to help me. Would you just stop yelling?" I flung myself back onto the bed, covering my face with my hands. I was so, so, tired. Tired of everything.

Zack finally stopped his irate pacing. The rage had slipped from his face. He sat down beside me and his apologetic expression seemed sincere.

"Do you at least have some way of protecting yourself if the monster guy tries anything?"

"Yeah, I put pepper spray in my purse after he confronted us and punched you."

"That's something at least." He took my hand and I let him hold it. "I'm scared for you. There's so much neither of us know. What if something happens to you? I don't think I could live with myself."

"I get that. But I can't lose anyone else." I looked down at our hands. "He's the reason."

"The reason?"

"Why I came out of my haze. Why I started to live again. The reason I became myself again."

"I figured," Zack said, his face stoic.

"I think you and I need to talk about us, and I will take some time to figure out what I want ... but at the moment it's simply not possible. All right?"

"Yeah, okay." He plastered a smile on his face, and hurt shot through me at the hurt I'd caused him. "Anything I can do to help you figure out that what you want is me?" he forced out.

I laughed. "Help me buy a new vehicle, maybe? I'm leaning towards a truck."

"A truck, eh? Felicity will be heartbroken."

"I know, but she'll just have to go to another good owner. Right now, though, I really need to study some biology, so ..."

"I get it. I get it. I'm getting lost." Zack gave me a hug that was longer than a friend hug, but I didn't call him on it.

The next day I didn't feel like studying after dinner, so I opened my laptop and pulled up the document I'd created to organize the different things I needed to make this rescue work: sand, salt water, a large aquarium tank, a truck, a trailer to tow the tank behind my truck, fish and other things Wyn ate, gas money, and food for me. I couldn't bring a trailer back to my aunt and uncle's place. I'd never be able to explain it. As it was, I'd have to tell them I was going to visit Josh for the weekend or something, although we'd actually be leaving sometime in the middle of the night. There was an empty lot down the road. That was the only place I could think of that would work for storing the trailer and to have the aquarium tank delivered.

I picked up my cellphone and entered the first number I'd recorded on my rescue document.

Can I pull this off? I couldn't help but think as I waited for someone to pick up.

"Great Price Car and Truck Rental. How can I help you?"

The next night, as I was struggling to work my way through all the word definitions I needed to know for my English final, there was a knock on my door.

I glanced around my room—a moderate amount of clothes were strewn over the floor, no underwear, though, and even though papers covered my desk I knew the lists I'd made regarding Wyn were still tucked into my backpack.

"Come in."

Andrew walked in. He looked strange, not uncomfortable really, more wary.

"Do you have a minute to talk?"

"I guess," I said.

"I know that traditionally it's the father who leads the girl ... *Ahem.*" Andrew cleared his throat. "Er ... woman ... graduate in the Grand March up at the university. Would you like me to stand in for you? I know it's just walking down the stairs and around the path showing off your dress, but I thought ..." He trailed off.

I'd planned on asking Aunt Jocelyn, but I hadn't gotten to it, and I definitely hadn't given Andrew a second thought.

I stayed silent, not sure if I could be polite. Andrew stared at me, concerned. "Valerie, where is all this animosity coming from? I know it's been more than rough for you this past year, and I've tried to give you the space you obviously wanted. But—" He crossed his arms, his body tense, then seemed to think better of it and uncrossed them again. "You seem to be more open and conversive with Jocelyn than you have been in a long time, yet there's still this huge cloud of something between us. What's the problem?"

Andrew's face was open, honest, like he actually cared. *Fine.*

"The problem?" I *tsk*'d my tongue. "You borrowed thousands and thousands of dollars from my dad to open your own practice. And then not only did you not open the practice, and go to work for someone else, but you never paid him back. And then there was bad blood between the two of you for years and then he *died*! You really think I can forgive you that easily when it was your fault there was this huge feud between you and him, and all that stress in our home while we grew up?"

Andrew's face had gone white as I talked. He reeled back.

"He didn't tell you?" Andrew whispered.

"Tell me what?"

"Your father and I went to lunch three days before he died. I paid him back the money. We made up. We weren't perfectly okay, but we were on our way there."

I blinked. "You what?"

Andrew gingerly stepped around some of my clothes on the floor, then pushed a sweater aside and sat on the corner of my bed.

"I'm sorry," he said, and he really meant it. His shoulders were slumped and his voice was regretful and full of sorrow. "I never should have assumed your father told you about our lunch. And you and I haven't really talked enough for me to understand why you were so angry with me."

He sighed like he was Atlas with the world on his shoulders and ran a hand through his hair. Who was this man? Most of the memories I had of him in the years before my parents' accident were of him and my dad fighting behind closed doors, of Jocelyn talking and reassuring him and holding him back after a shouting match with my father. Everyone in the family knew what it was about, the yelling was too loud not to. I stared at Andrew, incredulous that he'd actually apologized.

"The reason I never opened a practice was because I lost the money your father gave me gambling."

What? I gaped at Andrew in shock, waiting for him to continue. I had no words for this.

"Shortly after your father gave me the money, Jocelyn and I had a monster of a fight." Andrew clasped his hands together, staring at a spot on my floor. "We didn't know it at the time, but she had severe post-partum depression and it took its toll on our relationship. I remember pulsing with anger and for some reason heading to that casino five streets over before you hit the bridge.

"I don't know why I used the business account that night. But I did. And even though I'd never set foot in a casino before then, I couldn't stop." Andrew's whole body shuddered, and then he looked back up at me. "I was proud and stubborn, so I refused to tell anyone where the money had gone. I couldn't admit my weakness. Not to anyone, but especially not to your dad. I regret it more than I can say—especially all the time I lost with him.

"David was such a stand-up guy, and he'd helped me ... but somehow that only made it worse to tell the truth. It took me a year to finally admit to Jocelyn that I lost the money gambling. I hadn't gambled again because I'd lost so much, but it wore on me. I didn't want to work and our money started dwindling." Andrew looked away again and seemed far away, reliving old memories maybe.

I shifted in my chair, trying to calm my pounding heart. All the fighting had been over this one secret.

"Long story short, Jocelyn and I both got help. And even though it took us over a year, we saved up the money to pay back your dad. I didn't really feel like I could tell him the truth until I could give him back the money. I'm sorry if you hate me, or if it's going to take you a long time to forgive me, but that doesn't mean I ever stopped caring about you, loving you. You're my niece and I don't always have the answers and I sure as hell made one huge mistake that cost us all a lot. But ..." Andrew's gaze was tender and contrite. "I'd like to walk with you in the Grand March this Saturday, and I hope that even if you can't find it in you to forgive me right now, that maybe we can start making steps towards that."

I blew out a breath and tried to wrap my mind around it all. Yes, he and my dad yelled a ton about it, and he was an absolute jerk. And yes, it had been bad blood in the family for years—but he had tried to make it right.

I cleared my throat. Twice. "I need some time to process all of this, but yes, you can walk with me in the Grand March." I laced my fingers together and rocked a little bit on my chair. This was awkward, but I didn't want to shove his apology and confession back in his face. "Aunt Jocelyn has some swatches from the dress shop that match the colour of my dress. Ask her to help you find a tie or something in that shade, I guess." My uncle's smile was genuine and my heart lifted at his joy.

"Thanks, Uncle," I said. He smiled even wider and the lines around his eyes crinkled.

"You're welcome." He and I both stood. He reached for me and gave me a small one-armed hug that still smacked of the awkwardness between us, but was a start at least. After I heard my door click behind him, I turned back to studying, my brain buzzing with all he'd told me.

During my lunch hour on Friday a couple of days later, I decided to drop by the pool to ask some questions before my afternoon classes (which were mostly just review for finals anyway). When I got to reception I was happy to see someone I knew personally manning the desk.

"Hi, Linda," I said. "Do you have a few minutes to answer some questions for me?"

"Sure, Valerie—but you probably know as much about this pool as I do. What do you need to know?"

"Well, I'm writing a research paper for school, and I thought I'd write about this pool and how it compares to others in the city. I've been able to write most of it, but I have some specific questions."

"Sure—and if I don't know an answer we'll find someone who does. What's the first question?"

"How many lifeguards do you have working here in total?"

"Close to sixty. I can get the exact number for you, though, if you need it."

"No, that's fine." *It was just a filler question.* "Um, next question. I know you empty the pool to clean it once a year.

How long is the pool empty for, and when will that be happening this year?"

Wyn had told me his captors had put him in a barely large enough tank in an office while the pool was cleaned the previous year. This year it should be in November too, but he'd also heard a few comments from swimmers and lifeguards about emptying the pool for renovations as well. We needed to know an exact time for both.

"Normally the annual cleaning is in November, but with the renos it'll be emptied in just a few days."

"Uh, what?" I blinked.

"Yeah, they have to empty all the pools for the construction they're doing. They were going to empty it in a few weeks, but as it turns out they're ahead of schedule so they're closing it early. This Monday, in fact."

"Monday? Like, this Monday?" My voice squeaked so bad I sounded like a gangly boy in the middle of puberty. "Like not even seventy-two hours from now Monday?"

"Yes, there's a notice on the bulletin board there." Linda pointed across the entryway. "The pool will be closed for about a month, but then it will reopen so much better than before. The big sign out front has more detail. Didn't you see it?"

"That sign's about this pool?" My voice rose another half an octave. I didn't know it could get that high.

"Yeah. As a matter of fact we were going to print up another notice to tape to the doors just today. What's the matter? You don't look so good, sweetie. Why don't you sit down? You have to take things easy. Your accident wasn't that long ago." Linda patted my arm in a caring way before I turned and went to sit down on a bench.

Three days. Not even. Less than three days.

We were out of time.

They were going to empty the pool in three days.

-CHAPTER TWELVE-
Hysterics

This had to be what the Hulk-guy had meant when he said that I couldn't talk to Wyn for long. The pool was going to be emptied in three days, so they were moving Wyn. They'd take him who knows where and I'd never see him again. My breath came in great wheezes, and I was sure the ladies behind the desk wouldn't leave me alone for too long. To them, it probably looked like I was having a fit. My hands shook and I clenched my teeth shut. I jerked myself to a standing position and stumbled to the door.

I managed to hit the unlock button for my car and to open the door, but even as I fell into the car I didn't realize I'd opened the wrong door and was in my back seat until my face hit the smooth material there. Tears ran down my cheeks and I screamed and screamed. I felt my own hot breath push back into my face. I punched every space of material I could find, again and again. When I realized I'd left the door open, I hooked my foot in the door handle and slammed it closed. The force of it shoved me to the floor. I covered my face with my hands and tried to stem my tears as horrid scenes played in front of my eyes. I could kill Wyn trying to save him! He could only be out of water for so long. I was only one person. At least that kid had help when he'd tried to free the whale.

Enough! I yelled at myself.

I needed someone to tell me what to do. I pulled out my phone and dialed Josh before I even thought about it.

The phone barely rang and he answered. "Hello?"

"Hey," I said, unsuccessfully trying to keep a hitch out of my voice.

"Valerie? What's wrong?"

"I ... I'm just under a lot of stress right now and need someone to tell me I can handle it." I gave a little laugh. "I need a cheering section if you will. I'm trying to deal and I'm not very good at it."

"Valerie, you're more than capable of doing anything you want to." Josh's words were strong and I could sense the love in them. "I've seen you deal with more and do more than a dozen different girls twice your age. No matter what you're dealing with or stressing about, I'm sure you can handle it." There was a long pause as I let the words settle in my brain. "Do you want to tell me what you're stressing about?" Josh finally asked.

"Just ... normal high school stuff, I guess." *When there's a merman trapped in the local pool.* I cleared my throat. "Thanks for telling me all this, Josh."

"You're welcome. And I'm glad you felt like you could call."

"I didn't really think about it," I said. "My fingers pushed the buttons before I knew what was happening."

Josh laughed with me. "Regardless. You're amazing and talented and determined, and I know you can conquer whatever the heck you want."

"Okay, now that's laying it on a little thick." We both laughed again.

"Are you gonna be okay?" he asked.

"I think so." Saying it made it feel more real, like I really could do this and come out the other side. "Yes, thanks again. I should go, though."

Josh slipped in a few more encouraging remarks before I hung up.

I was still cramped on the back-seat floor, and my thoughts churned as I spun my phone in a circle with my fingers, the phone edge hitting my knee each time it swung around.

So many things could go wrong. Wyn would be discovered. Silhouettes of nondescript men racing into the pool, capturing Wyn, attacked my mind. They'd put him in some government facility. He'd be hooked up to all sorts of machines and they'd study him. They'd pull him apart to figure out how he worked, or worse, torture him to find out all about his family and his race. I couldn't, I *wouldn't*, let them take him. Josh's affirmations of my capability rang through my head. I was the one who had to set Wyn free. I knew he was dying, and his captors either didn't know or didn't care. If I didn't save him, he would die. There was no one else.

My eyes dried and my breathing slowed as my resolution grew and hardened. I pulled myself up onto my back seat. Even as my resolve to free Wyn and bring him to the ocean solidified, another course of action occurred to me. *Should I expose him to the public?* If I told the world about him, there'd be many alongside me to fight for his life, but others would want to study him, and still others would consider him a threat. Maybe it was too much to hope and believe that there could possibly be any scientists out there with good intentions, who'd actually let him live and set him free. *No. The risk's too great.* I wouldn't tell anyone else about him.

With the pool being emptied in three days, what were Wyn's captors' plans? Would they leave him in the pool to be found? Would they move him to that tiny tank in the office? Keeping him in a small tank in an office for a month didn't seem plausible. I rubbed my temples. All I had were more questions than I had answers to. And the more I thought about it, the more I realized the biggest threat to Wyn's safety was his captors. Transporting Wyn, keeping water on him, not being discovered—these were all minor concerns. What if they discovered what I was trying to do? What if I got Wyn free, only for them to capture him again before we made it to the ocean? I had no idea how many men were behind Wyn's continued imprisonment. I'd just have to act—move him and take him to the ocean and pray that we could keep clear of them. There was nothing else I could do.

His captors didn't appear to want him found any more than I did, or they would've revealed him already. And they'd fed him for over a year, so logically they needed him alive. They probably wouldn't notify any authorities if he went missing, so if I could avoid them, maybe there'd be no other obstacles. So it was simple. I had to do everything before his captors moved him. I climbed into the driver's seat, but didn't turn on the car. Could I pull this off? I needed to dive. I needed to think. I grabbed my keys and stumbled out of my car. Pumping my arms hard and pushing my legs, I sprinted the length of the parking lot and back. My breathing was fast and blood pumped in my ears. Adrenaline rushed through my veins. I had work to do. I slipped back into my car and drove so haphazardly through the streets that the cops would've stopped me if they'd seen me.

I skipped my last two classes of the day because there was no way I could sit through reviews with Wyn's life at stake. I went to the library and used the Internet there to make a list of every single option I had for aquarium tanks and trailers, across the Lower Mainland, Kamloops, Salmon Arm, and all the other cities throughout the Okanagan Valley. I needed to buy a tank *now*, and they had to be able to deliver within the next twenty-four hours. Once I finished my list I went outside to make my calls.

By the time I'd got to the fifth one, I was beyond discouraged. No one had anything on hand that I could get in such a short time frame. By the twentieth call I was resisting panic.

Finally, on my twenty-eighth call, I hit jackpot. I'd have to pay an absurd amount of money to get the tank here so quickly (the company was based in Vancouver), but at least I had one. I scanned my list of needed items again, and realized that I'd have to secure the aquarium tank to the trailer somehow. The only option that came to mind was to pack strong boxes and blankets around the bottom of the tank to make it as stable as possible.

I moved on to trying to buy a trailer and called every place in town. No one had anything for the next day. It was too close to the end of the month. And I couldn't go pick one up from another town because I had no one to drive my car back with me. I could buy the truck first, maybe, and then go pick up a trailer. Looking at the time, my heart lurched. My aunt would be out of the house to pick up the kids from school. This was my small window to rush home and find anything I could use to stabilize the tank.

Half an hour later I had a pile of boxes and extra blankets I found around the house stacked in front of my closet. I also had half a garbage bag of sand that I'd dug up from the alley behind the house. I hoped we wouldn't be stopped on the way to Vancouver, but if we were, I needed something in the water to pass it off as a kind of microorganism science project. I'd plugged in my phone as it was pretty much dead from all the calls I'd made. I checked my list again. I still needed to get ropes and bungee cords to secure the tank in the trailer if I ever found one. I'd take as many as Andrew had and then buy some more if I needed them. Now all I had to do was buy a truck, find a trailer, and transport a three-hundred-pound merman to the ocean. Holy fish on a cracker.

Public swim was almost over and I stubbed my toe rushing to get into my bathing suit, but I had to tell Wyn. I darted into the water and swam over to where he was by the bulkhead.

"Hello." Wyn smiled.

"Hi. I don't have time to sugar-coat it, because they're going to kick us all out in a moment. We have to leave tomorrow."

"What?"

"I'm breaking you out tomorrow."

"Heard I you. But why? We need more time. We have to—"

"I know you wanted to plan everything out to the last detail, but we're out of time." I was treading water and whispering, forcing myself not to freak out. "They're emptying the pool on

Monday. You told me that when they cleaned the pool last year they moved you into that small tank in the office the night before. Let's hope they plan the same thing this time and aim to move you on Sunday, because I'm moving you tomorrow night. I probably would've even tried tonight but I couldn't get a tank that quick. I had to empty my wallet just to get the one that's coming tomorrow."

"Three days?" Wyn's face was taut with worry. "How can I let you do this? There is so much risk and stress. And what about university for you in the fall? Cannot let I you spend all your money on me."

"Don't be ridiculous. I can get student loans. As for the stress?" I turned and clutched the edge of the pool. "I'm not about to give up and let you die, or let your captors forgo the small tank and take you to some distant secret location. I have no way of knowing if they'd even bring you back here or not. This is our best and only opportunity to free you and get you back to your family and your people. You do want to go home, don't you?"

"Yes, of course."

"Then this is how we've got to do it." I glanced around, hoping no one was watching me.

"But—"

A shrill whistle sounded. Public swim was over.

"I have to go. I'll be here at eleven-thirty. Hopefully when I get you to Vancouver, it'll be around three in the morning Sunday. Too late for the bars to be open and too early for a lot of people to be around. Bye." I climbed out of the pool and speed-walked to the changing room without looking back. One way or another everything would happen tomorrow night.

As I was leaving the building I heard a scuffling noise behind me. For the second time I found myself on the ground, my head spinning. I looked up to see the hulk of a guy who'd captured Wyn towering over me again. Before I had time to say anything, he grabbed my arm in a viselike grip and jerked me to standing.

"You've got a lot of nerve. We know you know there's renos in three days. Don't be getting any ideas."

No! How did they know about me trying to get Wyn out?

"If you're smart you'll leave well enough alone. Don't try and play the hero, you got that? Or I'll beat you till you're black and blue." He shook me, my neck snapping back and forth. I could've sacked him and told him to shove it, but maybe they wouldn't consider me a threat if I played the scared little girl.

"Yeah ... yes." I gulped audibly. "I understand."

"Good." He let go of my arm, throwing me back. "Don't try anything." He jabbed a finger at me.

I nodded feebly and started towards my car.

I kept my facial and body expressions the same all the way to my car and as I drove away. He, no, *they*, needed to think I was too scared to do anything. The creep had said *"we* know," so there was at least one other person in on the capture. Resolve hardened in my mind. No matter what they were planning for Wyn, I'd get him out first. Tomorrow was it. It was a cliché, but it was literally do or die time. I had no doubt that if I got in the way, Hulk-guy would harm or kill me. But I cared about Wyn too much. I wouldn't sentence him to death or a life of captivity, not when I could do something to prevent it. The death of my grandfather, my parents, and my brother and sister, had all been out of my control. This I could do something about. I wouldn't lose Wyn, too.

Standing in the entryway back at my aunt and uncle's, I pressed my forehead to the cool door and tried to focus on my breathing. I'd stopped at a car dealership on the way back. I needed a truck and had money for the down payment, but they wouldn't sell me one. Apparently I was too young and didn't have the credit, or a job for that matter. If I wanted a truck I had to have a co-signer on the contract. I had no idea whether all dealerships were the same, but I had a sinking feeling they would be.

"Valerie, is that you?" my aunt called from the kitchen.

"Yeah," I answered. "I just gotta do some research. I'll be in the den if you need me, 'kay?"

I barely heard my aunt reply in the affirmative as I closed and locked the door to the den behind me. If I couldn't get a truck from a dealership I'd buy my own from one of those pre-owned private sale type websites. There had to be someone selling a truck for less than the seven thousands dollars I had left.

I had only scrolled through the first list of options when there was a knock at the door.

"Zack and Heather are here for you," Aunt Jocelyn hollered. What the heck? Why were they here? I had to get a truck, like now.

I walked into the entryway and Zack was standing there in a smashing tuxedo with a sky-blue cummerbund and bow tie, a corsage in his hand. Heather's elegant canary-yellow dress billowed out around her, one corsaged wrist holding up her skirts. She was towering over me in the stunning nut-brown three-inch heels I'd helped her pick out the week before. My feet stopped dead. I was rooted to the spot, my mind refused to work.

"What the hell are you wearing?" Heather's voice broke through my stalled brain. Her hair was swept up in a gorgeous chignon knot, her makeup done to perfection, and glittering jewellery blinded me from her ears, neck, and wrist. *Uh-oh.*

"I've been calling and texting all afternoon! Where have you been?" Heather's voice wasn't just accusatory: it was lethal. "Obviously you missed your rehearsal for your hair this afternoon. But please, please, do *not* tell me you forgot that the three of us are all doing pictures at Riverside Park?"

"Uh ..." I said. Any and all things grad had fled my brain when I realized there was less than three days to free Wyn, but Heather's eyes were on fire and there was no excuse I could give her, especially not the fact that I was trying to buy a truck. "My cell died. I had to leave it in my room while I went out. I'll ... uh ... I'll just go get it from my room and put my dress on, I guess." I turned and fled up the stairs even as I heard my aunt explaining my actions.

"I didn't even notice her hair wasn't done when she came in. I just assumed she'd gone to her hair appointment this afternoon. I knew the pictures were today ..." I cut off my aunt's voice as I closed my door, leaning against it and inhaling air like I'd just swam fifty metres. *Holy hell.* Grad was tomorrow.

Three hard bangs sounded on the door behind me and I jumped away from it.

"I'm coming in, Val." Heather's powerful voice ripped through my door. "I don't care if you're decent or not." She pushed into my bedroom and then looked back out in the hall. "She's dressed, Zack. Come on in."

And then they were both in my room surrounded by my

clothes, mess of papers, and unmade bed in all their yellow dress and black tuxedo glory.

"What's going on?" Heather's voice held all the authority and power of any lifeguard at the pool. "Do you need help?"

"It's not like you to forget something like this," Zack chimed in. "What's happening?" They both stared at me so intently I felt like there should've been a two-way mirror behind them and a table between us.

I groaned. "This isn't something you guys can help with. I'm not getting anyone else involved."

"Involved?" Heather's voice was pointed. "What is it you're not telling us?"

Stupid slip. My hand twitched towards my ring out of habit. "Um ..."

"Look at me," Heather commanded. I obeyed—and regretted it instantly. Heather always saw what I was feeling. Now that it was barely twenty-four hours before I attempted to rescue Wyn, I was barely holding myself together. Being confronted with Zack and Heather's questions, the stress was too much, and suddenly I was fighting back tears. I fell back against my bed and slid down to the floor.

"What on earth is wrong?" With a swishy rustle Heather came over to me and gently put a hand on my shoulder. Her anger had vanished and concern was all that was there.

"Everything is so dang complicated," I said, staring at Zack and wrapping my arms around my knees. That next moment stretched out and became an eternity, as the enormity of what I was about to do broke over me. I had come too far. Neither of them would accept anything less than the truth, and I didn't have it in me to lie convincingly right now anyway. I had to tell

Heather about Wyn and the entire race of mer and tell Zack
that I had to try and rescue Wyn in two days. If I couldn't trust
them, who could I trust? I had no truck, no trailer, and I was
falling apart trying to do this on my own.

"I have to free him," I said.

"Free him? Him who? What do you mean?" Heather asked.

"Wyn. He's a merman."

-CHAPTER THIRTEEN-
Escape

"He's a *what*?" Heather said.

Zack didn't say anything at all. He just raised an eyebrow as though asking, *are you sure you want to do this?*

I sighed and dropped my head back to rest on my bed. "It's true. Wyn's a merman. He was kidnapped and he's being held in the TCC Pool." I stared at the ceiling. "Because of the renos, his captors may or may not be moving him somewhere else, which means my only chance to free him is tomorrow night, but I haven't found a truck to buy, and I still need a trailer, and apparently I totally spaced on grad."

"A merman? Like with a tail and everything?" Heather shrieked. I probably shouldn't even have continued. She needed some time to process the whole half-human, half-fish thing.

"Yes, he's got a tail. And he's amazing and he's dying. I have to save him."

"A *merman*?" Heather's eyes looked a little crazy. She was starting to scare me. "Ummm. Okay. Obviously you wouldn't make something like that up, considering how easily proved or disproved it would be, but I'm having a little trouble sorting it all out in my brain." She flopped down into my desk chair with poof of crinoline and a rustle of satin.

I lifted my head to stare at Zack. Why hadn't he said anything or reacted at all yet?

He returned my stare. "How come we can't see him when he's underwater?"

I sighed and rubbed my temples. "Merpeople are invisible underwater. You can only see them if you've touched one: it changes your physical chemistry. Above surface, as you know, anyone can see them—"

"Them?" Zack interrupted, shock plain on his face.

"Yes, *them*. He's got a family and a life in the ocean, Zack. There are upwards of two million merpeople living in the oceans."

Zack's eyes bugged out, and he sat heavily on the floor, his tuxedo jacket jutting out at weird angles. "I can't believe there are that many."

Heather had bolted to her feet, holding up her hand. "Wait, wait. Slow down. *As you know*—as in *Zack* knows? Are you freaking kidding me? Zack's met him? He's actually *real*?"

I nodded wearily.

Zack seemed just as uncomfortable. "Yeah, I've seen him. I confronted him about the danger he's putting Valerie in. I tried to stop her from visiting him—but you can see how well that worked." He shook his head at me. "You have to free him in the next two days?"

"Yes. The pool is going to be empty for a month because of the renos, so his captors will have to move him. I can't leave him anymore than I could leave either of you."

"Captor-*s*?" Zack asked.

"We know there's at least two. No idea if there are more than that."

"What's your plan, Valerie?" Heather said. "How are you going to free this merman?"

"So you believe me?"

"Yes and no. You wouldn't lie about this, and Zack's met him, so I kinda have to. But I don't think I'll be fully convinced until I see him with my own eyes. You haven't answered me, though. How are you going to get Wyn to the ocean?"

"Uh. There's a large aquarium tank that Wyn can fit into being delivered to the empty lot down the street at noon tomorrow. I was going to have the delivery guys load it onto a trailer and truck, both of which I was trying to buy today. I was going to go to the pool to get Wyn about eleven-thirty, drive to Vancouver, and use a park's boat launch to let him into the ocean."

"Do you even know if the parks and boat launches are open that late at night?" Zack said.

"I hadn't even thought of that." I closed my eyes and clenched my shaking hands together.

"Listen, Valerie. You need our help," Heather said, her voice determined.

I looked back and forth between them and then stood so suddenly I startled Heather.

"No! I can't let you guys do this for me. I can't let you risk the danger. That guy said he'd as good as kill me if I tried anything. I won't—"

"He threatened you again? After he confronted both of us?" Zack growled. "Where is he? I'll—"

"You'll what? Tear him limb from limb?"

"I don't care!" Zack yelled. "I can't sit by and let someone threaten your life and allow you to take all the risks. That guy deserves to be locked up for life. You're not doing this on your own. We call the police. Now."

"He's bigger than an NFL linebacker—and he's not working alone. They probably have guns and who knows what else? You really think you can handle someone with a gun? And what exactly will we tell the police? We can't expose Wyn, so what?"

"Well, I—"

"Cool it, Zack," Heather interrupted, then turned back to me. "You don't have a choice about whether or not we help. This is about saving Wyn, so let's get going." Heather's calm assurance forced its way into every crevice of my brain. "We've been up here a long time talking, and we can't do anything until tomorrow—so tonight we have to take grad pictures and act normal. Tomorrow we'll all do the Grand March and stay for a few songs at the dance, then we'll tackle freeing the merman."

I nodded and watched Zack bite back whatever he wanted to say. He had stopped yelling but I heard him grumble, "I won't let him hurt you," as he left the room so Heather could help me into my dress.

Heather pulled my hair into some semblance of a formal do with two small French braids in the front and the rest of my hair in curls from my neglected curling iron. She kept up a constant flow of meaningless chatter for which I was grateful. I started my makeup while she was doing my hair, and then she touched up and perfected my face. Once I put on my bold sapphire-and-pewter jewellery I was a little shocked at how gorgeous I felt. I tried to revel in the feeling and ignore the worry in my stomach for Wyn.

A friend of Heather's mom was a professional photographer and she took over two hours' worth of pictures of our trio. I'm not sure how natural my smiles looked, but Heather was constantly tickling me so maybe there'd be a few good ones. I didn't expect to laugh but I underestimated Zack's ability to be a dork. He did some great slapstick à la the Three Stooges, who I'd forgotten he was such a big fan of. He had me in stitches with his antics, and near the end of the photo shoot, Heather blasted music from her phone and we all took turns dancing together. I had the two best friends in the world.

Afterwards, Heather directed us all to go home, change, and then we'd meet at a local diner to "plan this whole mess," as she put it. Once I'd gone home and changed, I told Aunt Jocelyn where I'd be, asked her not to wait up and promised I'd check in once I got home. Soon I was slumped down in a booth at the diner with Heather and Zack, exhausted from having to act so calm and normal.

I pulled out the lists I'd made of what I needed, what I had, and what still had to be done. "The biggest problems are that I can't buy a truck and that I couldn't find a trailer to buy, either."

"What about all the water delivery trucks around town? Couldn't we transport Wyn in one of them?" Zack asked.

"Yeah, I didn't think of them. But we'd have to steal one, wouldn't we?" I licked my lips.

"I don't think we should do anything illegal if we don't have to," Heather put in.

"Well, if that's the case, the solution to not having a truck is obvious," Zack said.

"I didn't want to ask. You love that truck."

"That doesn't mean I can't help you. It's in great shape and will do the job, which means the biggest problem is a trailer, right?"

Just then the waitress came and we all took a few seconds to order some of their all-day breakfast. Once she was out of earshot I turned back to Zack.

"Yes, if we use your truck we should still try and get a trailer before the tank is delivered at noon tomorrow, but everything is closed now and who's gonna be open on a Saturday? Plus, I called pretty much every place in town already."

"Do we need a trailer?" Heather asked.

"Yeah," I said, giving her a *duh* kind of look. "How else are we going to get a ten-foot tank to the ocean?"

"Why not just put it in the truck bed?"

"It'll break, won't it? And huge as Zack's truck is, I don't think the tank will fit."

"If you're packing it with blankets and stuff, I don't think it will matter whether or not it's in a truck or a trailer," Heather said. "Plus the tank might fit if we leave the tailgate down and tie it in. Don't you think so, Zack?"

"Yeah, should do ..." Zack said, his expression thoughtful. "The bed of my truck is eight feet long, so with the tailgate extended it should just work. And this way you won't have to buy a trailer, Val."

"You guys really think that will work?" I'd torn my napkin to shreds while we talked. The pieces were scattered all over the table, like splotches of white paint if I were painting a blizzard.

"You're the one who said you were finding it tough to find a trailer," Heather said. "And it's possible that Zack's truck might absorb more of the impact of the road than any trailer. Who knows?"

I nodded, frantically trying to think of another solution, *any* other solution. I hated trusting Wyn's life to a truck, a tank, and some bungee cords. Our food arrived and the conversation turned to specifics. Zack spent the better part of the meal searching the Internet to find the optimum boat launch for freeing Wyn. I'd originally thought of going to Stanley Park or even Vanier Park in Vancouver, but Heather pointed out there'd be a lot more traffic and people in the big city. So Zack suggested Surrey, a smaller city a little south of Vancouver. Mud Bay Park in Surrey seemed to be our best bet. This plan just had to work.

Although I'd expected to toss and turn all night with worry, I zonked straight through the night. All those hours of visiting Wyn must've finally caught up with me. I woke the next morning and set to work straight away, folding all the blanket and sheets I'd haphazardly thrown in front of my closet and stuffing them in the boxes I'd collected. The fewer trips I had to make to the empty lot the better.

Partway through my task, I heard a small knock on my bedroom door. I opened it a crack to see Sasha standing there.

"Why didn't you eat breakfast with me?" Her look was more than a little inquisitive. "What're you doing?"

"Oh, I had a late night—and now I'm organizing and cleaning my bedroom," I said.

"Mom says you're not that messy, so what do you hafta clean?" Her curiosity was totally gonna kill me.

"Uh, well, I want to be extra neat and tidy so that when I start university in the fall I can focus that much better on studying. Besides, my room really needs it. Look." I opened my door a bit more so she could see all the different papers scattered everywhere and the piles of sheets and blankets.

"Wow, that *is* messy."

"I'll be down soon, 'kay?"

"Okay." Seeing Sasha demand answers from me, I knew I had to get everyone out of the house somehow, at least for a few hours. They'd all be around for grad tonight, but there was no way I'd be able to take all this stuff to my car without getting bombarded with questions. Looking out my window, the nice weather offered me a solution.

I headed for the kitchen with two twenties in my hand. Aunt Jocelyn was helping Michael make cookies for his school's bake sale on Monday. Uncle Andrew was playing a board game with a few more of my cousins in the family room.

"Hey, Uncle Andrew, everybody, come into the kitchen, please."

I held the money behind my back as I watched them all troop in.

"Aunt Jocelyn and Uncle Andrew," I said, looking at them and praying they wouldn't kill me for bringing up the idea in front of my cousins without clearing it with them first. "I thought it would be really fun if you took everyone to the park to play this morning." I pulled the money out from behind my back. "And then bought fried chicken for a picnic on me!"

While my cousins cheered and tried to decide which park, I pulled my aunt aside. "I've just got a lot of homework that's kind of overwhelming and with finals pretty much here, it would be really nice if I could have the house to myself for a while. I hope that's okay?"

"Not a problem. In fact, I think it's a great idea. Keep your money, though. Put it into your tuition fund."

"All right. Thanks, Aunt Jocelyn." I gave her a hug. "Oh, and by the way," I said more loudly so everyone could hear. "I'm going to visit Josh this weekend after the Grand March. I'll be coming back Sunday, but I'm leaving super late today, so I won't see anyone after the big dance tonight, okay?" Most of my cousins shrugged, but Sasha came over and hugged me.

"Will you play Candy Land with me on Monday, then?"

"Of course." But I didn't know if I *would* be able to. Who knew what would happen tonight? In fact this might be one of the last times I saw them ... *Good grief! Cease and desist, already. Hold it together!*

"All of you, go get your things together for the park," Aunt Jocelyn said. After a few minutes of uncontrolled din, everyone clambered into the van and they pulled out of the drive.

Once they were out of sight I went straight to the garage, grabbed all of my uncle's bungee cords and ropes, stacked them by the front door, and went back upstairs to grab a box to pack them in.

We had all the supplies we needed in Zack's truck and pulled into the empty lot with five minutes to spare. Pacing up and down beside the truck, waiting, I pulled off my puzzle ring and fiddled with it. It was the first time in a long while that I'd taken it off. Before I'd finished the puzzle a third time, a large white cube truck pulled up. A guy with a clipboard stepped out of the cab.

"You Valerie?" he said.

"Yes."

"Sign here."

A man wearing a ball cap got out of the truck too, and after I signed, both men moved to unload the ten-foot tank.

"Where do you want it?" the clipboard guy asked.

"On the bed of this truck here." I was glad to see there were foam panels cushioning the glass in the cardboard box once I pulled it open.

The cube truck kicked up a lot of dust as they left.

Heather and I looked at each other, resigned. Then all three of us set to work. It took two long hours in the sun to arrange everything so that we felt the tank was secure. We got off the top of the box and took out some foam so we had access to the tank. We wedged all the blankets and sheets in around the box, then tied and bungeed the whole mess down. We all had different ideas about the best way to tie it securely. The only thing we could agree on was that the rope couldn't go over the top of the tank because Wyn needed to be able to get out on his own if he needed to. We must've used over a hundred feet of rope. By the end we all had rope burns from tightening knots and more than one curse had been uttered by each of us.

It was two o'clock when Zack said he'd go to his place to fill the tank with water.

"My parents are both working until like an hour before the Grand March, which is"—he looked at his watch—"five hours from now. Four hours should be ample time to fill the tank."

"Do you want help?" I asked.

"No, no. I can handle it—and besides, Heather said she'd flay me alive if I didn't kick you both out of here for your hair appointments at two-thirty." Zack smirked, a laugh in his eyes. He was so good. *They* were so good. This was our Senior Grad. Formal dances weren't huge in Kamloops. There were no proms or homecomings, so this was kind of it—and yet, here my best friends were, tearing their hands apart to help me.

I struggled not to let my emotions show. What would I do without these two? Heather grabbed my arm and we rushed back to my aunt and uncle's house, where we'd left her car.

"Hey, guys," I said, as I walked in the door. "How was the park?"

I listened to all the different excited stories and responded appropriately, but my mind was with Wyn and what we were about to attempt. Heather and I would be getting ready at her place, so I ran upstairs to jump in the shower and gather my stuff before we headed to the salon. The whole MacPherson clan was going to meet us up at the university for the Grand March. The original plan had been for Heather, Zack, and I to go out for a fancy dinner with a whole crew from the grad class, but I'd kiboshed that idea when we hashed out details at the diner. There was no way I could manage being normal and putting on a happy face for dinner, the march, *and* the dance, when Wyn's life hung in the balance.

I'm not sure how Heather managed it but she worked some sort of miracle magic with unicorn hair or something and rearranged our mani-pedis, hair, and makeup to all be squeezed into three hours.

And I tried. I really tried to enjoy it all. To chat and visit and just be two senior girls going to grad, but I wasn't there. I know Heather understood what had me so preoccupied and made my answers to her chatter so ditzy and out there. It felt wrong to be dressing up and getting glitzy, while figuring out how to save a life.

When we left the salon, Heather made sure to grab samples of both our lipstick colours so she could reapply after we ate. Her phone chimed as she started the car.

"Zack texted. Both his parents changed plans and have to meet him up at the university, so we should go to his place once we're ready, and we'll order in something to eat."

"Sounds perfect," I said, as she started her car. Part of me wanted this afternoon to go by slow, because then I wouldn't have to face what would happen if I screwed up tonight, but another part of me wanted all the dresses, makeup, and hair to be done with. In the end, time went incredibly fast, but my head was filled with sickening images of Wyn being shipped away for study in some lab, wrecking the fun of it.

I did up the clasp on my pewter necklace, admiring its brilliant sapphire leaves, as Heather finished lacing up the back of my dress.

"So I told Greg I wouldn't be going to the big grad party with him after the dance." Heather's voice was slightly hard.

"Oh yeah? How'd he take it?"

"Not great, but we're okay. He was pissed at first, but when I told him you're in the middle of a crisis and need to go to Vancouver tonight after the dance, he relented a little." Heather shrugged. "We still haven't even talked about what'll happen this fall when I move to Vancouver, but we'll have fun tonight. And then ... I guess ... I'll help you and Zack free Wyn. Still can't believe he's a merman."

"I know, right? When I first saw him I thought I was hallucinating because of my head injury. I was totally convinced I was going insane."

Heather laughed and adjusted her dark gold bangles. "Well, you still might be. A merman is one of those things you can't really believe until you see it. Sometimes not even then."

We were ready for the dance but I still had to face the oohs and aahs of Heather's parents when we went downstairs for pictures. And as much as I loved them and had become close to them over the years, I was coming apart at the seams. No, I was dried paint flaking off a canvas. I started pulling in breath after breath. Faster and faster. I couldn't get enough air with the stupid built-in corset in my dress. What if we didn't get him out in time? What if we were stopped by cops? What if his captors figured out what we were doing? I leaned over, bracing my hands on my knees. *What if he died?*

"Val, what is it?" Heather's hand on my back did nothing to calm me. I was hyperventilating.

"Here. Breathe into this." A green paper bag from some jewellery store was shoved in my face.

A few breaths into the paper and my gasps slowed slightly. A few more and I sank to the floor, wrinkling my taffeta.

"What if we can't save him?" My whisper was barely audible. "What if I've sentenced him to death because his captors will kill him when they find out what we've done?" I expected tears to come, but my eyes were dry. Maybe from terror.

"Hey," Heather called to me from a long way away, and then I felt her hands on mine, pulling me up. "We've done everything possible to plan and hash out every detail. You care about Wyn, I get that, but don't think for one second that if it comes down to it I won't drive to Hawaii and back again to help save this merman. Got it?"

I nodded.

"We're going to take a ton of pictures, we're going to dance and get some use out of these killer dresses, and then we will save him." Heather practically hummed with determination and her energy seeped into me.

"Well, loan me some clothes then, because I won't want to go back home to change after the dance." We would do this. We would save Wyn.

"I parked the truck behind the guesthouse," Zack said, as we walked into the kitchen of his parents' barely-less-than-palatial mansion after I'd endured the picture taking. "We can hang out there after the dance until we need to go get Wyn."

The dark cherry wood and gourmet appliances in a kitchen the length of my entire childhood home had been intimidating when our trio was in its beginning stages, not to mention the interior decorated with ten-thousand-dollar couches and three-thousand-dollar vases, but now it was homey and familiar. I voted for Chinese food and both Heather and Zack agreed. Maybe the mix of salty and sweet with the soy sauce on my dumplings and the plum sauce on my egg rolls would calm my churning stomach. No such luck.

Greg picked Heather up, and Zack drove me up to the university in his dad's Jag. I don't remember much of what happened during the parade of graduates down the stairs and around the path. My mind was too full, going over every possible eventuality and every detail of our plan. I know I enjoyed seeing my uncle's face as he took my arm. I know I didn't trip on my tall pewter-coloured heels. I know there were a whole bunch of flashes from cameras all throughout the march and a huge roar of sound as we came to the place where Aunt Jocelyn and the cousins were camped out. We did the whole roundabout three times, and then there was the first dance with your escort and then another with your date. After that, Heather found me and dragged the MacPherson crew, me, Zack, and his parents to some corner under a tree for tons more pictures with all of us, including her family and Greg too.

And then Aunt Jocelyn told me they were going because the little ones had to be put to bed.

Sasha was the first to hug me. "I love you, Valerie."

"I love you too. See you Monday."

"Be careful," she said. I nodded and said goodbye and got hugs from everyone else. As they turned to leave I saw Sasha watching me intently, her tiny brow furrowed with worry. Despite the smile on my face, she seemed to know I was as fractured as any moulded, coloured glass art piece my mother would construct.

The next hour I danced along with Zack and Heather and the rest of my grad class, but my soul was at the pool.

At one point, Zack did manage to draw my attention—by speaking of Wyn.

"He's a good guy, you know," Zack whispered, and my mind lurched back to my best friend and his hands that I was holding. "Wyn, I mean. He probably could've killed me if he wanted to, especially after I insulted him. But he obviously cares about you. You're right to try and save him."

"Thanks, Zack. That means a lot." I smiled, grateful.

"Oh, and by the way—you do know you look absolutely gorgeous tonight, right?" He twirled me out from him and then pulled me back into his arms. "Your dress is like water. The lights make waves on it. But maybe you did that on purpose, eh?"

"Yes." I looked away from him, far out past the crepe paper and gaudy balloons, settling on the ocean I saw in my mind. "Even my dress has to be about the water." I squeezed his hand, then let go and turned at the sound of Heather's voice.

"All right," she said. "It's time."

The aquarium was covered with a tarp, indistinguishable in the back of Zack's truck. He'd already dumped the salt in and only filled it three-quarters full so it wouldn't overflow once Wyn got in. After some discussion and rehashing of details about where we'd fill up with gas and the route we'd take to the boat launch, Zack said he was hungry again so we all traipsed into the guesthouse to make a frozen pizza. I have no idea whether the pizza we ate was outstanding or horrible. I could've been eating cardboard. *We're doing this.* I sat on the barstool at the island in the modern, stainless steel-filled kitchen, and asked Zack for paper and a pencil. My drawing wasn't great, but my hands had to do something and my mind was too active for my puzzle ring. Zack and Heather's on and off talk was fuzzy in the background as I created sketch after sketch of ocean scenes, merpeople, and Wyn's face. It was ten. Then ten-thirty. Then eleven and we left.

I went into the pool first, leaving Heather and Zack with the truck.

Wyn was waiting, worry etched into his face more deeply than ever before.

I held up my hand to ward off questions.

"My friends Heather and Zack ... you know who they are. You've seen them and heard me talk about them. Can you trust them?"

"Yes, suppose can I. Why?"

"They're helping me. We have to use Zack's truck to transport you. Come on. We've got a long drive ahead of us and no time for introductions." I turned back to the door, but Wyn's voice stopped me cold.

"Heather knows?"

"Yes," I said, turning back. "I couldn't get a truck or a trailer fast enough and Zack has one, plus Heather has been keeping me sane as we've done everything needed to get you out of here and to the Pacific."

"Made you a promise. And yet break you it so easily." Wyn's voice was laced with more menace than I'd ever heard. "Why should I trust them?" His voice thundered over me and ricocheted off the pool walls. "Your life was in danger. That is the only reason the secret was revealed to you!" He surged out of the water, grabbed my arm, and yanked me down.

"What did you expect me to do?" I screamed back.

"It was a promise! My family, my people—better die I, than harm come to them." He dropped my arm so fast I staggered back and fell hard on my butt. He turned from me with a wordless yell of agony, clutching his arms to his chest. And then he turned back to me, his face such a mask of anger I didn't recognize him. His voice dropped. "Made you a promise to never reveal this secret. And yet the boy was led here and you told the girl."

That's when Heather and Zack burst through the door.

"We heard yelling—" Heather stammered, before her eyes bugged out at the sight of Wyn on the pool deck in all his rage and glory.

"Ummm ..." I stood, brushing my hands on the seat of my jeans. "Wyn, Heather. Heather, Wyn. And I guess you already know Zack." My voice shook terribly, and it was all I could do to point from one to the other. "And ... and I'm sorry. I should've asked you before I told anyone else. I did promise."

"All this shouting because Heather and I both know about you?" Zack glared at Wyn, who returned the angry stare, silent and stoic, like some majestic but frightening statue.

Heather shook her head like she was getting rid of a nightmare. "So let me get this straight. Val has been stressing to the point of hyperventilating, ruining what should be the happiest time of her life after excruciating heartbreak, and busting her butt to try to save *you*, and the first thing you do is scream at her for revealing your presence to her two best friends? Whose help she *needed*?" Heather's voice beat into us, not unlike a small hurricane.

Wyn looked shocked to be challenged by her, and in the face of *her* anger, seemed a little smaller.

"If it was really such a big deal that she told us, why haven't you done anything to free yourself before now? There's the door." Heather thrust a hand towards the back door where the truck waited. "We know one of your captors brings you food in the night. Why not, I don't know, bash his head in with your tail or something and make a break for it?"

Wyn's body shivered, all fight gone, like when he first told me the chemicals were killing him. His eyes were full of hurt, sorrow, and defeat.

"They told me if ever tried I to free myself they would start killing humans." His voice was low, pulled from him with great effort. "Yes, there is a river out that door that leads to the ocean which humans have spoken of, but it is miles away. Would I be visible to everyone while trying to get there. Couldn't risk I anything until Valerie's life was at stake. Then she would not stop coming to see me, despite the danger. What could do I?"

"There are a lot of things that could've been done

differently," Heather said after a long moment staring at Wyn, "but we're wasting time. We gotta go. Now. Will you let us save your life?"

Wyn's face was bare. I had no idea what emotions or thoughts were going through his head, but he moved towards the exit.

I rushed ahead and pushed the door open as far as it would go. Wyn supported his weight on his arms, his tail behind him, and moved out into the light of the street lamps.

"Can you climb into the truck on your own, or do you need us to help you? I'm not sure if we can lift you," I said.

"Should I be able to do it on my own. It is no different than the cliffs Faorin and used I to climb," he said with a slight huff. Apparently his anger was still simmering.

Wyn pushed up onto the middle of his tail, grabbed the side of the truck, and pulled himself up until his head was level with his hands. With a grunt he flipped his tail up onto the tailgate, keeping most of his weight on his hands and from there, he pulled himself into the tank. There was a huge splash and water soaked the cardboard, blankets, and sheets.

"Are you okay?" I called.

"Yes," he said, popping his head up over the edge of the aquarium and staring down at me.

"We're going to tie a tarp down over the tank so that it will be harder for anyone who sees us to know what's in the back of the truck." Wyn's face blanched slightly, but he nodded. Riding in the back of truck would be unnerving enough, but to be blind too? I fought back my anguish. There wasn't anything I could do. He couldn't be seen.

Once Zack double and triple checked all the knots, we were

on our way. I don't remember much about the drive. Mostly lots of neck twisting to look back at the constantly snapping tarp and wringing my hands and fingers so much that they fell asleep. Heather and Zack asked question after question about Wyn and his world. Answering them kept me only partially occupied. Marker after marker passed on the road as the highway flew past us.

Fifteen minutes outside of Hope my stomach started to churn. The headlights of the truck cut through the darkness like a beacon, but my hands turned to ice even as sweat ran down the back of my neck.

I interrupted one of Zack's questions. "Take this exit into Hope." I pointed at a sign. "I wanna check on Wyn."

"Why? What is it?" Zack said.

"Do you think something's wrong?" Heather asked.

"Just do it. And pull over somewhere as soon as you can."

Zack pulled into the first residential area we passed, and stopped in a back alley where most of the houses' lights were out.

I slipped on the gravel as I hurried out of the truck. Rushing to the tailgate I pulled at the knots tying the tarp down.

"Wyn," I called and banged on the end of the tank.

"Valerie ..." His voice was full of pain and I could barely hear it.

There was a small section between the edge of the tarp and the beginning of the cardboard and blankets where you could see the glass of the tank. I couldn't see any water behind that glass.

"Wyn!" I cried out and then covered my mouth. I'd been way too loud. My hands trembled and the knots in the rope refused to come undone. Heather pushed me away and finished untying my knot just as Zack got his side undone. I shoved the tarp back and scrambled up to look in the tank. I stared at the chalk-white form of Wyn slumped against the glass.

There was barely an inch of water in the tank.

-CHAPTER FOURTEEN-
Race

"The water's gone," I hissed, wanting to scream.

Zack immediately climbed up into the truck bed and examined the tank.

"There's a large crack and a hole in one of the corners. How'd this happen, Wyn?" Zack said.

I rushed to the cab and grabbed the two water bottles we'd brought. I poured them over Wyn. As the water washed over him he was able to reply.

"Don't I know. Heard I a crack when we hit a bump at the beginning." His voice was so weak. I blinked back tears. "Tried I to call, but the noise was too loud."

"We did hit a few potholes before we got on the highway in Kamloops," Zack said.

"I'm so sorry, Wyn." How could I think this would work? "This is all my fault."

"This merman is not dead yet." His voice was quiet, but he chuckled a little. "Just get me some water."

"There's a car wash one neighbourhood over," Heather said, her gaze focused on a search window open on her phone.

"Wyn, can you last a couple more minutes while we drive there?" Zack asked.

"Yes." His voice was laboured, but stronger than it had been.

"Okay. Let's go," Zack said.

Heather and I quickly retied the tarp with loose knots while Zack started the truck. Heather guided Zack to the car wash with the map on her phone, and we were there in three short minutes. Thankfully, it was a self-serve. Zack pulled into one of the bays.

I threw some coins into the washer wand and then pointed it at the inside of the tank so that the water splashed onto Wyn. Heather dug down through the blankets to find the hole, while Zack looked for his duct tape that was stashed beneath his seats somewhere. Once Zack found the tape, he cut through the cardboard and foam with his pocket knife. Heather grabbed a dry towel from the edge of the truck bed and tried to dry off the glass as much as she could so the tape would stick. I watched the water level rise, hoping the tape would hold and keep the water in.

I heaved a sigh of relief; the tape was holding.

"Zack, there's another box of salt in my bag."

"Right," he said.

"We'll leave again as soon as the tank's full, but I think we should tape the edge of the tarp part way up the back window so that we can monitor the water level as we drive," Heather said.

"Good idea." That would help, but I still couldn't be too positive. "If I tap loudly on the back window, move your fingers above the water so that I can see them and know you're fine. Got it?"

Wyn moved his tail feebly, gave me a wan smile, and

nodded. He'd been without water for so long. *When he finally gets to the ocean, will he even be able to swim?*

Neil watched it again from the beginning, filing his nails as he did. The video was low quality and didn't have the ability to zoom in, but he saw what he needed to. One boy, two girls. The merman moved into a truck that could be seen through the open door.

The phone rang, shrilly.

"Yes?" Neil said, expecting to hear that it was done.

"There's a problem. I … uh … fell asleep at the wheel. I just crashed into a tree," Doug stammered.

"You what? Will the car still start?" Depending on Doug was sheer idiocy. He had to be coached on everything.

"Let me check."

Neil heard the sound of an engine choking and struggling and then finally turning over.

"Yeah, it runs," Doug said, panting like he'd just run a mile. The fool had already cost him almost a year of setbacks in building the new holding tank—and now he could cost Neil everything.

"My guy will hack the traffic system and see where their truck goes. Just start driving. Fast. I'll deal with you later." Neil shut his phone with a snap.

Seal had given him orders that the abomination with a tail had to be kept alive. They'd been given significant compensation to make sure the fish never got back to the ocean, but other parties had come forward. It was no longer as lucrative to let the creature live.

Seal needed someone to blame for the beast's
death. The girl, in her panicked rescue
attempt, would be the scapegoat for a fatal
crash, if Doug actually succeeded. Doug had
been supplied with a poison not tested for in
autopsies and if any of the inconveniences
survived being run off the road, he knew what
to do. All Seal would know is that the girl had
wrecked her truck trying to rescue the
abomination. There would be no remains to look
for or find. Neil stood, smoothing his
immaculate white tie. He couldn't afford to be
seen anywhere near this enterprise. The
recompense from the experiments and the
necropsy would be worth any eventuality.

It was another two hours. Instead of answering Zack and
Heather's questions, I asked that they talked while I listened. I'd
turned halfway around in my seat to watch the tank through
the small gap we'd made, while Heather pulled the written
directions for where we were going out of my bag and guided
us there. I wanted to tap on the window every five minutes to
check on Wyn, so I'd see him wave if he was okay, but controlled
myself and only tapped every fifteen minutes or so.

When I finally saw the open space of Mud Bay Park I
unclenched and stretched my hands. We'd made it. We were at
the ocean. The water hadn't drained again, and we were about
to put Wyn back in the Pacific. We headed for the parking lot.
We were pulling in when a small black car with two huge dents
in the hood and a smashed-in passenger door charged into the
lot, too. Who would be here at three-thirty in the morning? The
car zoomed past, then whipped left and stopped right in front

of us. Zack slammed on the brakes, preventing a crash by inches. A man stepped out of the car. Our eyes were glued to the black gun he was pointing directly at us.

"You've been a lot more trouble than you should've been," the massive thug said. How could he possibly have found us? Vancouver was huge and there were a zillion places to access the ocean.

Not only that ... how had he known that we were moving Wyn tonight? Fear gripped me. To play the scared little girl to throw him off was one thing, seeing him level a gun at me after he threatened my life was another.

"Get out of the truck." He motioned with the gun.

None of us were a match for a gun. I knew Zack had taken a few self-defence classes, but I sincerely hoped he wouldn't try anything. The far apart lights in the lot made strange shadows, but I could still see that the gun was equipped with a silencer. Even if by some miracle someone heard the shot, we were in the middle of the park at three-thirty a.m. No one would come running. My mouth was dry, my hands clammy with sweat. Was he going to kill us? If yes, why hadn't he done so already? The three of us stood close together beside the truck.

He leered. "Move behind the truck now."

We obeyed. My fear intensified when I saw Zack's furious expression. *Please don't do anything, Zack!* I tried to make the thought stand out on my face.

"You," Hulk-guy pointed the gun at Heather. "Untie the tarp."

Once the tarp was untied and removed, we could all see the tank. The large space we'd cut open to fix the hole was enough to see the water and sand within it. I knew I was the only one who could see Wyn underwater, but my body still tensed with the stress. There was enough water visible for me to see his distraught face.

"Well, now. I think I have an idea what's in there. But I'd like to see him myself before I kill you all."

"If you're going to kill us, why didn't you just shoot us in the truck and be done with it?" Zack said, his voice clipped with contempt.

"If I did that, then I wouldn't be able to get in and drive that truck away now, would I? This has to look like a car accident, not murder."

Hearing our deaths discussed in such matter-of-fact terms made it seem more real than even having the gun pointed at us.

"Now, what do I have to do to get you to show yourself, merman?" the captor said. "Provoke you? Insult you? Show your ugly face, you revolting piece of squid." He waited and his face hardened when Wyn didn't appear. "Fine. I'll shoot her first then, shall I?" He pointed the gun at my face. My eyes locked on Wyn's. His horror and pain made my heart ache—then his expression changed to rage.

"No," I cried, stepping forward.

That's when both Wyn and Zack decided to do something. Wyn propelled himself upward with all the strength of an angered merman, water splashing all over the pavement. He looked as though he were going to tackle the criminal to the ground. Hulk-guy turned towards Wyn—and Zack rushed forward and grabbed the gun with both hands, pushing hard to force the barrel upwards. With a *pffew* the gun went off. I lurched forward to stop them, help them, anything. Zack placed a foot behind the guy's ankle and shoved—hard. Hulk-guy dropped and another shot ripped through the air. White pain flashed through my hand. With a ghastly crack the captor's head hit the pavement and he was still.

The gun should have been louder. It should've gone off with a deafening bang. Something loud and big, because the damage it caused was massive and horrific. One of the bullets had gone into Wyn's gut. His face twisted in pain and he fell back. The glass of the tank shattered beneath him with a sickening crash. I panicked as I watched the blood pour out of the wound. Wyn's blood was a strange dark green colour. It spread across his stomach, seeped into the blankets, and mixed with the broken glass around him.

-CHAPTER FIFTEEN-
Surviving

Wyn's been shot. No. No. This wasn't happening. It couldn't be happening!

But it was.

Blood streamed from between his fingers, and he futilely strived to hold back the dark green tide.

I felt a tugging at my hand and looked down to see Heather binding my right palm with bright blue material. The searing pain barely registered as my red blood turned the cloth a strange purple. *Wyn had been shot.*

"The second bullet grazed your hand," Heather said, a slight tremor in her voice. She tied off the ragged strip from her T-shirt with a sharp pull, and then turned and yelled at Zack as she rushed towards Wyn. "Quit standing there like an idiot and put pressure on that wound! Give me your sweater."

Wyn cried out as she pressed Zack's black sweater into his injury.

"It hurts, I know. Sorry," Heather said.

I walked slowly over to them, as if slowing my steps would slow time, make this horror not a reality. "We need help."

Heather's eyes were wide as she kept up the pressure. "*I can't fix this. We need a surgeon. We need your brother.*"

I'd been immobile, staring at the green blood oozing through Heather's fingers. But the idea of help, the idea that we could still save him pulled me into action. I yanked out my phone, but my hands trembled so bad I couldn't get to Josh's number fast enough.

"Here," Zack said, grabbing the phone from me. I had eyes only for Wyn. His dark blood covered both his and Heather's hands. They could've been holding a wad of seaweed in the strange light, instead of trying to keep Wyn from bleeding to death. *Oh God, help! Save him, please!*

Heather looked up. "Valerie, feel along his back. Is there an exit wound from the bullet?"

I did as she said and found a rough circular hole, and saw blood pooling beneath him. As I brushed the ragged skin, Wyn gasped in pain.

"Sorry, sorry," I said. I pushed Wyn's hair off his forehead with my bandaged hand because my other hand was now covered in his blood. "Yes, there's an exit wound, and there's also a lot more blood." My voice cracked but I pushed through. Heather needed to know this.

I heard Zack swear. "Josh isn't answering his phone. I've called three times. I can't reach him."

"Then we take him to Josh's place anyway." Heather's voice was steely. "Even if he doesn't have proper surgery tools, I'll make do, and we can clean up and explain later. I won't let him die."

"I'll break the door down if I have to," I said, "because I won't let him die either." I shoved Heather away and replaced her hands with my own. "He's mine."

The sweater we were using for pressure was soaked. I looked up and caught a look between Heather and Zack, but we didn't have time for anything but Wyn. "Josh's house is in Surrey, probably a good twenty minutes from here," I said. "We have to get moving—and watch the glass, it'll cut him."

"Once we're gone, I'll call 911 for that—" Heather let loose a string of four-letter words. "I won't have his death on my conscience."

Turning away from them I looked back at my merman's face. "Wyn, we need to stop the bleeding. Can you hang on?"

He nodded with great effort and I saw how pale he'd gotten in just a few short minutes. "The metal ..." His voice was laboured but full of urgency. I heard Zack brushing away broken glass as we pulled Wyn to the truck. Heather grabbed an extra blanket, soaked it in the ocean, and draped it over Wyn's tail, while I focused on him.

"Just breathe," I whispered.

"You need to ... ah!" Wyn clutched at my hands. Blood poured over our fingers, and with a jerk and a yell his body went limp. I cried out and would've kept crying, but Heather forced my hands to start lifting and shifting Wyn's heavy body and tail.

It took all three of us to heft him into the truck. We covered him with the tarp and I started to settle next to him, but Heather said, "You can't sit with him. It's illegal. We can't afford to be pulled over." I gave Wyn's hand a squeeze, while Heather bound his wound as tightly as she could and I slumped into the front seat of the truck.

My tears blurred all the city lights into lines. I dug my nails into my arms to keep from sobbing outright. Heather's conversation with the 911 dispatcher was short. I heard a crunch and then saw a broken phone fly past my face as she threw it out the window. The blood from the slash on my hand was staining my arm red. I finally had time to notice it: the pain was intense.

At last we pulled into Josh's townhouse complex. Zack backed the truck in and we pulled Wyn down and up to Josh's front door, looking around the whole time for anyone who might see us. I tried the door and it was locked. I was raising my foot to kick it in, when Heather cleared her throat. She reached behind the mailbox on the wall and pulled out a key. My mouth dropped open.

"Josh told me where his spare key was in case there was an emergency with you," Heather said, her expression sheepish. Any other time I would've been furious, but it didn't matter now.

"Whatever," I said. When I heard the lock click, I shoved the door open.

"I guess we'll have to operate on the table in the kitchen. And we'll need more towels or blankets soaked in water to keep him wet," Heather said as we pulled Wyn farther into the house.

"Who's there? What's going on?" Josh appeared in the hallway, rubbing his eyes and wearing only his boxers.

"What are you—? Valerie?" If the circumstances were remotely different, I would've laughed at the expression on Josh's face when he saw the three of us pulling a merman on a tarp into his house, but my hands were covered in blood and nothing was funny. "Is that ... is that a mermaid?" Josh's eyes were wide and the large gulp he took was audible.

"Merman—and why the hell didn't you answer your phone?"

I yelled. "We had to bring Wyn all the way here with an open wound!"

"I guess I slept through it. I just worked a twenty-seven-hour shift—"

"He's got a through and through bullet wound," Heather interrupted. "He needs surgery. *Now.*"

"This is Wyn." I looked right at Josh as I said it. He reeled back as though I'd hit him.

"Uh ..." Josh shook his head slightly and then became a lot more businesslike. "Okay." He pulled on a T-shirt. "Do any of you know how his anatomy might be different?"

We all shook our heads. I'll say this for Josh. He sure took things in stride.

Wyn was lying on the table. Wet towels Zack had soaked and brought from the bathroom covered most of his blue scales. When Josh palpated the wound to gauge how bad it was, I had to look away.

"There's something unfamiliar here that the bullet sliced in half," Josh said, "and a nick to his liver, but the rest of his organs seem fine." Josh picked up his scalpel. "I'll have to open the wound further. Heather, pour water and wipe away blood whenever I say." I stared at Wyn's face, willing him to make it through this.

"The blood flow is slow. Was it this slow from the start?" Josh asked.

"No," Heather said.

"I don't think that's good," Josh said. "Here's hoping I don't accidentally castrate him or something," he added in an undertone, and then cleared his throat. "Valerie, you need to monitor his pulse, and keep a hand to his mouth to make sure he's still breathing, while I stitch him up. Zack, bring the large flashlight from that drawer. I need more light."

I quickly found the throbbing point of blood in Wyn's neck; his breath was light on my hand. Once Zack was holding the flashlight in the right place Josh began to operate, meticulously cleaning and concentrating, while Heather wiped away more and more of Wyn's blood. A number of minutes later, Josh's shoulders seemed tenser and his brow was scrunched up.

"I've fixed the nick to his liver as best I can, but I can't ... I don't know what to do!" Josh spoke quickly, the stress in his voice evident. "This tube that's been cut in half comes down from somewhere, but if I cut him open enough to tell where, he'll bleed to death. I could try to reconnect it, but would that even solve the problem? His anatomy is so different. I just started my surgical residency a few months ago. I'm barely comfortable doing minor surgery on a human, let alone a life-saving operation on a fish-human hybrid. If I do this wrong he'll die! I ... I can't, Val." Josh's hands trembled as he pulled them back, turning away.

Josh had given up.

-CHAPTER SIXTEEN-
Revelation

"No, you can do it, Josh," Heather said. "I have faith in you. You know enough to save him." She gazed at Josh with intense ferocity.

"Don't give up. He has to live." Zack sounded broken, like he was trying to be tough, but failing.

"Save him, Josh." My words were rough and choppy. "Please. I know you can. He can't die!" I turned from Josh back to Wyn. His face was still. It was there, feeling Wyn's blood pumping beneath my fingers as he drew closer and closer to death, that I knew. In that one moment, I finally admitted the truth to myself. Seeing Wyn on the edge of death, facing the possibility that I might never again hear his voice, I knew I couldn't live without him. I'd been so focused on saving him, I hadn't realized I was falling for him. He had to live! He meant more to me than anyone else. All thoughts of the hows, wheres, and whens were far away. He wasn't just mine, he was my love, and that love consumed me. The sheer force of my feelings should have healed him.

I turned back to Josh, my eyes blazing. If he faltered, I'd take the needle from him and operate myself.

"Do it! Save him."

Whether it was the look in my eyes, or the tone of my voice, I don't know, but Josh turned back to Wyn.

"Try looping in from behind," Heather said, "and then twist the needle back and around to seal off the wound with a running stitch when you connect the tube."

We all looked at her, astonished.

She shrugged. "I wanna be a vet, remember?"

It wasn't long before Josh finished the last stitch.

Wyn was still unconscious. His striking face paler than I'd ever seen it.

-CHAPTER SEVENTEEN-
Home

After the last stitch, Josh wanted to seal up his work so that it was airtight. He was worried about possible bacteria in the ocean water.

"But he lives in salt water," I said, "and I've seen how healing it is for him. I think we should leave the wound open."

"Maybe," Josh said. "Why don't we pour a little salt water on the wound once we're back at the ocean and see how it reacts?"

I nodded. It would have to do. We simply didn't know enough about Wyn and mer anatomy to do anything else.

"Wait," Heather said. "We can't go back to Mud Bay Park. There might be an ambulance or even police. We have to go to another beach."

"What about Blackie Spit Park?" Josh suggested."It's one town over in White Rock, and there's a boat launch so we can go right up to the water."

I agreed, the closer the better. Wyn had been out of the water way too long. All four of us worked together to get Wyn back into the truck. We all squeezed onto the bench seat and I tried not to yell at Zack to drive faster. My neck got sore with how many times I wrenched around to stare out the back window at the tarp that covered Wyn. Finally, finally, we were back at the ocean.

We lifted Wyn's limp body out of the truck bed and settled him with his torso on the sand and most of his tail submerged in the ocean. Heather, Josh, and I crouched around Wyn. Zack stood, keeping a look out.

"We'll test how his wound does with salt water now," I said.

I scooped up a handful of water and poured it over Wyn's stomach. As the salt water ran over Wyn's stitches, the wound began to bubble, fizz, and hiss, like we'd just poured acid on him. I yanked my hands back and stopped pouring the water. My eyes swept over to look at Josh. His eyes were wide with fear.

"I don't know." His shoulders sagged. "I just don't know."

Wyn had looked horrible after the surgery. Now he looked even worse. His skin was a stark white, his lips bloodless and cracked. I frantically put my fingers to his neck and felt for a pulse. His breathing was extremely laboured. His heartbeat weak. The pool that was my soul froze over in fear.

A minute crawled by.

Then two.

Wyn's breath grew more and more ragged, coming out in strangled gasps. Long seconds passed before each breath.

No!

When it was a full thirty seconds between breaths, Josh and Heather glanced at each other, anxiety written on both their faces.

No. No. We're not at that point yet. I won't give up.

"Come on, Wyn. Please. Open your eyes. Feel the water." I

clutched his hand in both of mine. "Listen to me, Wyn. Hear my voice. You can't die. You can't." My tears poured freely down my face. "Come back, Wyn. Come back! Focus on my voice. *Listen!*"

And then with a flash I couldn't see Wyn anymore.

My vision was obscured with an image of an arm reaching towards Wyn. The hand moved forward and pulled down a section of Wyn's wrist cuff, revealing a small flat compartment that held three small leaves.

The hand took one of the leaves and crumpled it over the stitches on Wyn's torso, then scooped up some water from the ocean and drizzled it over the wound. One finger massaged the leaves and water together, making a jelly-like substance.

The image left my vision as suddenly as it had appeared. I shook my head and realized I was trembling. My hands were clenched tight, full of sand. I didn't know when I'd let go of Wyn. Heather, Josh, and Zack were staring at me, looking confused. I grabbed Wyn's wrist, pulled open the small compartment in his cuff like I'd seen, and found the small leaves. Taking one I broke it into tiny pieces and made the jelly substance over the stitches, the same way I'd seen it done.

"Valerie, what are you—?"

"I don't know, Josh. I just hope this works."

Within seconds of applying the jelly, Wyn's breathing evened out. His chest rose and fell in a slow rhythm. He inhaled deeper and deeper. I clasped his hand again.

A low moan escaped him and my heart leapt into my throat.

"Wyn? Wyn, can you hear me? It's Valerie. Are you okay?"

"Hear I you," his voice was raspy and barely audible. Wyn was alive!

All my breath left me in a short little laugh. We'd done it.

"How are you feeling, Wyn?" Heather said.

"What can we do to help you? Can you swim?" Josh said.

Wyn let out a laugh of pure joy, and I felt my eyes tear up again. He was safe.

Wyn's tail flicked in the water, and his fingers traced the wound on his stomach, touching the mixture there. He raised his hand to his face, staring at the gel on his fingertips.

"Who ... did this?" he asked.

"I stitched your wound," Josh said.

"I made the salve," I said. "I used one of the leaves from your wrist cuff. Should I not have?"

"It is the only way to stop ... metal poisoning for any mer." Wyn's voice was breathy. "Once metal is inside us, it leaches out a poison and shuts down our lungs. The bullet was gone ... but the damage was done."

"An image appeared in my mind showing me what to do, so I did it," I said and shrugged. Wyn was living and breathing—and was no longer a prisoner. That's all I cared about.

"Help me to deeper water, please," Wyn said.

Zack and Heather lifted his tail, while Josh and I guided his body into the water. When we were in the ocean up to our waists, Wyn said, "Can I swim on my own now, think I."

And he could. I watched him moving with the waves and wanted to cry with the sheer joy of it. We'd done it. We'd set Wyn free! He could swim and laugh and see his family again.

Above us in the early morning sky, a cloud rolled in front of the sun—and with the shadow came an equally unwelcome thought. With the long and anxious trip down to the coast, Wyn getting shot, and then Josh operating on him, I hadn't even considered our impending goodbye.

If I had thought about it ... I probably would've run in the other direction. The pain was too much to bear. How could I let him leave when I loved him like this? The clouds shifted again and the sky on the horizon brightened a little.

"It was nice to meet you, Wyn," Heather said.

"Yeah, I'm glad we could help." Zack shoved his hands in his pockets.

"I guess I'll have to hear the whole story from my sister later." Josh smiled. They all turned to go back to shore. Then it was just me and Wyn.

I looked at him. Would I ever see him again? Was this a forever goodbye?

"My Ajana." Wyn's voice was tender and soft. "Saved you my life, more than once. Can I never repay that. But will I always be in your debt. My family needs me. Must I go home. It will be long before we will see each other again. But will I come back again to see you at the winter solstice. If however, need you my help ..." Wyn opened another small compartment in the wrist cuff that didn't hold the leaves, and pulled out a tiny whistle made from a shell. "Will I swim to within a distance that can I hear this whistle once a month at the full moon. Will I wait to hear your whistle for one hour after the moon has risen." He passed the white shell to me. I gingerly took it in my hands. The small oblong shell had flecks of blue in it and shimmered in the half-light. I shivered. The ocean was cold, but held that familiar comfort I was used to from the pool.

"It is too cold. Will I leave you now. Farewell, Ajana." Wyn kissed my forehead. "Lasar aie eneese. Mooneese fras toram."

"Wyn, wait. I ..." *I love you. Stay here with me. Don't go to your family. We're home when we're together.* I sighed. "Be careful."

He touched my cheek and gave me a smile. With a flick of his tail he pushed farther into the ocean, then dove straight into the under curve of a wave. The ripples from his wake disappeared as the next wave rolled in. He was gone. The abruptness left me reeling.

He had come into my life and had now left as suddenly as my family. I hadn't prepared for the goodbye, for the hole left by his absence. I tried to console myself with the fact that he could go to those who loved him and tell them he was alive. I waded towards the shore, and the sand sucked at my feet, as though begging me to stay. Before reaching the beach I turned back and looked out to the horizon.

The waves lapped at my feet and lights danced behind my eyes as stronger morning rays reflected off the water. I imagined I could see the silhouette of Wyn in the distance, but I couldn't. My tears flowed, blurring the line between ocean and sky.

Valerie's Choice

I have to do it. I have to call him. The emails are getting more threatening. The last three months have inched by. Now, waiting for the moon to rise, I close my eyes. The ocean air stirs my hair, making wisps of it cross and re-cross my face. I force my lungs to move in and out with a slow rhythm. My feet are still and heavy on the worn wood of the dock, my limbs stiff and straight. I concentrate on the smooth, delicate shell whistle in my palm, the jagged scar from the bullet taut and ugly beneath it. Do I truly need his help? Will I call him or won't I?

Everything that has happened up to this point feels like a blip on the way to my real life: telling Josh I was moving to Vancouver four days after Wyn left, camping out on my brother's cramped couch for a week before finding an apartment (a ten-minute bus ride from the ocean), applying to Simon Fraser University in Vancouver and being accepted for the January semester, doing physical therapy day in and day out, trying to regain full use of my hand, training and working on the diving regime Coach had set out for me, and working at a video store ...

My new life is all about the lunar cycle, and I track it

methodically. The little moon symbols on the tattered calendar at work draw my attention even when I don't want them to.

That first month when the full moon rose, I stood on the dock, but left the whistle in my purse. To keep my hand from straying, I clenched it at my side as I waited out the hour. When it was over, I let out my breath all at once. I hadn't given in. And yet tears stung my eyes. The stark reality of my disappointment shocked me. My desire to see Wyn waged war against the part of me that knew he was helping his family—his words echoed in my head. *Call if you need my help.*

During the second month's full moon I struggled with my willpower again. I was pulled with the swiftness of a paint stroke to the ocean. The dock and the stretch of beach where I'd said goodbye felt more like home than the drafty apartment I lived in.

The shell whistle had glinted up from my hand, tempting. *If you need my help.* This small thing was my chance. How could seeing Wyn again be a negative thing? Was it so wrong to want to see the man I loved? *Not man: merman.* And there it was, the reason we'd never be together. We were too different. Hell, we weren't even the same species. I had no idea whether or not we were even physically compatible. Physicality, however, would be a moot point if he didn't love me back. A single tear slid down my face when the hour passed. I'd hesitated too long. Wyn would not hear me, even if I could bring myself to call him.

And now, month three, and I am back again, warring with myself once more. Three weeks ago, the emails started. Demanding information on Wyn. They came every few days. Then every day. Then three or four times a day. I had no idea how they got my email address. I deleted the account. Even changed my cell number for good measure. I received more emails at my new address three days later. The most recent one was gruesome in its graphic detail of how they would hurt me if I didn't comply soon.

Am I really so selfish? Will I pull him away from a family that desperately needs him because I feel alone? Because I can't deal? They haven't done anything yet. He'll be coming in a few months for the solstice, but ...

I stare at clocks everywhere, for hours at a time—work, the gym, the pool, my apartment. It has become a personal contest to see how long I can resist glancing at the time. Those first weeks after Wyn left, it was a few hours between glances. Then it was an hour. Now, only minutes. Yesterday, I looked at the clock every five minutes.

Wyn's last Farlan greeting to me echoes faintly in my head. I'm losing him. I can't quite recall his tone or the nuances of certain sounds and syllables. *If you need my help.* They can follow through on their threats, hurt me, but what could Wyn possibly do about it? I need to hear his voice again. I have to know that he's real, that I haven't simply imagined everything that happened—and is happening.

I look at my watch, only ten minutes left. Gazing at the still pattern in the full moon, my vision blurs. I clutch the whistle to my chest and collapse onto the dock. My knees hit the wood hard, jarring my body. More tears run down my cheeks, falling to the dock and sliding between the boards to join the salt of the waves beneath me.

I'm not strong enough. I can't carry on without him. I can't deal with them. It won't matter if he's angry with me. I need him now.

I close my eyes and blow the whistle.

Acknowledgements

It took, most assuredly, a huge team of people to bring this book to life. My family, my husband, and my kids did so much to give me the time I needed to get this done. Not to mention putting up with how many times I babbled on about imaginary characters in my head, and would gaze off into space in the middle of a dinner or a date. You all support me in so many ways, and I couldn't possibly come up with the words to thank you enough.

Tim, your overwhelming, constant support and encouragement is why I can write. Thank you, forever.

Mom and Dad, without you this book would not have been possible. Thank you for believing in me.

Buckets of thanks to the numerous beta readers and "writer in residence"s that brought this book from the super rough draft it was seven years ago, to the amazing, shiny book it is today. Sarah Johnson, Danita Maslankowski, Amber Sulymka, Lindsay Tizzard, and Vanessa Pierson, thank you for your input and time. Emily Olsen and Melodie Smith, you helped shape those important first chapters. Thanks to my fabulous structural editor Ev Bishop who brought out the best in this book and these characters, and truly helped me see what my brain had forgotten or ignored. Thanks to the great David Antrobus as well, my copy editor, who combed through this text with a fine tooth comb and made sure my text said what I wanted it to. Completely happy with the fab cover design by those at Deranged Doctor Design.

Thank you to all the wonderful people who backed the kickstarter for this novel, so that it could be published properly. You people are just plain awesome. A special thank you to Sherry Bateman, Don and Kasandra Mathieson, Tracey Oliver, Leslie Barker, Stan Johns, Kent Van De Veer, Alexandra Swenson, Rebecca Frazier, and Melissa Branchflower for their amazing support.

And to Andrew Sorenson, who after seeing chapters from my first novel in grade nine, said "I know you're going to be a published author one day." It was the burst of confidence I needed as a young teen to keep on writing and working.

About the Author

Danielle Mathieson Pederson is oldest of five children in her family and a part-time working mom of two children. She's been married to her sweetheart Tim for nine years and they live in Kamloops, British Columbia, Canada. She loves discovering a new book, and keeping up with all things geek. You'll typically find her reading a novel, wearing gorgeous earrings and a geeky cartoon T-shirt. She thrives on writing, and in addition to the current Mer Archives series she is working on, she has three different blogs, does book reviews and writes screenplays, short stories and the occasional poem. She has had several poems and short stories published. Find out more and read the latest from the world of Lasera at:

www.dmpederson.com